D1212027

Also by Elena Lappin

Foreign Brides

The Nose

Elena Lappin

The Nose

PICADOR

First published 2001 by Picador
an imprint of Macmillan Publishers Ltd
25 Eccleston Place, London SW1W 9NF
Basingstoke and Oxford
Associated companies throughout the world
www.macmillan.com

ISBN 0 330 37116 9

This novel is a work of fiction. Names, characters, places, and incidents
either are the product of the author's imagination or are used fictitiously.
Any resemblance to actual persons, living or dead,
events, or locales is entirely coincidental.

1 3 5 7 9 8 6 4 2

A CIP catalogue record for this book is available
from the British Library.

Typeset by Intype London Ltd
Printed and bound in Great Britain by
Mackays of Chatham plc, Chatham, Kent.

To my family: I *know* you'll never learn to be quiet when I'm writing, so keep up the noise and the happy turmoil. I love you all.

In memory of my father-in-law, Ben Lappin, with love.

. . . and in a few moments Raphael was rescued from obscurity and appointed to the editorship of the *Flag of Judah* at a salary of nothing a year.

Israel Zangwill, *Children of the Ghetto: A Study of a Peculiar People (1892)*

There is nothing so difficult to arrive at as the nature and personality of one's parents.

William Maxwell, *Time will Darken It (1948)*

Dr Carl Moss was a big burly Jew with a Hitler moustache . . .

Raymond Chandler, *The High Window (1943)*

1 Amateurs

To the Editor:
Mrs Natasha Kaplan
The Nose
PO BOX 9191
London N3

Dear Sir!

Whilst I am not Jewish myself, I really sympathize with the terrible fate the Jewish race suffered due to Hitler's malicious policies. I have written a moving poem about the above. Although you have rejected nine other poems of mine, I trust you will find this one suitable for publication in your worthy magazine.

Yours sincerely,
Nigel Pearce

The Jewish Fate

Through the forests
through the wood
you had to go
on trains, on foot.

A crying mother
a caring bloke
one by one
went up in smoke.

But have no fear.
You are still here
here in my heart
one giant tear.

~

To the Editor
For Publication

Dear Mrs Kaplan,

I write to complain about the consistently tasteless covers of the recent issues of The Nose. *They are tasteless and shocking. I would also like to add that they are very disgusting. In fact, the winter edition which showed an orthodox and a secular Jew locked in an obscene embrace was so bad I had to remove it from my coffee table so as not to upset my wife. I am sure most of your readers, myself included, would prefer to see a picture of something we can all be proud of on the cover.*

Your loyal subscriber,

Dr Joshua Rosen

P.S. Not For Publication: I enclose an artistic photo of my fourteen-year-old granddaughter Shoshana lighting a shabbat candle, taken by myself. My wife agrees that it would make a lovely cover.

~

Dear Editor, Shalom!

I am a famous Jewish storyteller here in Darwin, Australia, where I live. I would like to submit the enclosed story, 'Moses Spills the Beans', for your consideration. A friend has recently been to London and told me about your magazine. Please send me a copy when you publish my story.

Very truly yours,

Izzy (Israel) Chizzick

~

Dear Natasha,

Here's the promised excerpt from my forthcoming novel. Please excuse the scribbles and do let me know about any editing changes.

Best,

Mordecai

~

Dear N,

I am telling you, as a friend and supporter, to watch your back. They're likely to knife you one day. They've done it to Held – they can do it to you.

Cordially,

C

~

Another day's post. After a year on the job, Natasha knew how to distinguish the good from the bad, trash from treasure. She read it all, every single letter, postcard, poem, story, separating them like egg whites from yolks. Perfect simile, she thought: the tidy yellow tray contained a small pile of material she liked and would one day publish in *The Nose.* The white tray was an ever-growing, shapeless mountain of badly written, peculiar manuscripts, soon to be sent back to their authors with a polite rejection slip. At its peak was a card she had misplaced, one that should have gone into her (blue) correspondence tray. In tiny, convoluted handwriting it read:

Dear Natasha,

Don't forget to ask someone to write a piece about Danny Rubinstein. (I suppose you know he died this week?) He is (was) a very, very important writer, though perhaps long before your time. You must not lose sight of Held's legacy – don't make him turn in his grave!!

If you're stuck, I'd be happy to do a nice obituary. As you know, I have it on file.

Ever yours,

Charles

Charles Sugarman was a compulsive writer of obituaries. Every living Jew in Britain with a minor or major literary accomplishment to his or her credit could count on having a half-sycophantic, half-malicious obituary filed away in Sugarman's computer 'for future use'. These were kept meticulously up to date, so that one could safely die at any time and be sure that Sugarman would not forget to mention any recent developments in one's life and work. It was not entirely clear to Natasha whether Sugarman was the most effective gossip in London because he had to know everything for 'professional' reasons, or whether he got into the obituary business because he could only live vicariously through others. Even the most benign exchange with him would be relayed to the entire world and invariably return to its source in a substantially altered form. Sugarman misunderstood and misinterpreted almost everything one said.

Her reply to this card, as he no doubt knew, would be negative. Natasha abolished obituaries from her very first issue. She had made an early decision to leave Jewish necrology to the *Jewish Weekly*, a dedicated purveyor of the Anglo-Jewish lifecycle. She hoped Sugarman would have safely passed on by the time the *Weekly* needed an obituary of Natasha Kaplan. She knew he would say things like '. . . in spite of being an unknown American housewife and writer living in London with her Gentile husband, she was permitted to take on our most precious publication and gamble with the founding fathers' unique legacy; in hindsight, one has to admit that the magazine was none the worse for it – but there were those who claim she was allowed to go too far . . .' Natasha had no intention of turning in *her own* grave.

Sugarman was one of the Midgets, as she called the thirteen trustees who published *The Nose*. Her first encounter with them had been at her job interview – her 'nose job interview', as Tim put it when she told him what she was up to. 'You want to edit a *Jewish* magazine? You must be nuts, but hey, somebody's gotta do it, and it would help pay the mortgage,' he'd said. They lived two largely separate lives – Tim disappearing daily and nightly into the dark tunnels of the tube, working as a cop for the London Underground, and Natasha spending most of her time looking after Erica at their small bungalow in Southgate. It was when Erica pointed out, drily, that both she and Daddy had jobs – she went to school and Daddy was a policeman, but Mummy was unemployed – that Natasha decided to start looking at ads in that Monday morning's *Guardian*.

She had never heard of *The Nose*, not even under its more sombre and better-known subtitle *An Anglo-Jewish and International Review of Letters, Culture, Religion, Zionism, and the Arts, including Ballet*. ('Nose', it seemed to her, stood for NO Subject Excluded.) It had a very limited circulation, and a tired, poorly designed look. Yet it had charm, and reminded her of those old journals she would sometimes leaf through at the British Library, where she liked to go searching for unusual manuscripts. Natasha's predecessor (the magazine's founder) was a kindly and almost penniless old man who did all the work himself, with the help of occasional freelancers. When Held died (Sugarman's obituary appeared not only in *The Nose* and the *Weekly*, but also in a couple of broadsheets), the magazine teetered on the brink of collapse, with guest editors filling in, unenthusiastically, for about a year. At a critical moment, the Midgets managed to secure a small grant to pay a new editor's salary and decided to advertise the position.

The ad made it look and sound (almost) like a proper job ('World-Renowned Scholarly Journal of Jewish Letters Seeks Talented Editor, Salary Commensurate with Experience and Commitment to Jewish Values'), but as soon as Natasha entered the dingy, windowless storage room at the back of a small pet shop in Finchley where the interview was to take place, she knew that something was out of whack. She had expected to see a dusty, decrepit, book-lined office with leather-padded oak chairs and a huge mahogany conference table. Instead, she was invited to squeeze into a folding metal chair and face a jagged line of elderly, very serious-looking men and one youngish but no less solemn woman. The round plastic table in front of them barely supported a heap of papers and a dozen styrofoam cups containing foul-smelling coffee. Natasha had absolutely no idea who these people were – for all she knew they represented the intellectual crême de la crême of Anglo-Jewry – but she took one look at the scene and made an instant decision to forget about being nervous and not to take it seriously, not even for a second. She would enjoy the interview like an audition for a bad play, and then walk out into the daylight and get on with her life.

The first interviewer she noticed was, in fact, Charles Sugarman. She immediately nicknamed him the Flasher because, with his crumpled suit and oversized spectacles, he reminded her of the man who once exposed himself to her on the tube. This was many years ago, when she was in London to do some research and took the Piccadilly Line almost every day from Finsbury Park to Bloomsbury. One day, between King's Cross and Russell Square, she looked up from the magazine she was reading and found herself staring at a penis that seemed to belong to the animal kingdom. She didn't remember it in exact anatomical detail, but the electrifying display of majestic size and a variety of primary colours was firmly implanted in her mind. As was the man's face: the happy, somewhat apologetic grin, which quickly became menacing when she decided to jump up, and, after a brief salvo in juicy American English, slap him across the face. The ensuing commotion made sure that both Natasha and the flasher (whose short-lived moment of glory was clearly over) were taken away by a young policeman for questioning as soon as the train reached the station. She didn't know what happened to the man, but the young cop's name was Tim Parker and he took her breath away by actually *blushing* while writing down her official statement for the police (' . . . the man's veiny hand glided gently and self-consciously up and down his very large, wilful penis which seemed to reflect all the colours of the rainbow . . . no, I could not describe the colour of his eyes . . .') and it was only a matter of days before she got to know *his* (not as magnificent) penis.

The flasher's lookalike, Sugarman, kicked off the interview by asking her why she came to live in London.

'It's a long story. Mostly for private reasons, and because of a book I was writing at the time.'

'According to your CV, you have only one publication, a mystery novel called *Mrs Cohen's Last Supper.* I assume it has Jewish content?'

'Well . . . the victim, the detective and the murderer are all Jewish. But it's not what I would call an ethnic novel. I mean, it sold pretty well, for a first book.'

Sugarman, who had already cleared his throat in preparation for his next question, was interrupted by the only woman among the trustees. She spoke very fast, as if in fear of forgetting to say something important.

'Why do you want this job? What would you change about our magazine?'

'Everything,' Natasha shot back, just as fast, her own low voice in marked contrast to the high-pitched falsetto of her interlocutor.

Suddenly, she felt a tangible silence in the room. It was not an uncomfortable silence – it felt more like a sharp, deep, collective intake of air. She thought of moving her chair a small distance away from the wobbly table and uncrossing her legs under her short black skirt, like Sharon Stone in *Basic Instinct.*

After a brief pause, the trustees subjected her to a noisy avalanche of questions, competing with one another in trying to get her attention. She gave short, almost indifferent answers, like the most popular girl in high school fending off a swarm of nerdy suitors. It was almost fun, and the initial unpleasantness was gone. But she remained convinced that she would never see them again and declared, in answer to one trustee's question about any new contents she would like to see introduced to the magazine, 'I think you need a Jewish centrefold. You know, like in *Playboy*? It would definitely give your circulation a big boost.'

There was another silence, and then, to her surprise, a great deal of cacophonous laughter. They thanked her and said they'd be in touch.

Much later that night, at around midnight, Natasha's phone rang. She quickly spat out a mouthful of dark German chocolate when she heard the man's voice: 'Robert Taub, Chairman of the Trust.' He was calling to offer her the job of editor. It had been far from a unanimous decision, he added, in fact she won by only one vote. But the general feeling was that she had the right spirit and energy to take on *The Nose* at this difficult time, especially in view of the fact that there had been no other applicants. Was she interested? And could she work from home, like her late predecessor, Franz Held?

She was. She could. As soon as she put down the phone, she speed-dialled her brother Philip's number in New York. He was still in his office at the *Village Voice*, writing his regular gossip column.

'Isn't it a bit late over there? Is something wrong?' he asked in a slow tone, indicating that his mind was on other matters, but that he was grateful for the transatlantic distraction.

'No, listen, I just got a job! Editing a Jewish magazine! And I can do it from home, so it's perfect!'

'A *Jewish* magazine? What do *you* know about all that stuff? Just kidding – that's great, congratulations, but—'

'I just found out!'

'You just found out?! You mean, they called you at *this* time of night to tell you you had the job? *And* they don't have an office? Natasha,' he said emphatically, stressing every broad Brooklyn vowel, 'don't have anything to do with those guys. They're rank amateurs.'

2 Off-Screen

Philip, who was ten years older than Natasha, dealt with life like a razor-sharp military strategist, combining level-headed planning with quick intuition. He had been a precocious adolescent when she was only learning how to read, an opinionated Harvard graduate while she was still a confused, temperamental teenager. Natasha adored him. Her earliest childhood memory was of looking up, from her crib, at the smiling faces of her father, her mother and Philip, and suddenly *understanding* that he was *not* one of her parents, but something else, something much closer to herself: her brother. This excited her so much that she burst out crying.

When she was four, she emptied a garbage can over his head while he was talking to a friend in the kitchen. When she was six, she found his secret diary and scribbled funny faces all over it. When she was seven, she brought ten other little girls – she was having a sleepover party – into his bedroom in the middle of the night, lifted his blanket and told them to tickle his huge, hairy legs and the soles of his feet. But when she was eight and Philip was packing to leave for Harvard, she gave him a serious, adult look, told him she loved him, and begged him to please, please stay home.

He didn't, of course, and she grew up as if she were an only child, with a difference: she could expect a phone call from her brother almost every day, no matter where he was or what he was doing. Philip was very attached to his funny little sister, and missed having her around. They were kindred souls, and talked and laughed about everything. Philip always took Natasha seriously, and was not above discussing the latest Disney movie with her, or her puppy love affairs, or even telling her about his own. But their favourite topic had always been the Dynamic Duo, as they secretly referred to that embarrassing pair of perennial teenagers – their parents.

Sam and Alice Kaplan were a celebrated couple within the limited confines of the New York avant-garde film scene. He directed naive, semi-pornographic black and white movies in which she played wide-eyed, vaguely European innocents, often soaked to the skin under flimsy white tops. Sam thought of himself as an audacious version of Woody Allen (he even looked a bit like him), and never noticed that Alice was a bit too radiant for his grainy, dark films. His loving camera eye usually showed her under a solid downpour of heavy Manhattan rain. Off-screen, Alice was, by nature, a pensive, earnest woman who loved comfortable, slightly shabby clothes, kept an immaculate suburban home and read poetry in five European languages. But she could also switch off her quiet seriousness, without a warning, and be full of unrestrained laughter and piercing wit. She was unpredictable, and everyone loved her for it.

Sam accepted the housekeeping and the poetry, provided Alice remained committed to the perpetual whirlwind of mad activity he believed was a passion they both shared. They had parties to celebrate everything – not only finished movies, but barely articulated ideas for new ones. Sam would say to his wife, 'Listen to this one. A woman cop – you – catches a small-time mugger in the subway. There's a struggle, they become sexually aroused. She handcuffs him, almost tenderly. They're waiting outside the station for a cop car to arrive, it starts pouring and . . . Do you see what I see? Alice, baby, I think we've got a gem here. Let's have a party. I need some feedback on this.' An hour later, their large, tidy apartment would fill up with an immensely colourful, noisy, dramatic crowd of people who would bring with them a mildly toxic atmosphere and a sense of something very, very important taking place. At least, that's how it had always felt to Natasha, and for a long time even to Philip.

They also had parties to mourn their failures. Not that Sam ever considered any of his cinematic creations to be less than perfect, or his wife's performances in them anything but sublime; but it did happen, occasionally, that another avant-garde *auteur* had, inadvertently, made a film of more or less similar content to one of Sam's, at about the same time. Andy Warhol had done this twice, and each time, Natasha's father fell into a deep depression which, in turn, required a huge gathering of their closest friends to cheer him up and to convince him that there wasn't even a hint of truth in a vicious little review in the *Village Voice* which claimed that 'Warhol's most recent cinematic experiment proved that Kaplan's uninspired and repetitive attempts at film art are entirely derivative of Warhol's, and will never be in the same league'. The same review included a favourable mention of Alice Kaplan's 'finely tuned body-and-soul acting', with the well-meant suggestion that she 'would benefit from a less uxorious directorial hand'.

Alice kept quiet, and Sam pretended not to notice. But there was much truth in that comment, and they both knew it. Everybody knew it. Natasha had always been aware, even as a small child, of a peculiar twist in her mother's character. For some reason, Alice chose to act as an ultra-sensitive translator of Sam's erratic moods, as if he could only communicate with the outside world through her skilful interpretation of his mental games. Philip once said that 'Mom was to Dad like the bubble that comes out of a cartoon character's mouth or head, to show what he's saying or thinking'. In order to do this, Alice had to shrink a little in Sam's presence. She had to be receptive to his ideas about everything, including herself. They didn't always agree, and they did argue a lot; but the arguments were not about who was right and who was wrong, they were about the best way of realizing Sam's view of things.

Natasha simply did not know whether it had ever occurred to her mother to try out for roles in other directors' films, or even to stop acting altogether and do something different; the subject never came up. She had no idea whether her mother would have been happier without all that fuss and turmoil generated by her father. Alice had the ability to fill every space with her live-wire, dynamic presence; but that didn't make it any easier to get close to her quiet core. It had always seemed to Natasha that her mother's magic vitality was like a skilful, well-rehearsed performance projected on to a screen, but that her real mother was somehow behind or beyond that screen, as if it were made of steel rather than celluloid.

The gap between the two 'teams' – Kaplan parents and Kaplan children – had always been enormous, even though Sam and Alice were convinced that they had succeeded in creating an ideal family unit based on friendship rather than authority. In truth, Natasha and Philip were highly critical of their parents, and felt a little offended by their childishness. They couldn't really take them seriously, even though, as parents went, theirs were pretty entertaining. ('They're so immature,' Philip used to say. 'I feel like I'm older than Dad.')

Sam Kaplan had come to New York from California, the son of a prolific Hollywood screenwriter. When Natasha was growing up, her grandfather was still so much in demand that they very rarely saw him. She never heard much about her grandmother except that she had died when her father was only ten years old. Sam kept a framed black and white portrait of her on his desk, but never talked about her. Later, he added a slightly smaller photo of his father, making sure that the two frames did not face each other.

She didn't know her maternal grandparents at all, never even saw their photos. Alice was from Prague, but it sometimes seemed to Natasha that her mother came from nowhere at all. She had arrived in New York after the war, on her own, and was working as a waitress in one of the Village jazz clubs Sam used to frequent with his friends. Alice soon joined their group and, eventually, married Sam. They were both very young, and the wedding was just an excuse to have a crazy party which, as they still liked to boast, lasted a month. Sam's father couldn't come or wasn't invited – Natasha wasn't sure which; there was a large shoebox full of their wedding snapshots, all of which showed fuzzy takes of Sam and Alice surrounded by their laughing friends – never alone.

Philip's birth would have interrupted the shooting of his parents' very first full-length feature film – if Sam hadn't included it in the final scene. The film caused a minor scandal – this was 1954 – and became an instant cult hit. Sam and Alice Kaplan were now a well-known 'item', and, even though they moved to their apartment in Prospect Park, their flamboyant lifestyle attracted an even wider circle of admirers and hangers-on.

No one paid much attention to Philip. The apartment was always full of visitors, people engaged in passionate and wild discussions of this or that artistic project, and little Philip wandered among them with a frown on his freckled face, listening, watching, and finally arriving at the conclusion that he was better off on his own. Sam and Alice, too busy with their own lives, let him do as he liked. Even at six years old, Philip was considered old enough to be treated as an adult: when he asked to be left alone in the car while his mother went shopping, it never occurred to her to worry. It was a blissfully sunny spring day, somewhere in Brooklyn, the car was parked under a huge tree near a department store. People were walking past with shiny, new-season smiles on their faces.

What Alice didn't know was that after five, ten minutes of examining the interior of the pale blue Chevy and staring out of each section of the side window which, without the partition, formed a perfect half-circle, Philip had become so afraid that he let himself out of the car and, leaning against its hood, just stood there and cried. He had never been taught to pray, but he was praying. If his mother didn't come back, *right now,* something terrible was going to happen. He was sure of that because his fear had told him. But his mother didn't come. Instead, an older woman passing by with her grandson, who seemed about Philip's age, noticed the tears in his eyes and asked him if he was all right. When they heard that he was scared to be alone and was waiting for his mother, the little boy offered to sit in the Chevy with Philip to keep him company. The woman smiled as both boys climbed in the back seat, and waited outside while they talked, earnestly, about Chevys and other cars. The boy's name was Aryeh and he asked Philip if he, too, was Jewish. 'I think so,' Philip had answered and only many years later remembered that he had found this question soothing at the time. When Alice returned, she found no trace of fear or tears in her son's face. He looked happy.

By the time his sister was born, he had already had ten years of relative solitude behind him, and wasn't quite sure how to respond to Natasha. She responded first – by focusing on him rather than her parents, and following him around the house, trying to copy everything he did. But there was a big difference between Philip and Natasha: he was an earnest, sometimes melancholy boy and, later, man, while she had always been a goofy, giggly kid, usually in high spirits, often on the frivolous side.

The fun stopped when Philip left for Harvard. She began a mental countdown till her own graduation. Nine years. But when the day came, she realized that being away at college – even though she had chosen to go all the way to Columbus, Ohio – wasn't really enough; she wanted to put more of a distance between herself and her ageing but, in her view, still infantile parents. One day, she would. In the meantime, she studied an eclectic mix of subjects – a bit of English literature, foreign languages, some history – and even managed to write a moderately entertaining mystery novel in her spare time. She published it under a pseudonym, substituting Weiss, her mother's maiden name, for Kaplan. She didn't want to be associated with her parents' fame; she wasn't sure she was proud of the manner in which they had earned it.

Mrs Cohen's Last Supper was, miraculously, still in print when, eventually, she started applying for research grants and lowly teaching jobs which would take her away from the States. There had been nothing to hold her there; not one of her boyfriends – and there had been quite a few – had made her feel that it was necessary to link her life with his for any length of time. Her life: what was it about, exactly? It seemed faded to her, somehow, and patchy, like badly applied make-up. Perhaps it was the contrast with her parents' compulsive hyperactivity and Philip's focused self-awareness that made her feel empty, despite her very young age.

Two offers came through. She had a choice: a year in London to write her thesis on Victorian family values, or a year in Haifa, teaching English to future chemical engineers. She hesitated, and chose London.

If she hadn't taken that ominous underground train and met Tim, she would have had to find another excuse to stay in London when her grant expired. By the end of that first year – her thesis not only unfinished, but practically forgotten – she had no reason whatsoever to go back to New York. London had, to Natasha's surprise, filled some kind of void in her. 'Living here feels like reading a great book on a dun, rainy day,' she once said to Philip on the phone. 'I don't think I get that,' he'd answered, slowly.

3 Sussman's Pets

MINUTES OF A MEETING OF THE BOARD OF TRUSTEES

DATE: 12 October 199—

PRESENT: Robert Taub (Chairman)
Charles Sugarman
Yvette Moskowitz
Zygmunt Levy–Newman
Jonathan Warhaftig
Sidney Sussman
Joel Hirsch
Malcolm Blaustein
Lionel Myerson
Maurice Toledano
Baruch (Bruce) Shapiro
Natasha Kaplan (Editor)

APOLOGIES: Julius and Sidney Weintraub
SECRETARY: Sidney Sussman

Robert welcomed everyone back after the summer holidays and congratulated Natasha on a particularly entertaining summer issue (this opinion was seconded by all except Sidney Sussman, who stressed that he and most of his friends, family and business acquaintances did not feel like reading all that fiction).

REVIEW AND CORRECTIONS OF PREVIOUS MINUTES:

– Maurice Toledano's wife, *not* mother-in-law, has offered to promote *The Nose* and its editor at a special literary ladies' tea at her home in St John's Wood.

– Yvette had *not* promised to help with the tea.

– Natasha has participated in a conference on Jewish literature in Berlin, *not* Dublin.

– The minutes of the last meeting were taken by Sidney Sussman, *not* Sidney Weintraub.

The following agenda was then discussed:

1. EDITOR'S REPORT

Natasha informed us that Michael Fine and Stella Silverman have resigned from the editorial board. (She gave no reasons.) They have not been replaced. The editorial board currently consists of the following members:

Christopher Le Vine, Daniel Friedman, Jack Margolis, Susan Wilson, Janet Klein, Shlomo Cohen and Nancy Lichtenstein.

Sidney Sussman expressed strong interest in attending a meeting of the editorial board. Natasha ignored his request.

She reported that the autumn issue was going to be a few weeks late, due to scheduling difficulties. She wanted its contents to be kept secret, but did reveal that it would deal with Jews and crime. Robert said that was a good idea, but Yvette was worried it may lead to anti-Semitism. Bruce expressed his sincere hope that Jews would only be presented as victims, not perpetrators. This opinion was seconded by all except Maurice, whose brother has just been sentenced to six years in a French prison for armed embezzlement.

Natasha reminded the trustees (as if they needed reminding – S.S.) that the trial of Annmarie Goetz, the Nazi film-maker, would be starting soon. She will attend and cover it for *The Nose*. Yvette expressed the wise opinion that, as the trial was likely to go on for quite some time, this could distract Natasha from her editorial duties.

The editor also mentioned that she has made a number of significant contacts with potential sponsors. She will be dining or lunching with them (one at a time, presumably – S.S.) and will report on the outcome at the next meeting, if not before.

She said the financial costs of producing the autumn issue would be significantly defrayed by a large insert from a niche literary publisher, Corner Press. The price was still under negotiation, but she was hoping to obtain £1,000, or more.

OTHER MATTERS ARISING

Robert stressed that the financial situation, details of which can be seen in the attached Accounts, has once again deteriorated. He explained that this is partly due to increased costs of paper and printing, but also, unfortunately, to the editor's failure to economize on a number of expenses. This opinion was emphatically seconded by all, especially and most vocally by Sidney Sussman, who pointed out that it was hardly necessary to pay authors for their contributions to *The Nose*, as it is an honour for them to be published in it anyway. Malcolm reminded us that in Held's days, contributors were never paid. Natasha countered, somewhat sharply, that in Held's days, hardly anyone read the magazine, and that she had been hired, as she understood it, to make it more accessible and topical. According to her, this could not be achieved without paying good writers for good writing.

Jonathan, Charles, Joel and Lionel supported Sidney's view, pointing out that Natasha's approach is a tad too American.

Bruce objected, saying that, although he is American himself, he agrees with the majority view, and described the editor as 'extravagant'.

Sidney Sussman proposed a radical savings in the form of closing the magazine down in its present form and replacing it with a regular cultural newsletter, which he would be happy to edit on a purely volunteer basis.

This proposal was greeted with active interest on the part of most of the trustees.

The meeting ended with a gracious vote of thanks to Sidney Sussman for hosting the meeting of the board, once again, on his business premises.

~

Natasha finished reading the minutes and filed them away, with a sigh. There were few mistakes this time, Sidney had done a good job. She wrinkled her nose as she remembered his 'business premises': it was that dark storage room behind the pet shop, which, as she had discovered soon after her interview, belonged to Sidney himself and was called, simply, Sussman's Pets. The smell of assorted pet supplies managed to penetrate through a thick wall which separated the back room from the shop.

Scanning the names of the trustees, she tried to recall their faces, but it was all a bit of a blur. Even now, after a year of editing *The Nose*, she had trouble distinguishing one trustee from another. Most of them were older men in dark suits and gold spectacles, most of them had loud voices and tended to speak all at once. Zygmunt Levy-Newman stood out because he never said a word at any of the meetings. He never even smiled. His silence was a solid source of power and it was clear to Natasha that for some reason he was treated with great respect by the others. One day, she hoped to find out why. She also hoped to meet the Weintraub brothers, who had not attended a single meeting so far.

Bruce Shapiro was also different from the rest, but not significantly so. He was from the Bronx, a loud, burly man, and initially Natasha had assumed that for that reason alone he would be likely to support her more daring schemes. But he was anxious to blend in with the majority of the trustees, and always agreed with anything they said. He spoke with a peculiar accent, like an American actor auditioning for a part in a British film.

Maurice Toledano was the only man on the trust whom she found interesting and even a little exciting. He oscillated, unpredictably, between fiery melodrama and passionless melancholy. Natasha liked him both ways.

She also liked the chairman, Robert Taub, who was very kind and very, very weak, like an emasculated Godfather-figure. He wanted the trust to be one big happy family, and saw himself as responsible for *shlom bait*, peace and harmony among them all. Under his gentle guidance, belligerent trustees were mollified, nascent arguments resolved without evolving into major fights. But sometimes, when his concentration slipped – which happened every time he looked at Yvette or she looked at him – things would get out of hand, causing Sidney Sussman to mess up his minutes.

Sidney Sussman: a peculiar man. He had left the running of his pet shop to his daughter quite a few years ago, and now had a massive amount of time on his hands. This trust was one of many charitable foundations he had become involved with, and he seemed to love them all with equal passion: the Jewish Ramblers' Association, Kosher Mad Cow Disease Research, British Friends of the Haifa Zoo. (Natasha had heard that Sussman's wife encouraged him to 'keep busy and stay out of the house'.) But his commitment to *The Nose* was, nevertheless, inexplicably strong. So was the patience and exaggerated deference with which he was treated by his fellow trustees. Natasha knew for a fact that it was faked, and that they laughed at him behind his back. So why did they humour all his silly whims? Another little mystery.

Suddenly, Natasha made a decision: she would drop the mental nickname she was in the habit of using when she thought of the trustees. Instead of the Midgets, she would, from now on, think of them as Sussman's Pets. Or, at least, alternate between the two.

She looked at her watch. It was time to bring Erica home from school. Then drop her off at a friend's birthday party. Then call Tim, who would be finishing his shift just about now, and remind him to pick up Erica at six thirty, because she has a meeting in town. One of those dinners with a potential patron.

4 Give and Take

As she slipped into the elegant hotel lobby, Natasha stole a quick, furtive glance at herself in one of the large gilded mirrors: not a disaster, but, shit, her hair – too long, too blonde – was still wet from the blitz shower she had taken before leaving her house in a mad rush. She tried to tie it in a little knot, but failed. Making her way to her octogenarian host's table in the hotel restaurant, it occurred to her that the waiters must surely think she is a whore. And they wouldn't be totally wrong. A whore, of sorts, for *The Nose*: this had not been in the original job description, but the magazine was in dire straits, and it turned out that she was pretty good at fund-raising. Some of these old guys were quite charming, and some weren't even that old.

He stood up, with some difficulty. A frail man, with isolated wisps of white hair shooting out in an awkward pattern on his head and around his ears. Natasha inhaled, carefully, bracing herself for the usual odour she had come to associate with 'potential sponsors': stale, musty, fetid. In short, gross. But she was pleasantly surprised: Dr Hoffmann was surrounded by a fragrant cloud of expensive aftershave and cologne. He actually smelt nice! Phew.

'It's a real pleasure to finally meet you face to face, Dr Hoffmann.'

'Please, call me Ludwig,' he said, ceremonially. She had heard his German accent on the phone, but it seemed stronger now.

She smiled: 'If you call me Natasha.'

'It would be my honour, Na-ta-sha.' He pronounced her name slowly, as if he didn't want it to end.

'You are a fine . . . editor, if I may pay you a sincere compliment.'

'Thank you, Dr Ho— Ludwig. I'm glad you are enjoying the magazine.'

'I am. I am especially fond of your interviews. May I ask, Na-ta-sha, whom you will be interviewing next?'

'Well . . .' Natasha stalled. She didn't like to give away the contents of future issues, but she had the feeling this man could be very generous if she made him feel included in her plans.

'I have been promised an interview with the Chief Rabbi.'

'Ah,' he said, without much interest. 'I am not personally acquainted with him. But, you know, I am not at all involved with Anglo-Jewry. And Anglo-Jewry, I dare say, has never been much involved with the likes of me.'

She thought of the unusual letter on very fancy stationery she had received from him, about two months ago:

Dear Mrs Kaplan,

I have recently been introduced to your journal. Although I don't read very many publications any more, I have found yours a worthwhile read, and have now become a subscriber. I have even ordered a number of back issues.

I hope you will forgive me if, as a devoted reader, I will allow myself a small constructive criticism. Unfortunately, I find that the quality of the photographs you print does not quite match the high quality of the articles.

I have long been involved in professional photography; it would therefore give me the greatest pleasure to offer you the financial assistance you might be lacking in order to rectify this minor defect.

I would be extremely honoured if you would agree to have dinner with me in the near future in order to discuss my modest donation.

Yours sincerely,

Dr Ludwig Hoffmann

Their drinks arrived, served by a French waiter who addressed Dr Hoffmann by name and grinned at Natasha in a polite but meaningful way.

Natasha studied the menu. Bliss. She thought of the scrambled eggs Tim and Erica would be having at this very moment, in her cramped kitchen, and ordered an extravagant sequence of luscious French dishes. Dr Hoffmann looked at her a little quizzically, and ordered only a bouillon for himself.

'My digestion is not what it used to be,' he said apologetically. 'Not since the . . .' He paused.

'War?' Natasha offered, helpfully.

'Since my operation last year,' said Hoffmann, with a slight smile. Still, here it was: The Cue. There came a moment, during all her encounters with men and women of Hoffmann's generation, when they wanted to talk to her about their past. This was her favourite part. She could listen to them forever, soaking in story after story, linking them together and fitting them into the larger picture some people called history. She loved other people's stories because, as she had realized some time ago with her brother's help, her parents never talked about their past. Especially her mother, who, when asked about anything that happened to her a long time ago, would answer, harshly, 'Leave me alone. What was, was', or 'Who can remember', or 'Every person has the right to forget', as if she were being forced to reconstruct an unpleasant dream. One day, Natasha and her brother simply stopped asking those questions, even though, with time, they grew more curious, not less. Their self-restraint made Alice visibly relaxed and happy. She actually seemed *grateful* when they left her alone, and so they did. Yet the tension remained. The Kaplan family was cheerfully noisy, but the noise was always surrounded, and kept in place, by a great deal of silence, like a heavy boat in the centre of a soundless, invisible, but very powerful current.

But she was wrong about Hoffmann: the past was definitely not on *his* mind. He seemed much more interested in giving her the details of his surgery: the early symptoms of cancer of the colon, which he ignored, then several useless visits to local doctors, and, finally, a successful consultation with a German specialist in Hamburg ('my home town') and a masterfully executed operation in a luxurious clinic in Zurich.

'I am almost a new man,' he declared triumphantly, 'but only for an hour a day these days. I tire easily.'

So do I, Natasha wanted to scream. His medical report had taken her through all the courses of her scrumptious meal, which had somehow lost its charm. She was sipping her espresso, barely controlling her annoyance. So far, nothing had been said about Dr Hoffmann's supposed donation. She decided to take this aged bull by his fragile horns and bring up the issue herself.

'Ludwig,' she breathed. 'I was looking forward to hearing your expertise on the photographs in our magazine.'

'Yes,' he said.

'Well?'

This was getting ridiculous. The man was just staring at her, without saying a word.

'So-sorry, Na-ta-sha,' he muttered, with a start. 'Please forgive me. I am not senile, but I do lose my thread sometimes.'

Natasha excused herself and disappeared into the ladies' room. Clearly, Dr Hoffmann needed some time to collect himself. He looked a bit shaken, Natasha thought. Not as firm and lucid as he had seemed in the beginning. One day, I'm gonna be responsible for one of these guys' heart attack. Maybe even a string of them.

When she returned to their table, she saw that Dr Hoffmann had used her absence to place a cream-coloured cheque discreetly next to her coffee cup. She stared at it: fifty thousand pounds!!! The waiter cleared their table, widening his eyes when he noticed all the zeros. She caught his knowing smirk. Damn. Now I'm not just any hooker, I'm right up there with the best. Not bad for an hour's work. Kind of exciting, too.

'Dr Hoffmann, Ludwig, this is immensely generous. The trust will be exceedingly grateful. Thank you so much.'

'Please, Natasha, do not mention it, it's the least I can do. At the moment. I would be most delighted if you would use this sum to improve your printing technique. But let us not speak of this small gift any more. I would like to give you something else.'

He reached into his inside breast pocket, and extracted a small old black and white photograph of a young man.

'Do you recognize him?' he asked Natasha, expectantly.

She studied the picture for a few moments, and shook her head.

Hoffmann sighed. 'I thought so. But then, you are probably too young to have known him.'

'To have known whom? Who is this?' She was getting impatient again.

'Your predecessor, Franz Held. When I first saw your magazine and read the name of its founder on your masthead, I became very excited. I knew him, you see. I took this photo myself. I have a larger one at home, framed. We were friends, you see, a long time ago. Before the war, and . . . during. Then we lost touch. I pursued my career in Germany and elsewhere, he, so it seems, came to England. I had no idea. Eventually, my work and other circumstances caused me to move here, but it wasn't until I came across your journal that I understood that Franz and I had been living in the same city – London – without being aware of it!'

He seemed to have exhausted himself, but, no, there was more.

'I believe I have misled you a little, and I am sorry, Natasha. I am not a Jew, you see. I am German. But, sometimes, I am mistaken for a Jew, and this makes me happy. I hope you will not reject my donation now. And please,' he added, 'please keep the photograph in your archives. It is of much value to you, I am sure. If I leave it among my papers, it will only end up in a dirty junk shop one day.'

Natasha was speechless, for a change. This was a bit of history with a twist. But she slipped the cheque and the photo in the pocket of her blazer, and smiled at the old man.

'I . . . I will explain this to the trustees. They might want to get in touch with you. Would that be OK?'

'Of course. But I would like it better if *you* came to talk to me one day. I could tell you so much about Franz.'

Natasha nodded, as politely as she could. But the truth was, she wasn't interested. She never met Held, so why should she care? Having to deal with his surviving myth and compete with his past achievements was enough of a hassle.

'The picture I gave you was taken during the war. In Theresienstadt. Ah, here's my cab. Well, goodbye, Natasha. We shall see each other soon, yes?'

She nodded again, a little more vigorously this time. As far as she knew, Held had spent the war in England. Not in a concentration camp.

5 FSQ

Tim turned, slowly, into a narrow, claustrophobic alley just off Gray's Inn Road. It seemed miraculously far away from the main road's mad racket, but the stillness was eerie rather than pleasant. There was one particularly creepy little corner, almost hidden from sight, which he had to 'visit'. He stepped, gingerly, over a small pile of human excrement and saw, with some relief, that this popular cubbyhole was empty today: he didn't have to confront one of the regulars and talk them out of staying there. The tools of their trade were strewn around on the wet ground: muddy condoms, dirty chocolate wrappers. Sex and drugs. He'd seen them do it. He'd seen a lot during his five years with the 'Force'.

Contrary to what Natasha imagined, Tim did not always spend his working days in the sordid tunnels of the London Underground, hopping on and off crowded trains in search of nasty pickpockets and suicidal passengers. Many of his shifts, like this one, involved patrolling the streets around King's Cross, on foot. Sometimes he criss-crossed London in a squad car, with a partner, waiting for a tantalizing radio command to justify a bit of drama ('any unit, any unit, unconscious female at Victoria . . .'). The siren flashing and howling, mad speed, breathless arrival at the station, only to find and dutifully report 'it's not an unconscious female, it's a drunk, asleep on a platform, over . . .'. Some – though not many – of his mates were quite pleased to be mistaken for metro cops, their uniforms ('costumes,' as Natasha liked to tease him) being almost the same. But Tim was immensely proud to be a British Transport policeman. He had worked as a gardener, a carpenter and a postman, and had been good at all these jobs, but they left him with a feeling of deep boredom from about two in the afternoon. His father had been a highly respected superintendent at a tough east London police department, a rank he had come to naturally after a distinguished career in the military. He was retired now, but still an impressively robust, rugged man who never understood why his son made do with looking after other people's suburban lawns or delivering their mail. Didn't Tim know there was more to life than being safe? His son's stint as a carpenter left him particularly baffled: 'Jesus, Tim, that's the kind of thing you do on the side, we all do! A son of mine could put himself out a little more!'

These admonitory speeches were usually administered over a pint at the Whale & Gale, their local pub – well out of Tim's mother's earshot. Parker senior knew full well that Tim had been *forbidden* to follow in his father's footsteps: *she* had prevented it, without saying a word. Elizabeth Parker had always resented, even despised, her husband's dedication, his willingness to sacrifice everything, even his life, for the so-called common good – though not necessarily for his own family. Her always tired face was like a dark cloud, heavy with accumulated suffering. Growing up, Tim loved to boast about his father, but the truth was, he and his mother hardly ever saw him. And when he was old enough, she made sure he understood that if he ever married, his wife would be just as miserable and lonely as his mother had been, if he chose his father's vocation. Tim was no fighter. He could only please one of his parents, never both. He chose to appease his mother, having convinced himself that she understood him better than anyone. His boredom, he used to think, was a small price to pay for his mother's peace of mind, and for his own. As for his father's needling comments, well, he could live with those, no problem. He always had.

But he hadn't counted on a little epiphany which, one day, illuminated his life like a distant but powerful flash of lightning. He was standing on the slowly descending escalator at King's Cross tube station, watching the gently swaying, multicoloured wave of faces and bodies across from him, on the escalator moving upwards. A spirited South American rhythm emanated from below, and Tim had just decided he would reward the drummer with all the change in his pocket, when this urban idyll was suddenly cut short by a horrific slow-motion tableau: a woman holding a small child in her arms fainted and fell backwards, forcing the long row of people standing under her to collapse as well, like live dominoes. Someone tried to stop the escalator, in vain. There was chaos, panic, screams, until two uniformed men and one woman took control. Their calm voices and polite but determined instructions sent superfluous onlookers away from the scene of the accident. Ambulance workers were efficiently directed towards the injured. Tim's instinct had been to get involved and help, but the policewoman asked him to please move on. Within an unbelievably short period of time, things were back to normal. Even the drumming resumed.

Walking towards his platform, it had suddenly dawned on him that the uniformed men and woman were from the British Transport Police. Their work would have to be a much milder version of his father's supposedly dangerous job, yet it could never be dull. Tim had always been fascinated with trains, from toy ones to real ones . . . So, there it was: he would try to become a transport policeman. Why hadn't he thought of it before? For a brief moment, he was deliriously happy. Everything fell into place: for the first time, he could see how easy it would be to reconcile his parents' clashing expectations of him with his own dreams. But his next thought was tinged with sudden fear: would he be eligible?

As it turned out, twenty-three-year-old Tim Parker was model British Transport Police material. His physical strength helped him through basic training, and the first two years of learning the ropes under the firm guidance of an experienced tutor constable were more fun than he had ever had in his life. He loved seeing his mates every day, being a part of a team. He knew he had been accepted by them when he was awarded a nickname: Rosy Parker, for his initial shyness and frequent blushing. The nickname had been created by loud-mouthed, irreverent PC Ian Jones, who was soon to become his best pal and partner. Tim learned fast. He knew he was good at this stuff, all of it. He loved walking the beats at any time of day and night, and was ingenious at answering any number of FSQs (Fucking Stupid Questions) from passers-by with a genuine smile. He was just as good at conversing with toms and punters and pushers. He was particularly impressive at the gory work – accidents, violent attacks. He could even keep an immaculate little notebook, neatly recording every detail in its pre-numbered pages. One day, he hoped to make it into the CID and maybe, just maybe, get involved in some detective work as well.

His mother's prophecy had not come true: Tim had ended up with a wife who loved his police work, and couldn't get enough of his stories about what happened each day. In fact, he had to spice them up quite a bit to make his 'adventurous' career as a transport officer sound more exciting than it really was. Natasha actually read the *Police Review*, and, if he left it lying about, even his notebook. Then she would ask him strange questions, like: 'When you ejected the female vagrant from the Camden tube station, as you state here on page seven, did you make sure she had somewhere to go? Did you notice what she was wearing? Was she young or old? Did she have lots of plastic bags, and did you search through them? Did she have something to read? If she had asked you, would you have bought her a book? And, by the way, why did you eject her? Was she doing anything offensive? Did she smell? Do you believe in capital punishment?'

After each question, Tim would say 'FSQ' with a smile, and never answer any of them. But Natasha's interest in his job flattered him. It was another reason why, when he put on his uniform every day, he felt on top of the world. He felt great even when he was a little scared, like now. The alleyway was completely deserted. It was only two in the afternoon, too early for any serious action, and too late for whatever went on here last night.

Walking back towards King's Cross – he had to cover a couple of platforms at St Pancras and some bushes behind a car park – his radio came alive: 'Urgent message for officer Rosy Parker. You are wanted at home as per a previous agreement with your lovely wife, over.'

'Right, Ian, that's enough. You bored or something?'

'No, I mean it. No joke. She phoned to say you had to get Erica from a party. Has your day gone tits up? You want me to chip in? If you're busy, I'll gladly baby-sit and be there for your wife when she gets home. Some Ruby Rose deal, she said . . .'

Ah, yes, Tim remembered. Natasha had an annoying habit of leaving personal messages with his mates, no matter how often he told her they would only serve as fodder for more cruel jokes. Especially anything to do with *The Nose.* Why couldn't she work for a magazine with a normal name?

'Shut up, mate. We're fine. Anyway, where *are* you? I was waiting for you.'

'Tell you all about it. Over and OUT.'

Ian loved to shout his 'OUT's, and everything else. His superior officers were in awe of fearless PC Jones who saw right through all their godlike airs and the complex backstabbing that seemed to be a natural part of their daily routine. Tim tried to ignore the 'them' and 'us' structure that came with the police territory; the class system, as strong here as anywhere else, didn't bother him. But Ian was a rebel, always willing to stick his strong neck out, and if he thought that a chief superintendent's idea of how to organize a particular job was an LOB (Load of Bollocks), he would tell him so.

Tim worried that Ian, his favourite, if difficult, partner, would not last, not at the speed he was going. He was pretty sure he knew why he had been left waiting: Jones's fierceness and slightly menacing good looks invariably led to erotic encounters, of varying intensity, with attractive female victims he had helped in his capacity as British Transport officer. Tourists were especially spellbound by him. In fact, two of them had eventually become his wives – but that was some time ago.

Divorces were common among his mates. They were an over-stressed and oversexed group of people, at least the males. Tim wasn't sure about his female colleagues – maybe it was the same story. He thought about his own marriage: it was true that he had met his wife in exactly the same way Ian collected his women. Would they last? He wasn't sure. He thought they had a good life together. But . . .

Last night, Tim had admired the reflection of their two naked bodies in the huge mirror facing their bed (a kinky wedding gift from his colleagues): they looked good together, his long, strong shape next to her curled-up ball of soft curves, his dark, short-cropped head almost covered by the heavy curtain of her straight blonde hair. He wasn't sure why he'd suddenly said out loud what he was thinking at that moment – possibly because it had occurred to him before, or because he'd received more than his usual share of teasing at work that day, this time about his wife's origin.

'Natasha, are you absolutely sure you're Jewish?' he'd said, and regretted it the minute the words left his stupid mouth.

He was lucky; she was already half asleep. Maybe she didn't hear . . . . But she opened her eyes just a bit, and mumbled: 'Now that, Tim, is what I call a Fucking Stupid Question. F – S – Q. I mean, would I be editing a Jewish magazine if I wasn't? Q – E – D. And, by the way, your daughter is Jewish.'

Then she curled up even tighter into his armpit, and was now really asleep. Tim, on the other hand, was suddenly wide awake. It had never really occurred to him until that moment that he was the father of a Jewish child. What the hell did that mean?

Now, on his way back to the base, he thought, isn't life weird. You meet a woman who floors you with her incredible description of some sick geezer's superhuman dick, and before you know it, you are the father of that woman's Jewish child. Jesus.

6 Life Insurance From Hitler

Erica and Tim were both asleep by the time Natasha got home from her peculiar dinner with Ludwig Hoffmann, the crisp cheque still burning a hole in the deep pocket of her black velvet blazer. She gave each a noiseless peck on the cheek, inhaling Erica's delicious, clean fragrance and Tim's equally clean yet tangy scent. They mustn't wake up: it was almost midnight, and she could now look forward to several hours' work at her computer, hopefully uninterrupted. She changed into her pyjamas, made herself a strong cup of coffee and settled down in the dining room, one messy corner of which doubled as her office.

The computer and internet connection had been supplied by the magazine, though not right away: it had taken several long meetings with the trustees to discuss the pros and cons of using 'that kind of technology'. Held had managed without it, and it wasn't all that long ago; why change anything? What was wrong with delivering typewritten and sometimes even handwritten manuscripts to the printers, and doing the paste-up manually? When Natasha discovered that *The Nose* was put together in this antiquated manner, she informed the trustees that this had to change, 'as of today'. She did have a lot of admiration for the old-fashioned art of publishing, but she said it would be crazy to ignore the fact that these were the nineties. She had made enquiries, she said, and even the *Police Review* was published 'properly'. Yes, said the trustees, but Held . . . FUCK HELD, Natasha screamed inside her head, but out loud she had only said, quite calmly: 'Well, Held is dead.'

She thought they'd fire her on the spot – she had already noticed that the cult of Franz Held, the man who had created *The Nose* in the fifties, was still going strong. Then it occurred to her to add: 'If he were alive today, he'd be introducing those changes himself. I can tell, from the old issues of the magazine I've been studying, that he was a man of considerable vision.' 'Hear, hear,' chirped Yvette Moskowitz. She actually *chirped*.

This had been Natasha's first application of what she began to refer to as 'LOB strategy', in imitation of her husband's professional slang. It worked; amazingly, the strongest support for her ambition to modernize the magazine's production process came from Sidney Sussman himself, who had recently acquired a computer for his pet shop business, and another one for the paperwork he did for various charities. In fact, as he had taken a quick course in desktop publishing, he had volunteered to help Natasha with the layout and the graphics. She had turned this down, of course, as she had done with all of his offers of 'help' so far. One day she would have to let him do something, she thought, but it would have to be something innocuous, well outside of what she considered her professional domain. Maybe, she thought with a smirk, he could be her designated driver . . . Natasha didn't have a car, and Sussman owned a big, flashy red Mercedes. He had once given her a lift to one of the meetings; it felt like riding in a soft, soundproof bubble. But, ultimately, Sussman had not been the generous donor of Natasha's expensive computer. It was sent, mysteriously, by the Weintraub brothers, the two trustees who never attended any meetings and in whose existence Natasha had – almost – ceased to believe. Whoever they were, they had made her life infinitely easier by giving her this little toy . . .

Before she did any serious work, she always checked her e-mail – her private e-mail and the magazine's. Tonight, there were no personal notes, not even from her brother, but the 'letter box' for *The Nose* was bursting: thirty-two messages. The first one was from an Edith Heller of somewhere in the States who addressed Natasha as Dr Kaplan. Her formal note requesting rates and references had an attachment – several close-up photographs of the woman's nose, taken from different angles. Natasha giggled as she examined the magnificent beak, using her wonderful new graphics software to zero in on the slightly obscene area around the wide open, hairy nostrils. Great, now I'm surfing the net for nasal pornography, she thought, and sent the poor woman a brief note back explaining her error: NatashaKaplan@the.nose.mailmerge.co.uk was not the e-mail address of a British plastic surgeon. She couldn't help adding: 'Sorry to be personal, but, for what it's worth – I'd leave it be. Your nose has a lot of character.'

Natasha mused about the wonderful and strange intimacy of e-mail, until she opened the next thirty messages. They were from someone who called himself John White. Each one read, 'Your impure publication will soon cease to exist, like the rest of your impure race. See my website (www.whitewhitewhite-global.net) for details. Merry Christmas, John White.' Natasha did not delete these. On the contrary: she saved them in a special folder she called 'FILTH'. Its volume was growing slowly but steadily.

The last e-mail was from NettySurvivor@aom.com. She wrote:

Ms Kaplan

I have SURVIVED. You ask: How? I ask: Does it matter? Maybe I was in a camp. Maybe in a cupboard. Under the stairs. In a convent. In a forest. A cellar. An attic. Who cares? Maybe it wasn't me, maybe it was my mother. The only thing I want to say to the world TODAY is this: if I spent the war hiding in a cupboard, what happened to my EXCRETA? Please confront your readers with this question.
My identity shall remain unknown.

Yours,

Netty Survivor

Help, thought Natasha. Madness everywhere. She wasn't sure what to do with this one: answer it, file it, delete it? With a heavy heart she decided to do the latter. Then she changed her mind and forwarded it to Philip. He might know how to handle that sort of stuff.

Next to amazon.com, to check whether her book was still selling. Last time she looked (about a week ago) her sales rank was 365,782 – very, very poor. That must have been a fluke: only a month before that, it had reached a respectable 45,963. Natasha waited for the colourful page featuring her racy book jacket to fill her computer screen, and stared at the figures: today, the paperback edition of *Mrs Cohen's Last Supper* had a sales rank of 2,001!!! Pretty good, but it did not make sense. She scrolled down and saw another surprising new detail: twenty-two customers had submitted reviews of her book. Last week, there had been none. Her average customer rating was only one star out of five. Intrigued, she began to read the reviews, and found that they sounded surprisingly similar, in spite of the fact that they had been sent from different places ('a reader from Houston, Texas', 'a reader from Toronto, Canada', 'a reader from Hawthorne, New York' . . .) Under a headline screaming 'I FELT CHEATED!!!' or 'MISLEADING TITLE, DON'T BUY THIS BOOK!', the readers complained about how her mystery novel was not at all what they had expected: 'I bought this book because I liked the idea of a Mrs Cohen having her last supper, but found that she was just another Jew victim.' 'I was looking forward to reading about a dead Mrs Cohen. But this book is about finding and punishing her murderer. Disappointing and cheap. Dropped it in a garbage can at Penn Station.'

Natasha scrolled up a little and read that 'customers who bought this title by Natasha Weiss' also bought: *Mein Kampf* by Adolf Hitler, *International Jew* by Henry Ford, *The Communist Manifesto* by Karl Marx, and *The Protocols of the Elders of Zion*. Hence, by amazon.com logic, 'if you like Natasha's book you will also like *these* . . .'

She clicked on *Mein Kampf*. Hitler's sales rank was significantly better than her own – and better than that of most other books for that matter – 1,001. And he had 69 customer reviews (average number of stars: 4).

Natasha leaned forward (she hated wearing glasses, even when she was on her own) and began to read them. Some of the reviews called Hitler a misunderstood genius and heaped scorn on his detractors.

Others thanked the book for giving their life new meaning. Only a few (not many) described *Mein Kampf* as boring and/or dangerous. Most didn't seem to be aware of its place in the history of this century. History: there it was, again. It seemed to follow her everywhere. Did history, too, come with her job, like the long nights at the computer, the endless, endless meetings with the tireless trustees and the mercenary pursuit of sad sugar daddies?

She had not counted on getting *involved* in any of this when she'd applied for the editorship. She loved books and magazines and had thought it would be fun to try her hand at editing – and it was, when she was free to do just that. But most of her time was eaten up with . . . well, resisting *The Nose* and preventing it from taking over her life.

But it wasn't all bad. Hoffmann's cheque, for example: she couldn't wait to tell Sussman et al. and watch them *gasp* when she revealed the donor's identity. She figured they'd need six or seven meetings to decide what to do about it. And then there was the juicy matter of that lucrative ad she had mentioned at the last meeting. The artwork had arrived that morning, and it turned out that Corner Press was a small publisher specializing, as it turned out, in politically correct exotic erotica. Natasha was curious to see the trustees' response to the photograph advertising a book entitled *First Love, then Peace in the Middle East*. It featured a Semitic-looking nude couple seated between the humps of a camel, surrounded by a bleak desert landscape.

It would be good to talk to Philip about all this. But he was somewhere in California, on a short holiday with his new girlfriend. So she dialled her parents' number instead, knowing that her mother would answer at this time of day. Sam Kaplan would be in the park, walking their cat, as he did every day, his work schedule permitting.

'Mom, it's me. How—'

'Natasha. Darling. I'm so happy you called.'

Her voice doesn't age, thought Natasha, still crisp and serious and lovely.

'Is everything OK?'

'Yes. Absolutely. Your father is trying a new, silk leash for the cat, he thinks the old cotton one depressed her. He is taking a course in feline psychology.'

'Mom . . . I don't want to hear about the cat. How about you?'

'I'll tell you the truth. I don't know what to do with myself. Daddy is planning another film, but, frankly, I think we're both past it. At least I am. You know what I've been thinking, Natashka?'

Natasha's ears perked up. Her mother never used the tender Czech diminutive of her name unless she was about to say something of great importance.

'What?'

'I've been a shitty grandmother.'

'Mom, are you drunk?'

'No, darling, you know I never drink. Well . . . hardly ever. How old is Eritchka? Three, four?'

'She's almost eight, Mom.'

'You see! That's exactly what I mean. I don't even know her age. We haven't seen her for *years*!!'

'You saw her last summer, remember? I came in August . . .'

'Well, maybe . . . But that's not enough. Natashka, I've made up my mind: I want to be a proper grandma. *And* a proper mother, and mother-in-law! That's why I was going to call you myself. I'm coming. To London. But I don't want to be a tourist. I'll rent a flat – is that what you call them – or a room, somewhere near you kids, and I'll live there for as long as I'll feel like it. You do need my help, don't you, Natashka? You have the magazine now and with Tim's shifts . . .'

Natasha was silent. Then she said, 'Sure, Mom, we'd love it. But you can't get away with this.'

'With what?'

'Not telling me. The real reason, I mean. Why are you coming?'

'I told you, Natashka. Your father is working on a film. About the cat, working title *Chat Noir*. I was supposed to be in it, as the cat's sex slave, but I rebelled and so—'

Natasha cut in, with a smile which she knew could be *heard* on the other side of the Atlantic: 'Oh, come *on*. You used to be a better actress than this . . .'

Alice laughed. 'OK,' she said. 'I might as well tell you, you'll find out anyway, it's bound to be all over the papers . . . But don't ask me any questions, OK? I'm really coming to London because I am to be a witness at a trial. Have you heard of Annmarie Goetz?'

'Oh my God. Mom. What's your connection with that—'

'Darling, I said: no questions. I mean it.' Suddenly her voice had that impenetrable hardness again. Pure steel.

Natasha sighed. 'I'll look for a place for you,' she said.

'Don't worry about a thing. I've already found something, through an ad in the *London Review of Books*.'

'You read the—'

'You have no *idea* what I've been reading. I'll tell you all about it. I've been reading your magazine, as well! I never looked at it before, not properly, I mean, but now I read it cover to cover. I have some comments and suggestions, especially about your editorials – a bit long-winded, darling – but let's talk about it when I get there. Your masthead is interesting, by the way.'

'Masthead?' Natasha's end of the conversation was beginning to sound decidedly idiotic. All she could do was echo her mother's amazing statements.

'Yes, baby, you know, all the important names in your magazine. You have so many trustees! Any attractive men among them? You know, in case I get bored in London . . .'

'Mom!!'

'Just kidding, darling, just kidding. But you know, seriously now: the retired founding editor, Franz Held: what's he like? An interesting old man? I'm picturing a sprightly . . .'

'He's not retired. He's dead.'

There was a long silence. Too long, considering the upbeat – and long-distance – nature of the call.

'Mom? You there?'

'Are you sure?'

'What do you mean, am I sure? Of course I'm sure. Anyway, what—'

'Natashka, it's late, how come you're up at this hour? Go to sleep, darling. I'll be in touch when my travel plans are ready. Good night, sweetie.'

'Good night—' but her mother had already hung up. Far from being sleepy, Natasha was fully alert now. She remembered the old photograph Hoffmann had given her, of young Franz Held. Was her mother, of all people, about to join the huge circle of his admirers?

The computer was still on, but Natasha could not possibly concentrate on any more work. She thought, angrily, about her mother, who had managed to remain so completely secretive. As always. But this time, it wouldn't be for long – the trial was about to become a major public event. So why couldn't she have told Natasha what it was all about? What possible connection could there be between Alice and this Annmarie Goetz, the film-maker once celebrated by the Nazis, who, as had recently been discovered, had 'borrowed' Jewish men, women and children (all inmates of the Theresienstadt concentration camp near Prague) to play extras in an artistic feature film? They had been used for gruesome scenes which were enhanced by their authentic – their *real* – deaths. Natasha suppressed the powerful urge to redial her mother's number, and decided to go to bed.

Compulsively, she checked her e-mail one last time. There was just one note entitled 'SUBMISSION'. It came from Sidney Sussman.

Dear Natasha

As you and I are the only fully computerized members of the small extended family that is The Nose, *I've decided to e-mail you this little idea for an article. I think it would be interesting to conduct a survey among both Jews and non-Jews in this country, to see how they would answer the following question: 'Would you buy life insurance from Hitler?' I believe that a scientific evaluation of the answers we would receive will shed some light on a number of hugely important issues. I am sure I don't need to elaborate (although I would be prepared to do so, if you wish). I would be quite happy to undertake this myself, both the survey and the analysis of the results. I have already prepared a preliminary plan of action, and invested in some excellent software to help me with the statistics, etc. My survey would cover a very broad cross-section of the British population. I am looking forward to your speedy reply.'*

Yours,

Sidney S.

P.S. I am sorry to bring this up, but you have, once again, overspent your budget for postage and stationery by £12.39. Must you buy quite so many stamps?

Natasha's decision was instant. She answered immediately:

Dear Sidney

Excellent, inspired idea. Very important question. Go ahead. It will be an enormous task, but I rely on your thoroughness. Don't rush it, take your time. Our readers will thank you for it.

Best wishes,

Natasha

She knew that he would be waiting by his computer, hoping for a quick reply. He will not believe his luck.

She also knew that he would not mention the stamps again, not for a while.

When she finally climbed into bed and adjusted Tim's shoulder to make a cradle for her head, he woke up, briefly, and held her tight.

'Tim.'

'Hm.'

'Would you buy life insurance from Hitler?'

'Don't be silly. You know we can't afford it,' he mumbled.

As she drifted off to sleep, Natasha had a big smile on her face. At least here, in her own bed, she was safe from all that history crap.

7 Lice

Tim was long gone and his half of the bed cold by the time Natasha woke up. When he had a morning shift, like today, he was up at 4.15 and out of the house by a quarter to five. And she wouldn't see him in the evening, either – she had to meet with the trustees to discuss Hoffmann's contribution to *The Nose,* and that ad . . . Erica would spend the evening and possibly the night at her grandparents' house, just round the corner.

It was a handy arrangement. Natasha loved her in-laws. She thought her father-in-law was still a very good-looking man, and she could easily see Tim in him – the broad, muscular build and the roughly chiselled, strong features. And the smile – they both beamed when they smiled, though Parker senior never blushed. Their voices were similar too – a rich, mellow baritone, which could, very rarely, turn into a surprisingly loud bark of anger. But Tim had his mother's unusual, wide-set green eyes, which had been the main reason why Natasha had not been able to concentrate on recalling the eye colour of that flasher she was supposed to be describing to the dazzling young policeman . . .

Tim's taciturn mother was still a mystery to Natasha – they had a good relationship, she thought, without ever really talking about anything personal. When Tim's parents first met Natasha's parents, at the simple wedding that had been organized and celebrated at high speed and without much drama, Natasha had been afraid that the New York branch would – with some justice – be perceived as loud and insane by Tim's family. Well, if they were, it had never been mentioned or hinted at, in all those years she had been married to Tim. Everything was in order – no tensions, no pressures, no jealousies – Natasha's parents didn't even seem to mind that Erica was closer to her English grandparents. This, Natasha suddenly realized, could have been a temporarily and artificially blissful state of affairs, due to the distance between London and New York. But now, with her mother's imminent arrival in London for a longer stay, things could change . . . She didn't want to think about it. It was time to wake up Erica.

'Baby girl, wakey-wakey . . .'

'I've been awake for *hours*! Didn't you see that my eyes were open?'

'Erica, they weren't . . . OK, so you must be ready to hop out of bed!'

'Mum, I don't *hop*, I'm not a rabbit!'

Natasha laughed. She loved Erica's English accent, and the funny, sarcastic things her daughter said. She wondered if her grandparents really understood just how *sharp* this little girl was. She could be both silly and wise, all at once. And delicious, too! She had Tim's eyes and maybe, just maybe, a nascent version of Alice's charm. Natasha was ecstatically happy to be Erica's mother.

She put her arm under Erica's head, cradling it and rocking it.

'That's what I used to do when you were a tiny baby. You used to love it. Do you still love it?'

Erica giggled. She had an amazing giggle, deep and sonorous, like a perfect little tune. Now she really *was* awake.

'I missed you last night,' Natasha said, as she watched Erica struggle with her school uniform: short grey skirt, white turtleneck, navy blue sweatshirt. Thick black tights. She wasn't allowed to help – her daughter was very independent when it came to dressing for school. Actually she was pretty independent in every other way as well . . . 'I'm sorry I was home so late.'

'Where were you?'

'I had to have dinner with an old man.'

'Is he a good friend of yours?'

'No, I only met him last night.'

'Why?'

'Because he said he wanted to give a lot of money to my magazine.'

'Did he?'

'Give me the money? Yes, he did.'

'Oh goody! Can you buy me something? I really need . . .'

'Erica, it's not for me, it's for the magazine. I can't keep it!'

'Too bad.'

Breakfast was a swift affair – a half-eaten toast with butter – and soon they were walking down their long street, at the bottom of which was Erica's primary school, hidden behind a row of high evergreens and a black fence.

'Mum, I forgot to give you this note from Miss Foot.' Erica stopped and fumbled in the depths of her orange schoolbag. 'Here. It's about my lice.'

'Your what?!'

Natasha read the note, which informed her that, sadly, her daughter was found to be infested with headlice, like a great number of her classmates. The child was to be treated accordingly and not allowed back in school until she was free of live lice.

'OK, let's go home,' Natasha said, through clenched teeth. 'You really should have told me or Daddy.'

At moments like these, Natasha hated England. Lice! What a primitive place this was! She had never heard of such things in New York. True, they had cockroaches and she had seen a rat once, but headlice?! There was something medieval about it. Something permanent, too – she knew how hard it was to get rid of them. The conversation among the mothers in the school playground had recently turned to this sensitive topic, and various methods of delousing were discussed with great zeal. So far, Natasha had only half listened, convinced that it could not happen to *her* daughter. Erica's straight, honey-coloured hair was cut in a short bob – hopefully, this meant that she was *not* a lice magnet . . .

Back in their house, Natasha washed Erica's hair and, as she combed through it with a fine-toothed comb, she found disgusting, tiny grey-black insects wriggling their horrible, tiny feet in a desperate attempt to hold on to some fertile ground.

'How many have I got?' Erica asked, matter-of-factly. 'Amy had twenty last week, and Judy had twelve. Mark had one. I need at least five to join the Lice Girls – that's our secret club.'

By the time Natasha had thoroughly combed through all of Erica's hair, they had counted sixteen mature lice, two of whom were actually mating.

'But you still have some nits, and some baby lice I probably missed.'

'I want to keep those as my pets. I don't want you to kill them! That's cruel, Mum! Lice have a right to live, too. How would you feel if someone got rid of me, just because I am a sweet little baby louse? If *you* were my mother louse, I mean.'

'Oh Erica, shut up and get dressed again. Let's dry your hair and I'll take you back, with a note for Miss Foot. We'll have to do this every day from now on!'

Walking down the street towards the school for the second time that morning, Natasha remembered: 'Your New York grandma will be coming soon. And this time, she wants to live in London for a while, so we'll see her a lot.'

Erica didn't say anything, but Natasha could see that she was excited.

'Remember, grandma is picking you up from school today.'

'Grandma Alice? Today??' squealed Erica.

'No, she's not here yet. Grandma Beth.'

'Oh. OK. Does she have to take care of my lice?'

'No, no, I'll do it tomorrow. And you know what, baby? Let's not tell her about it. She might not want you in her house, in case she might get them. So try not to scratch.'

'Sure, Mum.' And she disappeared inside the school gate. Natasha watched her go in and turned back, for the second time that morning. Damn it, she thought. LICE!!! What if she had caught them herself? Her scalp *was* kind of itchy . . .

She decided not to think about it and get on with her work. She had to sift through another bag of mail, delivered to her from the post office box. And she had an editorial to write. What could she say about Jews and crime?

Her phone rang.

'Natasha Kaplan?' said a dry, impersonal male voice.

'Speaking.'

'Julius Weintraub.'

'Oh. We've never . . . It's a pleasure finally to speak to you.'

'Why is it a pleasure? You don't know me.'

Ah, thought Natasha. No LOB with this man. What a relief. 'No, I don't. But I hope . . .'

'I'm calling for two reasons. First, to inform you that my brother and I will attend the meeting tonight. And second, to put my brother on the phone. Just a minute.'

There was a bit of static noise and some muffled voices. Then she heard a voice as dry and impersonal as the first one, though perhaps an octave higher.

'Natasha Kaplan?'

'Yes, Mr—'

'Sidney Weintraub. We will meet tonight. My brother and I wanted to inform you of this, so as to avoid any surprises. We don't like surprises.'

Natasha could only utter, 'I see. Thank you for letting me know.'

'That's fine. One more thing: we approve of you. You are not Franz Held, this cannot be helped. But you have not ruined the magazine. So far. This is why we decided to donate the computer. Are you pleased with it?'

'Yes, thank you,' said Natasha, thinking, if I hear the name Held mentioned one more time I will scream. I will definitely scream. But she was intrigued. The Weintraub brothers were breaking with a long tradition by actually making contact with her. Now she was almost looking forward to tonight.

After that, it was quiet enough for her to read through the mail and to start thinking about her editorial. It had to be ready within two days, so she didn't have much time. *The Nose* employed a free-lance sub-editor, Karl Spitzer, an old, very cultured Berlin Jew whose English sounded almost completely German but was actually perfect. He had worked for the magazine since Held's days and asked for – and received – very little money for his efforts. Natasha admired his ability to rewrite almost completely the very badly written material they were often forced to publish, and enjoyed his perceptive corrections of her own sometimes over-elaborate prose. Spitzer was now waiting only for her editorial; everything else was ready to go to the printing bureau, which now also took care of the layout and graphics, all under the same roof. No more unwieldy galleys and manual paste-up.

The mail bag contained a bunch of manuscripts she had been expecting and only two letters. The first one was handwritten and a little sad because it was actually addressed to her predecessor, by first name:

Dear Franz!

Year after year, issue after issue . . . how much longer? Why did you always publish Charkovsky's stories but not mine? I will send you reminders as long as I live.

Yours,

....

The letter was signed by hand but Natasha could not read the signature. There was no return address, though the stamp had a recent local postmark. Second class.

She sighed and decided that it was clearly time to open a 'HELD' file. Didn't 'Held' mean 'hero' in German? Maybe she was being unfair to the old man – maybe she owed it to him to collect bits of memorabilia about his person. From time to time, the trustees organized a memorial event in his honour. What if she managed to compile a modest but moving profile of Held, based on letters like this one, and other mementoes? One of the old black file boxes stored under her desk was still empty. It would do.

For the moment, the box contained only the handwritten letter and the photograph she had received last night from Hoffmann. But Natasha had a feeling it would soon be filled to capacity, the way things were going. Everyone had something to say about the legendary Held, from praise (Sugarman: 'the man was a poet of ideals') to cautious criticism (Sugarman again: 'he could be harsh'). Well, now, instead of getting impatient with such comments, she would keep careful track of them and store the record of her 'research' in this box.

The second letter was from Nigel Pearce. This time, he sent no poetry, only a note:

To the Editor:
Mrs Natasha Kaplan

Dear Sir!

After many years of submitting my well-meant and heart-felt poems to The Nose, *I have come to the conclusion that poetry is not the right medium for expressing my deep feelings about the Jewish people. I have now decided to turn to science fiction, and am hereby sending you the first fruit of my efforts. My short piece is entitled 'One by One'. As you will see, it deals with the fate of a Jewish egg, frozen by a neo-Nazi doctor for the purpose of future 'genetic' research. I trust you and your readers will appreciate the sad implications. Thank you for your kind consideration.*

Yours very truly,

Nigel Pearce

Natasha got up and stretched, slowly, from her toes to the tips of her fingers, almost reaching the ceiling. She could feel every dormant muscle which had become sleepy and lazy ever since her life had begun revolving around her computer and her telephone. She needed exercise, badly, but when did she have time for it?

She dragged her feet to her bedroom and allowed herself the luxury of a very, very brief siesta. Siesta? Her watch told her it was almost three in the afternoon – and she hadn't even had lunch. Forgotten about it. Time seemed to stand still and night hardly differed from day when she was alone with her work. It was only when Erica or Tim or both made her aware that she had to do things with them and for them that she came back to reality. *The Nose* was a bizarre, shadowy universe, consisting of people living and dead, pulling her in so many different directions, sucking her into murky worlds which were completely foreign to her. Natasha often pictured *The Nose* as a maze that had no centre and no exit – in other words, a trap. Her connection with it was, basically, a silly coincidence. And yet . . . she knew, she definitely knew, that she was there for a reason. Natasha was a great believer in coincidences being governed by an underlying, invisible set of rules and patterns which, if deciphered, could ultimately explain everything. Even, or especially, *The Nose.* She'll uncover that hidden meaning, she decided, and then get out.

She looked up and saw herself in the oversized mirror by their bed. She had never liked it, but didn't say anything to Tim; the huge and wildly symbolic wedding gift from his mates had made him very happy. But sometimes, it was interesting to see herself – and Tim – from that startling vantage point; she was the proverbial fly on the wall, the bird's eye spying on her own intimacy. Right now, she saw a tired-looking, fully dressed young woman spread across an unmade bed. Natasha made another decision: her long blonde hair (it had only been *this* blonde for a year or so) would have to go. She would try a bob, possibly a reddish-brown one.

She forced herself to slide out of bed, with some difficulty: it was time to get ready for another big meeting at Sussman's pet shop. She felt a numbing exhaustion and boredom deep in her bones just thinking about it. The phone on her side of the bed rang five times before she found the energy to answer it. Her mother didn't notice.

'Natasha my darling, wonderful news. That flat is definitely free. I want to give you the address. How are you and Tim and our wonderful Eritchka?'

What's with those Czech diminutives all of a sudden, Natasha wondered. The answer came fast.

'Natasha, Daddy might come after all. Not right away, I'll be there first, but he wants to join me later. He is very interested in meeting some film people in London, and the ICA might do a retrospective of his – of our – old films . . .'

'Isn't he coming to see me? *Us*? His granddaughter?'

'Of course darling, why do you sound so upset? Is something wrong? You know you can tell me every—'

'Mom, Erica has lice,' Natasha interrupted her mother's breathless speech.

'What did you say?'

'I said my daughter has got lice. Headlice. Disgusting little insects crawling in her hair and it makes me *sick*!!! So if you want to know how I am, I'm terrible!'

'Darling, you're not crying, are you?'

'Yes I am!!' She was. In fact, Natasha was sobbing now, the tears running in hot little streams down her cheeks.

Her mother's voice suddenly changed. Its honeyed timbre gave way to a harsher edge.

'Listen to me, little girl,' she said almost sharply. 'Are you sure you're talking about *head*lice? You don't mean lice, you know, the kind that lives on the body, in your clothes?'

'No, Mom, 'course not. But why does it matter . . .'

'Headlice – that's nothing. Piece of cake. I'll tell you what to do. Listen carefully.'

And Alice Kaplan proceeded to explain to her daughter, in astonishing detail, how to tackle the pest that had invaded little Erica's scalp and hair.

'OK, honey? You got all that?'

'Yeah, I got it.' Natasha's tears had miraculously dried up while she had been listening to her mother's professional-sounding expertise.

'Mom. You're a licemeister. How come? I never had any. Or did I? I don't remember.'

'Oh, never mind. I want to know why you were *really* crying.'

Natasha wanted to scream: Because you never tell me *anything*. Because I don't know who you are, not really, or what's in your past that can make you any kind of witness at a Nazi war criminal's trial. But she only said, 'I really have to go now. I'm late for a meeting. So when are you coming?'

Natasha heard her mother sigh.

'Listen baby, when I get there, you and I will have a nice long talk, OK?'

'OK. Bye, Mom.'

On her way to the meeting (twenty minutes on a bus bound for Finchley), Natasha couldn't shake the thought that this had been the closest she had ever come to having what she considered a 'standard' mother-daughter conversation. And she had absolutely no idea why she had suddenly burst out crying. It was definitely *not* because of the lice.

8 Big Trains, Little Trains

'Mum, it's Tim. Is Erica with you?'

'Of course she is, love. I picked her up from school and she's had her tea and now we're watching a bit of telly. Natasha said that was OK. Isn't it?'

'Oh sure, that's fine. Can you put her on the phone please?'

'Hello Daddy. Where are you?'

'I'm working, sweetie. Actually, I just finished my shift. Can you hear the noise? That's . . .' Tim hesitated.

'I know. You're in a pub. You and your friends.'

Tim laughed. 'Well, actually, I'm standing just in front of it. How did you know?'

'Because it's Thursday night, Daddy. You always go to this pub on Thursday nights. It's called the White Horse, right? See, I knew it. Are you getting d-runk?'

For some reason, Erica always pronounced 'drunk' with delayed emphasis on the second consonant. It was a word she was in awe of, possibly because she didn't *quite* know what it meant. She had heard her father's stories about 'the drunks' he had to deal with every day on the 'big trains' (the railway) and the 'little trains' (the tube), and her friend Amy sometimes talked about her mummy 'getting drunk' and 'sleeping it off'. This had made Erica wonder whether her own mummy, who also liked to sleep a lot during the day, wasn't 'a drunk' as well. But her parents had reassured her that Mummy only slept in the daytime because she sometimes had to work late at night. Still, what if her Mummy drank whisky or beer while she was at her computer? She had once sniffed the contents of her mother's mug, but it had only smelt of old, yukky coffee, the kind she could sometimes smell on her teacher's breath after lunch-break.

Erica always protested that her father didn't have to use that baby language with her – why didn't he just say 'tube' instead of 'little train'? Tim had explained that he wasn't saying it that way because of her, that was just how he and the other transport policemen always talked. Still, Erica wished that her father would treat her less like a baby and more like a grown-up. She knew he didn't have a clue what sort of thoughts went through her mind. They weren't baby thoughts, that's for sure. Sometimes she worried about the world in her head, especially her very strange dreams – where did they come from? Daddy was no use, you couldn't talk to him about dreams. Mum was better – in fact, she loved it when Erica remembered something that didn't make any sense, or woke up because she was afraid. When that happened, Mum always stayed with her and they cuddled and talked forever, until the twisted images in her head didn't seem silly or scary at all. With Mum's help, they became adventure stories, with a beginning, a middle and an end, and Erica would always be the amazing hero to whom it had all happened. Actually, Mum liked to leave those stories a bit unfinished, and say 'And now, if you go back to sleep, you'll find out what happened in the end.' Her mum was fun. But Daddy . . . Daddy was . . . she couldn't describe what he was like. No one would believe her if she told them that she thought of her father as a tree, or a mountain. Really big and strong and solid. If Mum died . . . Erica was always thinking about what her life would be like if her parents died. If Mum died, Erica would make up a new one. It wouldn't be hard at all, she would have a mum in her head and she could talk to her and be with her inside. Daddy wasn't inside her head at all; she couldn't imagine him if he didn't exist. So if Daddy died, Erica knew *she* would have to die, too. She didn't really know what dying meant; maybe it was like disappearing under a giant drop of liquid white-out.

'How was school?'

'Horrible. Daddy, it's *school*!'

'You'll spend the night at your grandparents, and I'll see you tomorrow, all right?'

'Fine. Can I go back to watch *Neighbours*?'

'Bye, baby. You know I love you.'

'OK, Daddy, whatever. I mean, I love you too.'

She was gone. I miss her so much it hurts, Tim realized as he stood outside leaning against the wall of the White Horse, his head almost touching the entanglement of plants overflowing the sides of a heavy hanging basket, still clutching his mobile like a lifeline to his home. I never see her, I never see Natasha, what sort of life was this for a family? It wasn't so bad before Natasha started working herself, but now, with her insane and unpredictable schedule, their paths never seemed to intersect. Maybe his mother had been right after all and he should go back to being a gardener or something . . .

'Hey, Tim. Talking to a boyfriend? I heard you!'

Ian had crept up on him, noiselessly, which was no mean feat for a guy his size.

'My daughter, you idiot.'

'You sure?'

'Yeah, I'm sure.' Ian was clearly in the mood to bother Tim with his 'jokes'. But given Tim's strangely maudlin frame of mind, he wasn't likely to get very far.

'Come on, Tim, I know you're gay, just admit it. You can tell me, I'm your mate.'

'Oh shut up, Ian, I'm not gay.'

'Sure you are. Don't fight it, just come out with it . . .'

'But I'm not!'

'I *know* you are.'

'How do you know?'

'I saw you fuck a man. In Wicklow Street.'

Tim smiled. Now he knew what was going on.

'Oh. OK then, fair enough,' he said, with a laugh. 'That's evidence.' This was an old routine he and Ian had developed on one of their boring drives around London: how to make anybody confess to anything – all you had to do was put words in their mouth or convince them they had been *seen* doing the 'crime'. They called the game 'That's Evidence' and if you were forced to pronounce those words, you lost.

The laughter that followed his last remark was too powerful to have come from Ian alone. Everybody else had been hiding somewhere in the vicinity, pints in hand, listening in. How much had they overheard? Tim wasn't proud of his soft side. Not when he was wearing a British Transport policeman's uniform.

Red-haired PC Georgina West, also known as Red George, snuggled up to Tim: 'It's all right, give us a hug. You're the only one here with a heart. How's your American wife?'

Tim allowed himself a stiff embrace and did not answer. But Ian did.

'She's hot stuff, George, don't even try to compete. Tim's Yankee lady is not bad at all for a female skid. Get it? Female skid? Yankee Yid?' He laughed heartily at his own crack and did not see Tim's right fist until it came so close to his nose he could smell the sweat on his mate's white knuckles. But it stopped there before delivering what would have been a devastating blow, because Tim had heard the quickly whispered apology: 'Sorry, sorry pal, stupid joke, didn't mean it. Have a go at me if you want to. No? That's a relief. Phew. Have a pint on me, then.'

They all staggered back inside, laughing and talking, the brief, unpleasant flash of danger having passed, erased from their minds. Not from Tim's mind, though. This was not the first time Ian had voiced something of the sort, something he felt he had to defend himself – and Natasha – against. He always did so and never left Ian or anyone else in any doubt as to how far they could go in teasing him about his, by his mates' standards, unconventional marriage. But the problem with countering their sometimes gentle, sometimes lethal verbal blows was that Tim could see, exactly, why he *had* to be the object of their harassing remarks. He often thought those very same thoughts himself, if not about his and Natasha's situation, then about others.

Ever since the British press managed to sensitize the police to the idea that it was perceived by the public as racist, Tim noticed that his superiors, even at the BTP, had become aware of the need to counteract that bad image. What it really amounted to was a hell of a lot of extra paperwork: any encounter in the line of duty which could be interpreted or construed as mistreating a member of any ethnic minority had to be paid special attention to. Tim was not aware of having ever been guilty of an overtly racist attitude, at least not in his work. But he knew he *was* guilty of stereotyping people along racial lines (who wasn't?!) and didn't have a problem with using racist slang, just like everybody else. Rajvanis, nigels, jam spoons, shvartzes, four-by-twos . . . It was Natasha who had told him that shvartzes was, in fact, a Yiddish word for blacks which had entered cockney slang through east London Jewish vernacular – he'd thought that was kind of funny.

Tim joined Ian, Red George and Ed Walker, an older officer who was in charge of training the dogs they used to sniff out drugs. Tim liked Walker, and his job. Sometimes, he wondered whether he shouldn't show more interest in that sort of work, and maybe retrain. Erica would definitely love him for it, she was crazy about dogs. But he would miss the face-to-face encounters with people who were neither victims nor criminals, just innocent users of London's very tricky public transport system. Tim thought of the railways and the London Underground as poorly disguised death traps. It was faulty, inefficient, and therefore dangerous. But daily, millions of people, men, women, children, descended into the subterranean tunnels and boarded trains looking bored and tired instead of scared. Then, if bad things happened to them, their feelings came floating to the surface – and it almost always turned out that their daily travelling to and from work, school, theatres and restaurants was accompanied by a permanent, disguised mild anxiety or even real fear, not boredom. And for some reason, Tim loved to be the guy who made them feel better and safer than before, so that when they went back to their routine travelling, they would remember his solid, cheerful presence and feel secure. He had this inexplicable need to make everybody feel safe, but it wasn't because he felt so very safe himself: quite the opposite.

'I happen to know,' Ian was proclaiming loudly, 'that our Inspector Clifford is a two-faced bastard. He's trying to get rid of me, I'm too much of a hothead for him. But he won't say so to my mug, so he's playing it both ways. Giving me tricky assignments. Hoping to catch me making a mistake. He *wants* me to mess up. Do I give a fuck? No I don't. At the end of the day, he knows I'm the only guy he can send into dangerous areas. He couldn't have handled that Wembley situation last month without me! But I speak my mind and tell him what I think of him, he doesn't like that. Wanker. Got himself promoted on the basis of you know what? Hot air and a phoney accent! That, and letting his snooty bitch of a wife fuck the chief superintendent.'

Ian was an acknowledged master of CA – character assassination, a popular game among the 'troops'. He was usually right but had few supporters. Tim was his partner but stayed out of his disputes with the powers that be. Truth was, Ian was beginning to annoy him. Ed Walker, who always looked like he was about to say something but rarely did, would be a far better man to have around . . .

'What you guys don't get – especially you, mate,' said Ian, nodding in Tim's direction, 'is that this place needs a revolution.'

Walker suddenly woke up: 'What place? The White Horse? I agree. It should stay open all night, what do you say?'

Everybody cheered and laughed, except Ian. 'You poor bastards, you don't get it. You're all being screwed by the likes of Clifford. Is anyone here hoping to get promoted to his rank? Forget it, pal,' he said to no one in particular. 'You're not the right kind of *material.* Hard work and putting your naked backside on the line day in day out won't help you. This is England. Nothing ever changes and everybody stays where they are.'

'You're wrong,' countered Walker. 'I've been around, and you can take it from me, things don't stay the same around here. They get *worse.*'

More laughter, even from Ian who was too tired to resist the general mood of mindless hilarity.

'Hey,' he said in a conciliatory voice, 'I'm not blind. I can see the good stuff you get with this job.'

Everyone looked at him expectantly.

'You get to fuck all those ladies who just *love* our uniform! Have you noticed how they go for you, especially the ones who've been robbed or something? Tim, come on, tell us how you met your lovely wife. We can't get enough of that story! I keep forgetting – was it a big train or a little train?'

Normally, Tim wouldn't have minded going over the entertaining details of his first encounter with Natasha. But tonight, he didn't feel like hiding his oddly depressed mood behind a mask of crude jollity, just to please his mates. Tonight, he was in the mood to please himself. He hated himself for blushing when he said, as decisively as he could, 'Sorry, I gotta go. My lovely wife is waiting.'

This wasn't strictly true. Natasha was at a meeting which wouldn't be over until much later in the evening, but it had occurred to him that if he left now, he could go home, take a shower, change, and then surprise her by picking her up from that weird pet shop in Finchley. Erica wouldn't be home tonight. Who knows, maybe he and Natasha could even go out for a nice late dinner, or stay home and indulge in that rare pleasure – a bit of sex between two fully awake (and married) adults.

9 Zygmunt Levy-Newman Speaks

Natasha tried very hard to be on time, but she never, ever managed it. It wasn't entirely her fault – she couldn't drive and therefore depended on the terminally unreliable public transport system. Well, she *could* actually drive, but had never bothered making sure that her American licence was valid in this country, as this would have involved a driving test and Natasha couldn't bear being tested, on anything. She would rather endure endless bus, tube or cab journeys. This bus was almost always late. When it finally came, it would meander its way slowly through congested, narrow north London streets and wide, leafy avenues, as if it were taking its tired passengers on a sightseeing tour. She didn't mind; in fact, she enjoyed those unhurried bus rides, because they made her feel like a neutral observer: a tourist. She missed being a temporary visitor in London. Long ago – or so it seemed – she had been just that, and then, almost imperceptibly, she had become a Londoner. Not an American expat, like some of her former friends from the States, with a trendy little place somewhere in Knightsbridge or Notting Hill and a trendy life to go with it. No; through Tim, she had slipped into his lifestyle as if it had been pre-arranged, just for her, as if it were the most predictable thing in the world for a budding New York Jewish intellectual of solidly eccentric ancestry to end up in a placid, uncomplicated suburb of London, where most of her neighbours in similar 1930s semi-detached boxlike pebble-dashed two-storey houses and squat bungalows were charming Greek Cypriot minicab drivers or equally charming bankrupt Irish builders. 'Why do you live where you live?' Yvette Moskowitz (who resided in a 'gynormous', as Erica would call it, mansion off Bishops

Avenue) had once asked her. Because *you* don't, Natasha had wanted to say.

She looked forward to watching Yvette's mannered pirouettes which never failed to transform the meetings of the board of trustees into instalments of a cheap but very entertaining soap opera. Yvette had the disconcerting habit of addressing one man while fixing her hard smile and unblinking, wide-eyed gaze at another. 'Robert, I simply cannot agree to this if we do not form a subcommittee to discuss it further,' she would trill in, say, Lionel Myerson's direction. This allowed her to cover a double amount of territory in one go and was very effective in unsettling the emotions of not two but usually *all* of the trustees, who each expected to be drawn into her sphere of gently flirtatious attention. If she hadn't known it to be a bona fide publication with some serious content, Natasha would have to think of *The Nose* as one big Jewish playground. Playground? Wrong word. Well, maybe not – but if it was a playground, it was not a safe one. It was an old, shabby one, with broken swings and chipped slides. She remembered the sexy advertisement she was about to present to the trustees, and, inhaling sharply through her mouth – the smell of cat food made her nauseous – entered Sidney Sussman's pet shop via a creaky side door leading directly to the 'office'.

It appeared more crowded than usual, and Natasha could immediately see why: the Weintraub brothers had arrived, as promised. For some reason, she had visualized them as identical twins, but they hardly looked like brothers at all. 'Julius Weintraub,' said a booming bass belonging to a diminutive, clean-faced man with a burning bush of bright red curls. 'Sidney Weintraub,' echoed the squeaky tenor of his tall, bulky, dark-haired and heavily bearded sibling. The similarity between them, as Natasha immediately discovered, lay in their peculiar handshake, which consisted in lightly pressing the palm of their hand against Natasha's, without grasping it, their thumb stiffly projected into the air, like an unwanted penis. They looked more vigorous than the other trustees, and seemed to carry enough weight to silence even Sidney Sussman, who was unusually subdued this evening. The precarious balance of power among the members of the trust had clearly been disturbed.

'This is a special meeting indeed,' said Robert Taub, nervously, 'we have Julius and Sidney with us for the first time in . . .'

'For the first time, full stop,' said Julius.

'Yes, quite, thank you.' Robert was not sure how to go on. Natasha thought he might resign his chairmanship there and then, but he resumed:

'Before hearing Natasha's report, Sidney Sussman has a very important announcement to make. Sidney?'

All eyes were on Sussman, who was, at that very moment, munching very loudly on four or five biscuits he had just removed from the paper platter of pastries his wife would usually send along to all meetings. He spoke quickly, his mouth still full of unchewed crumbs.

'The autumn issue cannot go to the printers.' He gave himself time to swallow before continuing. 'Some of you may think Natasha's decision to dedicate an issue of *The Nose* to "Jews and Crime" may have been a little unwise, but let me tell you the problem is far more – *far more*! – serious than that. I'm talking about money, or rather, the lack of it. Put bluntly,' he declared triumphantly, finally returning to his more usual, louder self, 'we have spent this year's budget.'

'*We*?' asked several indignant trustees, in perfect unison.

Sidney was pleased with this response, which he had anticipated. He would respond, in turn, with a list of Natasha's fiscal misdemeanours. The same routine took place at every single meeting. When it happened the first time, Natasha had taken it at face value and felt responsible for the imminent collapse of the magazine which had been entrusted to her by such sage, dedicated men and one woman . . . But now she knew that this was simply an exercise: it was Sidney's way of asserting *his* power, and meant absolutely nothing. Nor did his mathematical calculations, which were more artistic than accurate, and were never questioned by other trustees.

'Sadly, Natasha has overspent her postage and stationery budget,' continued Sidney, 'by £12.39, which is £1.21 more than last month. This represents an annual increase of almost 800 per cent. Although I have repeatedly requested that I be consulted prior to the posting of editorial letters, this has not happened. The result is – bankruptcy. Or something bloody well near it.'

'Sidney,' intervened Yvette while looking intently at Julius Weintraub, 'may I suggest that we form a subcommittee to deal with this recurrent problem?'

'I am Julius,' said Julius Weintraub. How long, thought Natasha, before he, too, would succumb to Yvette's technique of 'confuse and rule'?

'But Sidney, surely even Held had to buy stamps occasionally . . .' said Charles Sugarman, in a conciliatory tone.

'I have a surplus of good, barely used paper and brown envelopes in my dental office, some of them pre-stamped, would that help?' asked Joel Hirsch, in a tremulous voice which betrayed his age rather than any emotion.

Joel, a placid, plump man with a perennially happy round face, had been introduced to the trust many years ago by Sidney Sussman himself, as a 'learned man well-travelled in European culture'. He had recently retired, rather late in life, from a business he liked to be known as 'a dental office'. In fact, Joel had spent many years dealing in multicultural dental waste. This was the stuff dentists extracted from their patients' teeth and sold, based on weight, to a representative of Hirsch D.W. Ltd (usually Joel himself). His job had consisted in travelling to certain European countries collecting these potentially precious amalgams and bringing malodorous bags containing the worst in Europe's teeth back to England, where he sold the purified gold to jewellers. Joel loved to tease his friends, male or female, by informing them that their valuable ring/earring/gold chain was just a recycled filling belonging to Herr Schröder or Signora Rossi. Over time, Natasha had become aware of Joel's role on the trust as the good cop to Sussman's bad cop, as the man who would try to soften his friend's often harsh words and tone of voice by proposing a useless but well-meant solution to the problem in question.

His generous offer to provide recycled stationery was drowned out by a noisy, disorderly debate which now erupted among the trustees, most of whom were anxious to offer their own ideas on how to solve the current money crisis (Baruch Shapiro – 'Don't print any pictures'; Maurice Toledano – 'Make all articles shorter and cut pages from eighty to eighteen'; Yvette – 'A subcommittee, *please*!'; Jonathan

Warhaftig – 'Are there any more biscuits?'). Sidney and Julius Weintraub looked on in amazement, occasionally shaking their heads in synchronized disbelief. Finally, Sidney Sussman raised his voice above the staggering noise level in the room and shouted, enunciating each word slowly and clearly:

'NO!!! NOT THIS TIME! THERE-IS-NO-MONEY-IN-THE-KITTY. NOTHING. NA-DA. *GUR NISHT*!'

Finally, there was silence – but not for long. Yvette, very briefly lost for words, her breath caught in the confines of her white silk blouse, exhaled very loudly and spoke thus: 'Surely, if all our subcommittees make a *conserved* effort, our plans will come to *fruitition* and the problem can be *salvaged*?'

No one ever corrected Yvette's malapropisms, and some of them even found their way into Sussman's minutes of the trust's meetings. Natasha knew that Yvette only said 'fruitition' when she was ready to indulge in creating a major crisis; clearly, the moment had arrived for Natasha to present her own dramatic news. She cleared her throat to control the itch to laugh and, sounding a little more pompous than she had intended, announced: 'Things are not as bad as they seem. Here's a cheque for £50, 000, which I have just received from a Dr Hoffmann. Dr *Ludwig* Hoffmann. He admires the magazine, used to know Franz Held and would like us to improve our printing technique, for example. A *very* generous subscriber . . .'

Natasha placed the cheque, face down, on the rickety table and waited for the trustees' response. It came instantly, in the form of several pairs of hands trying to grab the cheque in order to see, with their own eyes, that this was really true: this time, Natasha seemed to have pulled off the impossible – she had delivered something far more substantial than the usual few hundred quid that tended to be the result of her fund-raising dinners and lunches. FIFTY THOUSAND!!! Sidney Sussman's hand was longer and faster than all the others. He pulled the cheque towards himself, turned it over and examined it for quite a few minutes. Then he said, with some degree of reluctant pleasure in his gruff voice, 'Yes. We're saved. This will take care of things, for a while. But unless we can persuade Natasha's mysterious donor to do this again some time soon, it is nothing but a temporary stop-gap measure.'

With heavy sighs of relief, the trustees broke into happy smiles. Even the Weintraub brothers decided to abandon their grim demeanour and, one after the other, patted Natasha on the back.

Yvette said, 'I, for one, don't even want to *know* what Natasha had to do to . . . Let us be thankful!'

'Hear, hear!' seconded various cheery voices.

This, thought Natasha, was the right moment to complete her report. 'However, there is a catch. Dr Ludwig Hoffmann is German. German, not Jewish. Does it matter?'

'How old?' came the instant, shocked reply from several trustees.

'*Very* old,' said Natasha. 'Old enough to have been *there* and done *that*.'

'Money doesn't stink,' said Maurice.

'Oh yes it does,' said Robert Taub. 'We have a problem. May I have everyone's opinion, please? This is a serious matter.'

There followed a heated debate, in the course of which the Weintraub brothers declared that a Jewish magazine could not receive support from a German benefactor, however generous. Yvette countered that Dr Hoffmann may have been a member of the German resistance, in which case his generous *retribution* would be most welcome. Maurice repeated that money did not stink, especially new German money. Joel Hirsch agreed and said that it was in fact most appropriate for a Jewish magazine to receive help from a German, 'after what they did to us. I bet there is much more where this little cheque came from!' Yvette was suddenly beside herself with excitement. 'Oh my God,' she shrieked, 'if we make a *concerned* effort to target German donors, we could become the richest Jewish magazine in the world!' 'Particularly,' added Baruch Shapiro, with a meaningful glance at Joel, 'if we can establish that some of us are Holocaust survivors.' Baruch was hoping that Joel would pick up from there and chime in with his harrowing personal account, but Joel kept silent, his face stone hard. Malcolm Blaustein said you just couldn't argue with fifty thousand quid, and Lionel Myerson pointed out that the least a guilty German could do was support a bit of

Jewish culture. Charles Sugarman mused, with a deep theatrical frown: 'Aren't we all survivors of the Holocaust?' While everyone's attention was on the passionate debate about the moral acceptability of German money in the hands of a Jewish intellectual enterprise, Jonathan Warhaftig managed to consume the entire remaining supply of butterscotch biscuits. 'I just don't know about this,' said Sidney Sussman, with an uncharacteristic lack of certainty in his voice.

'Thank you all,' said Robert Taub. 'I believe that we have reached a consensus here. I will personally contact Dr Hoffmann and inform him that, although this is a highly irregular situation, we will be happy to accept his cheque, provided his credentials are . . . well . . . clean.'

'You will do nothing of the sort,' said a calm, measured voice Natasha had not heard before, for it belonged to Zygmunt Levy-Newman, the perennially taciturn trustee who never spoke. Until this moment. He had a European accent she could not place, and the very fact that he had spoken caused a stir among the trustees. They became very quiet, like schoolchildren whose boisterous chattiness had been interrupted by the entrance of a strict teacher.

'Natasha,' continued Levy-Newman. 'What we need to do is find out who this man is. You say he was a friend of Held's?'

'That's what he told me.'

'Hard to believe, but why don't you meet him again, and find out more about this Dr Hoffmann? In the meantime, let us hold on to the cheque without cashing it. It can wait.'

'But . . .' began Sussman, and stopped. Everyone knew what he was about to say: what about financing the printing of the current issue?

'I propose,' said Levy-Newman, 'that those of us who can afford to do so – and most of us can – contribute to a special fund, to be established forthwith, which will be used for emergencies such as this. I propose a minimum contribution of £1,000 each.'

The response was an embarrassed silence. 'How about . . . £500?' whispered Yvette.

Levy-Newman ignored her. 'Robert, will you take care of this? It will need to be formalized.'

With this he fell back into his usual silent pose, like an Indian chief who had said his word and expected it to be the final one.

But Natasha had one more thing up her sleeve: the advertisement. 'I have managed to negotiate a fee of £1,500 for a full page for the Corner Press, if we can place their ad on the back cover of the next issue. I don't mind doing this from time to time,' she said while she straightened the picture out in front of her, so that everyone could see it, 'but in future, perhaps one of you could take over the advertising? I'm not very good at it, and it's very time-consuming. Here is the ad.'

The trustees stood up and huddled around the mildly pornographic photo. There were a few chuckles, but they were in instant agreement: it was absolutely fine. Love and Peace in the Middle East? This was certainly the spirit of the magazine, and it would have been in tune with Held's philosophy. Only the Weintraub brothers frowned a little, but did not voice a protest. Natasha felt a bit embarrassed, and pleasantly surprised: the trustees were no prudes. She had underestimated them. She quietly decided to go ahead and place a cartoon in the next issue which she had not been sure of until this moment. It showed a diminutive Jewish husband being chased by his generously proportioned, busty and very angry wife, with the caption: 'All I said was give me two minutes alone with your breasts!'

'Any other business?' asked Robert Taub. 'No? Well, thank you all. This has been a very interesting meeting, and we all look forward to reading Sidney's minutes . . .'

'Oh my God,' said Sidney Sussman. 'I'm so sorry. I was so busy participating I completely forgot to take notes!'

'Can you do it from memory?' asked Robert, with a smile.

'I've done it,' said Jonathan Warhaftig, to everyone's mild surprise. 'I have written it all down. I always do, but no one ever asks me for my notes, as it's Sidney's task. Shall I do these minutes, by way of an exception?'

No one suspected that a few days later they would receive an absolutely faultless and complete account of the meeting. Sidney Sussman would not be pleased. But at this moment, there was nothing he could do except agree with Robert that he was not up to fulfilling his usual responsibility.

As the trustees left the room, one by one, Natasha found herself alone with Zygmunt Levy-Newman. He approached her, slowly, and said: 'If you have any difficulty with Dr Hoffmann, please speak to me. I will help you.'

What sort of difficulty did he have in mind, Natasha wanted to ask, but he had already gone. Were all magazines like this – full of annoying little mysteries? Did she *have* to know and understand them, in order to edit and produce eighty A5 pages of reasonably interesting reading matter every three months? Until now, she hadn't really cared. She had allowed those peculiar secretive things – like Sugarman's postcards about being 'knifed in the back' (what the hell did that mean, anyway? And did he really think she would take his ridiculous attempts at stirring up intrigue seriously?) – to accumulate, ignoring everything that didn't seem to have an obvious connection with her immediate task, which was to edit *The Nose*. But Hoffmann's cheque had obviously changed all that: she had been asked to investigate the man and his past, and his connection with Held. Natasha was nothing if not a thorough investigator. She would find out everything she could, and, as far as she could remember, Hoffmann was quite willing to speak to her. In fact, she now recalled, he had invited her to come and talk to him about Held. So she would.

She noticed Sidney Sussman waiting in the doorway, chatting with Yvette Moskowitz. He would, as he always did, offer her a lift home, and on the way bore her with his complaints about the cost of postage stamps and today, perhaps even discuss his analysis of Hitler's appeal as a life insurance salesman . . . As she bent over her papers which were still spread on the table, Natasha noticed a small dark insect which had just fallen out of her hair and on to the Corner Press ad. Oh God: a louse. A live head louse. She had been infected by her daughter!

Natasha picked up the louse and held it between the thumb and forefinger of her right hand. With her left, she gathered up her things and then moved towards the door. As she passed Sidney and Yvette, she shocked them both by giving each a little hug and even a friendly kiss goodbye: this was not their usual level of familiarity. Natasha had no idea why she had suddenly decided to plant the louse in Yvette's stiff perm. It was an impulse, and she felt positively evil as she left the louse hanging on to a bunch of hard curls at the back of Yvette's head. Sidney had no hair to speak of, otherwise she would have shared her private plague with him.

'Your husband is waiting outside,' said Sidney, still profoundly startled by Natasha's sudden display of physical affection towards Yvette and himself. If only he knew, Natasha wondered, what would he *think*? What would they both think? Would they demand that she give up the editorship of *The Nose* for spreading headlice among the trustees? Would this be the subject of the next meeting?

But, Natasha noticed, the louse had not survived the transplant: Yvette's hair was clearly too dry and hard to hold on to. The louse had dropped to the floor, and now lay hidden and dying under Natasha's heavy platform heel.

She saw Tim standing in the street outside the pet shop and smiled at him with surprise and relief. Now she was back in her own, sane world, the meeting already a distant memory.

10 Two Flies on the Wall

'Do you think I should give up my job?' Natasha asked Tim, for the third time that night.

His plan had worked, and his wish had come true: they had managed a quick late supper at Café Christina, a little Greek taverna around the corner from their house, and a few hours (hours, not minutes!) in bed. Christina, the young plump cheery owner of the café who loved to chat and distribute kisses to her customers, was just a little hurt when they rushed through the meal ('Not hungry today?').

Back home, they took their time making love, just because they could. Natasha cherished the way Tim concentrated on watching her and feeling her and feeding her alternating spoonfuls of tender and rough sex. Bit by bit, a delicate layer of bittersweet sweat would cover his entire body, like soft lacquer, from his temples to his toes, and it always seemed to Natasha that this dedicated lover, her husband, could not possibly be happy with her far more distracted presence. While she let her body play with Tim's, her thoughts wandered and could not be stopped; her mind was always in restless overdrive. She worried, occasionally, that he felt a little neglected in bed. But the mirror said otherwise; it framed a long shot of a contented naked couple, the man sitting up, the woman stretched out beside him. Who says a mirror in the bedroom is bad feng shui, thought Natasha. A quick furtive glance at this picture and I feel ready for more. She knew that Tim played the 'fly on the wall' game as well, secretly, making sure she never noticed, and without telling her how it made him feel. But, he, too, seemed re-energized after catching a glimpse of their reflection in the mirror, like a voyeur in his own bedroom.

Natasha saved her questions for the brief lulls in their rhythm. Tim never left a question unanswered – polite to the end – even if he thought she was wasting their precious moments together on silly chatter. But when he noticed that she had asked the same question more than twice, he decided to pay attention.

'What are you talking about? Why should you give up your job?'

'I don't think I can take much more of their crap.'

'What crap? What's going on?'

'Oh, you know. All those meetings, and the annoying, weird people I have to deal with. It takes up too much of my time. Of *our* time. And I think it's starting to drive me crazy.'

'Natasha, I think you're just tired. My job is full of crap as well, but so what? Most jobs are. Main thing is, do you want to do it? Seems to me Erica loves the idea that her mother is an editor!'

'So you're not upset?'

'Upset about what?'

'My mind being on other things all the time.'

'Is it? I hadn't noticed,' Tim lied.

'Thank God. OK, I'll stick with it. At least until I finish dealing with a little investigation I've been asked to carry out. There's this man, a German, who gave us a lot of money and I'm supposed to find out if we can accept it. Just in case he was – is – some kind of Nazi.'

'Oh.'

'Tim?'

'Yeah.'

'Aren't you interested?'

'Not really. Sorry.'

'But . . . OK, never mind. Listen, I forgot to tell you: my parents are coming to London. For a while. First my mother, then my dad. She is supposed to be a witness at a big trial . . . I don't know much about it. *And* she wants to help us! Can you imagine?'

They both laughed. The idea of Alice and Sam acting as anything but hyperactive *artistes* was a joke. Tim did not seem to have taken in what Natasha had said about the trial.

'Hey, now that Erica is older, maybe they can take her along to all their crazy events. You know, shows, parties . . .' said Natasha, imagining Erica having a great time and her and Tim enjoying a bit of a break.

'Are you kidding? We have no idea who they hang out with. If it's anything like their circle in New York—'

'What do *you* know about their circle in New York?' asked Natasha, with some indignation. The evening had been too idyllic so far, she was ready for a bit of a fight . . .

'Just what you and Philip told me: the drugs, the crazy characters, the orgies . . .'

'Tim, that was a very long time ago! My parents are old now!'

'So? I bet they're still the same. Look at . . . Mick Jagger!'

'MICK JAGGER??!! My parents are much older than Jagger!'

'OK, so David Bowie. No, I mean Tina Turner.'

'Now you're getting warmer.'

They were laughing again, but Natasha felt that Tim had a point: her parents could not be entrusted with Erica. Unless—

'What if they've changed?'

'Changed, how?'

'I mean, what if my parents have given up making strange erotic films, and have turned into perfectly respectable senior citizens?'

Tim looked at Natasha, and said nothing. She waited. She knew that if she waited long enough, he would give in and talk. He was getting better at that sort of thing.

'Truth is . . . If your parents did that . . . I mean . . . I wouldn't want them to change. I quite like them the way they are. You know. Fun. Yeah, they're fun. And it's great for Erica, too.'

'Hey, does that mean you like me the way I am, too? Or do you want me to change? Just say the word . . .'

The mirror averted its eyes as Natasha and Tim embraced one more time. 'One for the road' to send both of them, finally, off to sleep.

But only Tim slept. As always. After a while, Natasha wiggled out of bed and switched on her computer.

She was definitely addicted to this thing. Couldn't drop off to sleep without seeing the latest messages. But there was only one, from

Philip. Reporting that he was back from California, having dumped the girlfriend somewhere en route. They'd had a bitter political disagreement – she had suddenly and unexpectedly confessed to being a closet Republican. Philip's e-mail sounded angry and sad.

Natasha wrote back:

Sorry. But – didn't Mom warn you about her? You know Mom and her sixth sense about people's politics. Anyway. You'll bounce back. Don't you always?

News: Did you hear? THEY are coming to London. First Mom, then Dad. They are renting a place! I don't get it. Should I worry about this? And do you know anything about the Goetz trial? What's SHE got to do with it?!

How's work? Mine's getting complicated. Call me?

Your favorite baby sister

Her private phone rang within minutes of her pressing SEND. Philip was clearly intrigued.

'You're kidding.'

'I'm *not*.'

'They never told me! I talked to Dad this morning and he didn't say a word about coming to London. Strange. So what's this about?'

'Well, in his case, a retrospective of his old films at the ICA. Pretty exciting, don't you think?'

'I guess . . .' Philip's opinion of his father's artistic achievement was sceptical to say the least, but he did assign a certain historical value to his early work.

'What do you mean, you guess? It *is* exciting. Listen, for all we know our father was a revolutionary of the American cinema!'

'Natasha, you're getting carried away. Stop it.'

'You know what, I disagree. Didn't your very own paper recently run a series of articles on Dad's old films?'

'How do you know about that?'

'It's on the internet, genius. Plus, Mom told me.'

'And did she also tell you that those articles were mainly about her?'

'What?? No, she didn't . . . Same old story, eh?'

'That's right. Anyway, so I guess it would be *their* retrospective, not his?'

'Who knows . . . In any case, she seems more interested in my magazine than in the old film business.'

Natasha gave Philip a verbatim account of her recent conversation with Alice, not mentioning the bit about her daughter's headlice.

'So, what do you make of that?'

'Nothing.'

'Nothing?'

'Natasha, this is a long-distance call. Try not to be repetitive. All I know about the Goetz trial is what's been in the papers. What a story. I actually really wanted to cover it, but the *Voice* wouldn't see the point of paying for it. Idiots. But I intend to find out why Mom's a witness, don't you worry.' He sounded angry.

'And what about that other stuff? I mean, why should she suddenly discover her grandmotherly instincts – that's clearly a pretext for something else.'

'Like what?'

'How should I know? Though I have a feeling – and I could be wrong – that Mom might be rebelling. Finally.'

'Why should she be rebelling? Against what?'

'Philip, what's wrong with you? I thought we'd always agreed she wasn't happy with Dad's lifestyle . . .'

'Well, I'm changing my mind. I think she was. She is.'

'Happy?!'

'Yeah, happy.'

Natasha was momentarily lost for words. Philip was either being intentionally provocative, or . . . Or, she thought, he might be depressed by what happened in California . . .

'Do you want to talk about *her*?' she asked.

'No I don't,' he said, without missing the reference.

'Why not? I'm your sister.'

'And I'm your brother. It's over. No big deal.'

'Philip. I'm worried about you. Are you losing your touch? I mean, how beautiful was she if you could overlook the significant fact that she was a Re—'

'Natasha!! Shut up!!'

'I won't. Not until you tell me.'

Philip finally laughed. Their conversations were still exactly the same as ten, twenty years ago.

'OK, but only one thing. She was my dream woman, and she was black. From Washington, DC.'

'And a Re—?'

'Never mind about that. I was fooled. You would have liked her.'

'Maybe you could stop being so political?' asked Natasha. 'Maybe it isn't that important? I mean, if you really liked her . . .'

'Natasha, being a Republican is not about politics. It's about aesthetics. You've been an expat for too long. You don't get it.'

Natasha giggled, and suddenly realized that she hadn't felt this relaxed in a very long time.

'Philip, one more thing. My job . . . it's starting to get to me. There is all this weird stuff happening and I—'

'Sorry, Natasha, I really gotta go now. I'm interviewing someone in a minute. Send me an e-mail and keep copying me with those crazy messages you've been getting, I love them. Yeah, all those cranks. Talk to you later.'

I miss him so much, Natasha thought. We need to talk for *days* – and all I get is tidbits.

She sat at her desk for a moment, thinking about that huge pile of laundry she would have to attack in the morning. Or should she start now? No, that would be mad, even for her crazy routine. She would go back into her warm bed.

But instead, she pulled out the black file box from underneath her desk, and took out the photo of young Franz Held. It was more than a snapshot, she realized: it was a portrait.

The young man in the picture was of indeterminate age – he could have been in his twenties or his thirties, Natasha couldn't tell. Hoffmann would be able to help her – he had said that he had taken

this photo himself, so perhaps he'll remember the year. That would be a start.

She couldn't decide whether the man's expression was melancholy, sad or a little hard. No trace of a smile. Again, Hoffmann should be able to help her there.

The more she looked at young Held, the less she could pull her eyes away from his, even though this wasn't one of those portraits where the subject seems to follow you with his unblinking gaze. On the contrary: the man appeared to be staring at some invisible, distant point, at an oblique angle which made it impossible for one's eyes to intersect with his – as if he were avoiding a direct encounter. She traced the outline of his nose and his mouth with her thumb, and felt . . . What? What could she possibly feel by touching an old, brown, grainy piece of paper? But she couldn't deny that she had sensed some sort of *life* in that ancient photograph. She could almost see a thin, maybe sweaty body under the dark pinstriped suit and white shirt, could almost reach down below the confines of the photograph, imagine the man's hands. He would have had long, thin fingers, but his knuckles would be rough and would betray his habit of rolling his right hand into a fist and hiding it behind his back when he spoke . . . Natasha had always had a tendency to make stories come alive in her head; they usually began as something she'd seen or heard, something that caught her attention and wouldn't let go. Well, this picture had, finally, grabbed her attention all right.

She tried to imagine the moment in real time when the photograph was taken. She saw a young Czech Jew, Franz Held, being photographed by a young German, Ludwig Hoffmann. In Theresienstadt, which was a concentration camp! Did that make any sense?

Natasha couldn't picture the circumstances under which this happened. Were they really friends? Where? What happened then? Why hadn't she seen any other photos of Held? When she started working for *The Nose*, she had inherited a substantial archive of old photographs, but his picture had not been among them. Nor had it ever been reproduced in any of the old issues of the magazine, as far as she could remember.

So, her first question for Hoffmann would be pretty straightforward. And after that, the rest would be easy . . . She would complete the puzzle, slowly, taking her time. Maybe she would collect enough material to write a proper biography of the man? Some people thought he was important, so maybe his life story would be of interest to a publisher?

Natasha sighed. Who was she kidding. She didn't have the patience to work at a deliberate, leisurely pace. Her problem was that she had to know everything, *now.* As fast as possible. Still, it would be a great project. Writing and researching a biography couldn't be all that different from writing a mystery novel . . .

She put the picture back, face down. And reread the letter addressed to Held. About an article, or was it a story . . . What if she had it in her old file boxes, the ones she had been given at the same time as the picture archive?

Suddenly, she saw those very old papers in a new light. Until now, they were simply the remains of unpublished and hence, presumably, unpublishable material, but now they acquired new meaning: they were the magazine's history. Why hadn't it occurred to her before? But considering the fact that those files represented many decades of editorial work, they were surprisingly slim. Just two boxes full of papers, without any particular order.

Natasha could not restrain herself and began her first serious search in her new capacity as Held's self-appointed biographer. She tried not to allow herself to get sidetracked by other treasures – all those papers seemed like treasures now – and concentrated on finding anything resembling the vague description of the manuscript in question, or any writing in the same shaky, old-style European handwriting. After half an hour, she was rewarded with a few sheets written by the same or at least very similar hand. It looked much older than all the others, and was, possibly, the story she was looking for. Unfortunately, it was in German, and although Natasha's German was not bad, she would need time before she could decipher and translate this text. She removed the sheets from where she had found them and added them to her Held file.

She was just beginning to enjoy the idea of her new research when she remembered, with a slight shudder, that her first task was to look into Hoffmann's past, not Held's. Though there seemed to be a connection between the two, if the existence of the photograph was anything to go by . . .

Oh, enough of this shit, she said out loud. I'm going to bed.

'It's about time,' said Tim, who was just waking up. It was almost four a.m. He looked in the mirror and saw a rosy, fresh face – his own, and a grey, exhausted one – Natasha's. 'You're killing yourself, love. If you keep this up, you'll *have* to quit that job.'

'Not a chance,' mumbled Natasha, and finally fell asleep.

11 Natasha Needs A Method

'May I speak to Nastassya Kaplan, please?'

'Speaking.'

'Am I speaking with Natalie Kaplan, the editor of the Jewish review *The Nose*, etc., etc?'

'*Natasha* Kaplan. Yes.'

'Ah. This is Max Brass. You've heard of me?'

'No, I'm afraid I haven't, Mr Brass.'

'I have been a long-time supporter of your journal.'

'Oh, I'm sorry. Are you a tru—?'

'No, no, I am not on the trust. No time for that sort of thing. But I am a regular and very generous sponsor. There have been crises, as you may have heard . . . And I was always happy to help my friend Franz. I dare say that without my assistance, he would have had to give up a long time ago, and what a pity that would have been. For all of us. From time to time, I write little pieces, and Franz was always pleased to publish them.'

Natasha's ears perked up.

'Were you close friends?'

'Oh, yes. Very close. We've been through so much, you see . . .'

'Would you like to talk to me about your friendship with Franz Held?'

Damn, thought Natasha as soon as she'd asked the question. I'm not handling this well at all. I'm too obvious, too crass, too direct. I'll put him off . . .

'Why? That is not why I am calling at all.' He sounded annoyed.

'I'm sorry. It's just that I am very interested in my predecessor's history, as it is, to some extent, also the history of *The Nose*.'

'Well, Miss Kaplan, I would like to talk to you about something else. I have written a memoir, you see. You must have received it from my publisher quite a few months ago.'

'Sorry, I don't recall. What was the title of your book?'

'*My Way Out.*'

Natasha knew she had not seen it.

'Oh yes, I remember. A very interesting book.'

'Thank you. I do agree with you. I have received many compliments from some very valuable members of the community. The Chief Rabbi ordered twenty-five copies. The chapter I want you to print in *The Nose* is the one about my arrival in England, in 1939. But, if you prefer another one, we could discuss it.'

'I'm afraid I don't understand. Should I have received a letter from you about this? I don't recall seeing it.'

'Why should I write a letter? No time for that sort of thing. Writing my book was enough! Thank God my wife did the typing. Nothing else, of course. She's dead now, by the way. Chapter nine in my book.' He chuckled.

'Mr Brass, I will get back to you on this. What is your telephone number?'

He gave it to her – the first few digits pointed in the direction of Hendon – and hung up. Natasha dialled Robert Taub's office number.

'Robert.'

'Natasha.'

'Have you got a minute?'

'Of course, my dear. How can I help?'

'Who is Max Brass?'

She heard a sigh. Then: 'An old friend of the magazine.'

'Does he give us money?'

'Oh yes.'

'How much?'

'£125, every other year. From his wife's family fund.'

'Thanks. Have you read his book?'

'I have.'

'And?'

'Natasha, does he want you to publish something from it?'

'How did you know?'

'Well, we always have. We have a tradition of printing the work of loyal supporters—'

'You mean Held did?'

'Of course.'

'I have to read it first.'

'I'm sure you'll find it . . . interesting. Please do.'

'I'll see. Thanks, Robert.'

'Bye, my dear.'

Natasha was outraged. She wasn't about to publish some amateur drivel by one of Held's bosom buddies! Just because *The Nose* had some stupid 'tradition'. She was an editor, not a puppet of the trust!

But . . . what if she was wrong? What if Max Brass turned out to be a decent author? She scanned the shelf where she kept all her review copies for the book. It was hard to find – its cover was almost indistinguishable from about a dozen other volumes: red lettering on a black background and a black and white photo with an aura of post-Holocaust *tristesse* seemed to be the preferred style for Jewish memoirs. But, here it was. Natasha wasn't surprised to see that the publisher was a well-known vanity press. Still, that didn't mean anything – she knew how blind some commercial publishers could be, rejecting many a treasure. Her own novel had been turned down by seven publishers before it had found a home . . . She was willing to give Max Brass a chance.

There was an author's photo on the inside back flap, presumably taken many years ago. It showed a jolly man in his early fifties, big smile, no hair, bulging eyes behind thick, horn-rimmed spectacles, prominent eyebrows. The picture didn't match the man's phone personality at all. Or did it? She wasn't sure.

The actual book was another surprise. Each chapter – with headings like 'My Home in Vienna', 'My Home in Manchester', 'My Home in Hendon', 'My Mother', 'My Children', 'My Professional Life' – consisted almost entirely of photographs, with long, detailed captions and a page or two of chatty prose. In short, a family album.

Not publishable, of course, but Natasha loved other people's family albums, maybe because her own parents had never had an interest in keeping one themselves. There were always lots of pictures lying around their house, but no one had ever organized them in any order, or written any comments to explain the meaning of each photograph. Their family history didn't seem to matter to Sam or Alice. Natasha caught herself feeling jealous – Max Brass's family was lucky. She turned to chapter nine, entitled 'My Wife', and read:

> I was fortunate enough to meet Trudi Salzmann, my future wife, only a few weeks after my arrival in England. She was a beautiful girl (also from Vienna) and fell in love with me on day one. (Between you and me, she wasn't the only one!) Day two, I told her we were too young to marry, day three we became engaged. The war was hard but not so hard as when we would have stayed in Vienna. I could not join the army on account of bad eyesight, but I did my best to help my new homeland. Before the war was over, we were married anyways and never regretted it. Trudi is a good wife but also a good mother (see chapter six). She would have been a good daughter-in-law but my parents never made it out of Vienna (see chapter four). Her parents gave us a room in their flat in Manchester (see chapter eight) which almost broke our marriage. But when I started making a little money in my profession (see chapters ten, twelve and fourteen), we could live together properly. Now, we are grandparents (see chapter fifteen) and we enjoy a quiet life, thank God. My boys are in charge of the dry-cleaning business and doing well, thank God.

Trudi Salzmann had been an earnest-looking young woman. Quite attractive, in a very proper sort of way. As she matured in the photos, she retained her girlish figure in spite of all the pregnancies (they had four children) but gradually lost her seriousness, so that the last pictures of her showed an old woman who seemed to be laughing, not smiling, at the camera.

Before she closed the book, Natasha looked up chapter eleven – 'My Friends', hoping to find something about Held. She wasn't disappointed. Franz Held was mentioned as 'a dear friend', a 'wise man' and a 'great intellect', 'a very busy man who travelled a great deal'. But there was no photograph of him, nor any other useful information.

I couldn't publish anything this man has written, Natasha decided, but I *could* do something with those pictures. A sort of photo essay, showing a classic Jewish immigrant history – from Vienna via Manchester to London . . . Not a bad idea. And, given Hoffmann's insistence on using some of his donation to improve the quality of their printing, she could actually make it look quite decent. Maybe it would start a series . . .

This reminded her of the most important task of the day – she had to call Hoffmann and make an appointment to visit him. She'd been delaying that call. How was she supposed to tell him she had been asked to 'check his credentials' as a German?

His voice sounded more vigorous on the phone than it had when they met.

'How good to hear your voice, Na-ta-sha. Are you well?'

'Yes, thank you. I am calling to let you know that I have discussed your extremely generous offer with the trust.'

There was a pause. Then he said, 'And you need to know who I am before you can accept my money? Would that be right?'

Natasha laughed, relieved. Maybe she liked this man, whoever he was . . . 'That's basically it, in a nutshell. But there is more: I have some additional questions of my own. I have become interested in . . .'

'Na-tasha, how wonderful! Do I understand you correctly – you want to know more about my old friend Franz? I am so pleased – I must confess I was very disappointed to hear that you didn't know anything about him at all. He was such an interesting young man when I knew him . . . So different from everyone else around him . . .'

'That's exactly what I want to talk to you about. May I come and see you?'

Dr Hoffmann was absolutely delighted. Could not wait. They decided to meet on the following day, as he was about to leave London soon, for a few months. Natasha wanted to ask him when exactly he knew Held, but he had already hung up.

But, thought Natasha, I have to be prepared for this meeting. I have to know *something* about my predecessor. Where do I start? You're a crap detective, she said to herself. You have no method, no system, no *rules*. That's no way to investigate anything.

Who could she ask for help? Her brother had other things on his mind at the moment. Who else did she know who could think straight and keep his mouth shut? Tim!! Natasha felt truly inspired. Tim could help – it was his *job* to look for clues and to collect evidence! What a brilliant idea. She would talk to him tonight.

She forced herself to move away from her desk, and looked around. The house was a total mess. A basket with clean laundry waiting to be put away, two baskets with dirty laundry waiting to be washed. The kitchen floor was sticky, and the breakfast dishes still on the table. Her and Erica's clothes over every chair in sight – only Tim kept his modest wardrobe under perfect control: folded, organized, put away. She didn't know what to tackle first – she was too tired to do it all, and couldn't decide which chore should be given priority. This isn't *my* kind of life, thought Natasha, I was born to be idle, in a Russian-intellectual-aristocracy sort of way. I was born to read and write and talk. I shouldn't have to do that *and* clean a house . . . She wasn't even dressed yet.

The phone rang again. Saved by the bell, she cheered and did a little dance in the nude.

'Natasha, this is Chris,' said a serious, deep voice. It was what they called a 'posh' voice in this country, but she didn't recognize it.

'Chris?'

'Christopher Le Vine.'

'Oh, hi! We haven't spoken in ages!'

'True. I am phoning to confirm the time and place for the editorial meeting tonight.'

Oh shit, shit, *shit*. It had completely slipped her mind! The meetings of the editorial board were not as frequent as the trustees' meetings, and so she tended to forget about them. And they were important, more important than the other kind! Plus, she had been looking forward to having a quiet evening at home . . .

'Right,' she said. 'It's still the same time and the same place.' She would look up later what those were . . .

'You mean my place, eight p.m.?'

'That's right, Chris. Thanks for having us there.'

'That's no problem. See you later.'

Now that she knew that her evening would be ruined, Natasha went into overdrive. To the very loud tune and glorious rhythms of a hip-hop CD – her current favourite was 'Da Delivery Boy' – she dealt with the kitchen, then with one basket of laundry (the dirty one). The other one would have to wait. Hip-hop didn't go with clean laundry (or did it?).

Just before she was about to leave the house to pick up Erica, she noticed that the green light on her answering machine was blinking. She must have missed a call while she had the music on.

'Natasha. This is Sidney Sussman. Have you dealt with the German fellow? I need to know as this has an *immediate* impact on our finances. Please call me as soon as you can.'

'Natasha, Karl Spitzer here. Your editorial? I am still waiting. Everything else is ready. Though, as I hear from Sidney, there is no rush. You have my number.'

She ignored Sussman's message but felt bad about the second one. She had written a brief editorial about Jews and crime but had not sent it to Spitzer. Forgotten. How could she forget to deal with such an important thing? First the meeting, then the editorial . . . Maybe she really was losing her grip.

She glanced at what she had written. She had produced 600 words, had talked about crime and the Torah, about the Ten Commandments forbidding this and that, about Dizengoff's famous quote that Tel Aviv will be a normal city when it produces its first criminals (it didn't take too long), a joke about the Jewish mafia in the States . . . She had linked all these motifs together and come up with a cute text that was guaranteed to annoy Sussman and amuse or bore all the others. And, hopefully, the readers. This was pretty much the formula according to which she had been editing *The Nose.*

She would send it to Spitzer and let it be published, but her next editorial would be different. Her next editorial, if everything went according to plan, would surprise *all* the trustees.

Walking towards Erica's school, Natasha suddenly realized that the reclusive Karl Spitzer should know quite a lot about Held – he had been his sub-editor for many, many years. She was, finally, getting a tiny bit better at this detective stuff.

12 Leader of the Pack

The tube ride from Southgate to Kensington, where she had arranged to meet Ludwig Hoffmann at his flat, seemed endless, with frequent unplanned stops between stations, during which the driver sent muffled messages through the loudspeaker system about 'signal failures'. The late morning travellers on the Piccadilly Line looked as pale and sleep-deprived as at any other time of the day. Natasha had a book with her – one of the review copies for *The Nose* – but could not concentrate on the craggy poems by one s.m. kravitz. She gave up after the first one ('scrub me clean / wipe me hard / try telling pure lies without thinking / think impure thoughts without lying / I was a Jew / now I eat lard / . . .') and focused instead on the haircuts of her fellow female passengers. Natasha was fed up with her overgrown, wispy look and craved a drastic change – but to what? There were so many options. She imagined herself wearing that woman's wild curly red perm, down to her shoulders. Or this little girl's neat geometric bob – like Erica's. Or – hey, there's an idea – that man's incredibly short cut, no fringe, just a neat little lawn on her head – maybe she should even go green?

Her own reflection in the window opposite did not show the best-looking woman in the entire train. Not by a long shot. She wasn't even sure whether she still looked *young*: the dark glass and bad light managed to distort and age her features – her always sleepy, foggy eyes, confident, simple nose, a mouth Tim loved to tell her was 'really, really kissable' but Natasha herself thought of as way too plump: her face had been flattened into a warped caricature of herself. With her hair tied in a small bun she looked grim and almost middle-aged. But maybe that would be the right way to present herself to

Dr Hoffmann, for a serious, solemn discussion of an important slice of his, and Held's, past.

Or was she wrong to blame the glass? Was she not staring at a severely hungover version of herself? She had looked very different last night, at the editorial meeting. Alert. Relaxed. Happy. Her hair was untied and probably untidy, but it didn't matter; whenever the editorial board got together – about every three months – it felt more like a party than a meeting. The only whiff of formality would be generated by the host, Chris Le Vine, who liked to pretend to be all sorts of things, but was basically a very nice guy and a generous spirit.

He had a huge, ornate flat overlooking Hampstead Heath, where he lived with his partner Vladimir, a gorgeous Russian acrobat. For an acrobat, Vladimir was surprisingly lazy, and never budged from a fluffy red rug in front of the mahogany-framed fireplace, where he lay curled up like a cat reading Russian poetry, never uttering a word, never even stretching, his black hair reflecting the light of the gently bouncing flames. Natasha always felt like joining him there. What would they all say if she suddenly cuddled up to Chris's partner and closed her eyes, forgetting all about *The Nose*?

The editorial board consisted of two writers (Daniel Friedman and Susan Wilson), three academics (Chris Le Vine, Jack Margolis and Nancy Lichtenstein), one poet (Janet Klein) and one all-purpose Judaica expert and part-time political activist (Shlomo Cohen). The average age was just under forty, the average height just under six feet: all the men, except for Daniel, were exceedingly tall, and the women not far behind. Natasha had, of course, nicknamed the editorial group 'The Giants' in counterpoint to the secret name she had assigned to the mostly diminutive trustees.

Chris, with his prematurely white hair and conservative grey suits had the look of the elder statesman among them, but was in fact, at twenty-seven, the youngest member of the board. His wealth was inherited – not from his parents, who were still alive and well and only two streets away – but from an older sister, who had been a successful top model. She had died from a drug overdose.

Natasha knew all this because each editorial meeting began with Chris 'sharing' his family history with the others. The well-known art critic and lecturer was in daily therapy and suffered very badly when a session came to its programmed end. Each day, he begged to be allowed to stay and talk more, knowing that this could not be allowed. He would then engage any person he encountered throughout the day in 'therapy speak', talking to whoever was prepared to listen, thus extending the feeling of his morning session for as long as it was possible. He had lost many of his friends as a result, and reduced Vladimir to a silent, carpet-hugging Russian sphinx. When Natasha had invited Christopher Le Vine to help her shape *The Nose*, she had had no idea that she had made him very, very happy. He insisted on hosting all the meetings in his spacious home like lavish, decadent literary soirées, was full of creative ideas for the magazine and asked for nothing in return except a few minutes of introductory 'sharing'. Listening to the repetitive summaries of the results of his recent therapy was easy – he never demanded any response at all.

There had been no editorial board whatsoever when Natasha became editor of the magazine. When she realized that the trustees expected her to create *The Nose* all by herself, with frequent input from Sidney Sussman and, occasionally, some of the others, she quickly put together a small editorial collective to help her come up with inspired and inspiring ideas and give her feedback and criticism. (The issue on Jews and crime had been proposed by Daniel Friedman.) They were all busy people, but were willing to get together on a regular though infrequent basis and do some brainstorming. None of them, except for Shlomo, knew anything about Judaism, but all liked the idea of being involved in shaping a contemporary Jewish literary magazine. None of them had ever met the trustees (except for Janet Klein who was a distant relative of Charles Sugarman's) and most knew nothing about the magazine's past history.

Vladimir's contributions to the meeting were not insignificant: he provided large jars of red and black Russian caviar which they were allowed to consume in huge quantities, like jam, on aromatic dark bread. Chris supplied the drinks which were plentiful and very, very alcoholic. The drinking began slowly, during his introductory soliloquy, and gradually escalated, until Janet fell asleep, snoring, in her armchair. The others were able to maintain a barely coherent level of discourse. Shlomo never drank at all.

Natasha tried to remember the main topic of their conversation last night, but all she could recall was a passionate discussion, initiated by the usually taciturn Susan Wilson, about whether or not an unpublished poem by F. Scott Fitzgerald was anti-Semitic, or merely humorous. She – a huge Fitzgerald fan – had discovered it 'with a shudder' in an obscure collection of his poetry and did not know what to think of these lines:

If you have a little Jew
Beat him (when he sneezes)

Could it be a joke, Susan had asked, a game on words? Obviously, said the whimsical Janet (who was still awake) in a haughty voice, 'a Jew' sort of rhyming with the implied sound of a sneeze ('achoo'), nothing sinister about that. Especially if you devoice the 'dj' sound in 'Jew' and pronounce it with a sort of German accent – 'a Tshew'. But, argued Jack Margolis, why ridicule a sneezing, German-sounding *Jew*? Why not a sneezing, maybe even German-sounding Gentile? Because, said Janet the poet (awake but only just), it wouldn't have any *rhythm*. What sort of rhythm was she talking about, asked Shlomo indignantly, the hard, heavy, merciless, blood-curdling and ultimately blood-spilling rhythm of anti-Semitic innuendo? But, Nancy had countered with her sexy, laconic delivery, Fitzgerald had written those words *before* the Holocaust. That made a difference. Not really, objected Jack. There was a direct correlation between racial prejudice in the pre-war years, and what it ultimately led to. And let's not forget the pogroms, and the Inquisition . . . Vladimir had suddenly looked up from his Pushkin volume and whispered: 'Fijerrrad was not Nazi, or kozzak, he was Amerrrican.'

Natasha had repeated the poem, out loud, and found it pretty funny. As she had the unfortunate tendency to find almost everything pretty funny, she'd decided that she wouldn't be the best judge of Fitzgerald's little ditty, and kept quiet on the subject. Chris expressed the interesting view that if you could visualize the poem, or any statement, and come up with an anti-Semitic image – a vicious caricature – then it was definitely *meant* to be anti-Semitic and saturated with hatred rather than any kind of humour or compassion. Did that litmus test apply to Shylock, Jack had wanted to know. A new, heated discussion followed, and, again, Natasha had kept quiet. She was thinking of John White, and his e-mail missives. It wasn't hard to visualize *those*. Maybe this was the real reason why she always ended up saving rather than deleting them: John White's murderous hatred had a pictorial force, like a violent film one felt compelled to watch, repulsed, to the very end.

She remembered how Shlomo had suddenly jumped up on a gold-embroidered black leather pouffe and patted Chris on the back: 'You're a genius! That's exactly the kind of criterion I've been looking for. Let us not forget' – he'd addressed the others as if they were in a political assembly, or at least in Hyde Park, which her underground train was passing at that very moment – 'let us never forget how Marx – Karl Marx, the self-hating Jew – gave the world the most vitriolic anti-Jewish text with his essay "On the Jewish Question". Did he not say that the "worldly cult of the Jew is bargaining"? Did he not claim that "the secular basis of Judaism is practical need, self-interest, *money*"? Money, said Marx, was "the god of practical need and self-interest". He even had the chutzpah to talk about the Jewish law, of which he knew nothing. He called it superficial, its morality unfounded – governed by nothing but egoism. The worst anti-Semites are not the Gentiles who poke fun at our traditions. The worst anti-Semites are self-denying Jews, and Marx is the paradigm case. Why are they so vicious? Because they are desperate to free themselves of any hint of Jewish association, lest they appear tainted before the aristocrats, Christians, revolutionaries, Muslims – those to whom they are determined to prove their credentials.'

Just when Natasha hoped that Shlomo had finally exhausted himself, he'd jumped off the now heavily dented pouffe and continued his speech while circling the room, spilling the mineral water from his green glass: 'Did you know that the main organizers of the Spanish Inquisition used Jewish converts as the most aggressive informers and inquisitors against the Jews, that Lenin used Trotsky to throw the Bund, the Jewish socialists, out of the Third International? That Stalin used Jewish Bolsheviks to denounce Yiddish writers and Jewish cultural leaders? It's a well-known pattern and Marx is simply a particularly clear case . . . I have nothing against genuine dissent or against radicalism – you know me and what I stand for; I'm a radical venture socialist myself; but I just can't *stand* this form of self-debasement . . .'

Although Shlomo's passionate speech had failed to rouse the editorial group out of their alcoholic semi-stupor, it was generally decided that the little poem was definitely suspect – especially when Susan revealed that in the book where she had found it, it was followed by another untitled set of rhymes: 'I hate their guts / the lousy mutts'. Natasha recalled, vaguely, that Daniel Friedman had then suggested putting together an issue of *The Nose* around the topic of 'Famous Jewish Anti-Semites', and that everyone thought it was a great idea. Chris knew of a talented cartoonist who could illustrate the pieces.

Did they have a conversation about the Goetz trial? Probably, but Natasha wasn't sure. She could always call Daniel later to check.

Here was her stop. Gloucester Road. She picked up her bag – why was it always so heavy?! – and stepped out on to the platform, forgetting to heed the loud advice to 'mind the gap', and almost losing her balance. Why don't they just build the platforms to match the trains and vice versa, she thought, annoyed. Walking towards the exit, or the 'WAY OUT' as it was called in this country (had Max Brass been inspired by the exit signs in the London Underground for the title of his memoir?), she noticed a British Transport policeman in conversation with an old man sitting on the bench next to the chocolate machine. Natasha could see only the exaggerated grin on the old man's face; the cop's broad back concealed the rest of his body.

'I think,' she heard the uniformed man say very loudly and clearly, 'that I will have to arrest you.'

'Why's that?'

'Because you are very drunk and offensive.'

'How d-do you know? P-prove it.'

'Well, let's see . . . you just called me a dirty old cunt. I think that's proof enough. And we could measure the level of alcohol in your . . .'

Natasha could not control herself. 'Hey, why don't you check *my* breath for alcohol, while you're at it. And everyone else on the tube, for that matter. It's almost Christmas.'

The cop turned around, abruptly, and now there was a grin on *his* face. Tim's partner, Ian. She should have guessed . . .

'Natasha, love, was that a pass? You know I'd be happy to check your breath any time . . . And Charlie here is an old pal, aren't you, Charlie,' he said in the direction of the old man, who had used the brief interlude to disappear in the crowd.

'What are you doing so far from home?'

'Working,' said Natasha. She knew by now that pithy replies were the best kind as far as Ian was concerned.

'Working? Here? Does Tim know?' Ian winked at her but refrained from placing his large, heavy hand on her shoulder.

'You look tired, love. Is Tim not letting you sleep at night?' He winked again. Then a quick thought shot through his mind – 'I bet you've got lovely tits' – and before he could stop himself, he realized he'd said it out loud.

'Fuck off, Ian. I gotta go.'

'Hey, hey, I was only kidding. In an appreciative sort of way . . . Oh, shit, here I go again. You know I'm your husband's best mate. If you ever need anything . . .'

'Well, as a matter of fact . . .' said Natasha, hesitating for a brief moment, 'I do have a little problem. I seem to have lost my ticket . . .' This was true. It was probably somewhere in the deep entrails of her huge bag, but she didn't feel like searching for it. And she was already a little late.

'No problem, love, let me escort you out of here. It might cost me my job, but, what the hell . . . See how good it is to have friends in high places? Not that the BTP is such a high place . . . In fact, at the moment, I find it a little low . . . and how is your own Ruby Rose?'

'My what?'

'Your *Nose*, darling, I thought our Timid Tim had been teaching you a bit of cockney . . .'

'Fine, thanks. Hard work. Well, bye, Ian. Say hi to Tim if you see him today,' she said quickly and left him standing by the bottom of the stairs leading to the lift. She couldn't know that his eyes remained glued to her back until she disappeared out of sight. If she had turned around, she may have noticed that Ian was looking at her with hunger, but also with concern.

Ludwig Hoffmann's flat occupied the entire top floor of an elegant building at the end of a quiet cul-de-sac. It was as she had pictured it – arranged with immaculate taste but with an obvious disregard for detail, a strange combination. His greeting was short and formal; he was clearly anxious to start talking, and led her into a large study, where he (or someone else? a wife? a housekeeper?) had set a little glass table with tea, coffee, a crystal carafe with mineral water and some pastries. There were no armchairs, only chairs. And those were uncomfortable, as Natasha discovered when he invited her to sit down.

'Well,' he said with a chuckle, 'shoot, as you young people like to say. What would you like to know?'

'May I take notes?' asked Natasha.

He smiled. 'Is your memory so bad? In my youth, I had to remember things without ever writing anything down, no repetitions, either. Too dangerous. In fact, that was how I first met your . . .'

'My predecessor? Franz Held?' Natasha was elated to have been given such an easy opening.

'No, my dear. Your mother. And I'm not . . . mad,' he added when he saw Natasha's expression of outrage and disbelief. Why was she wasting her time on this *alte kacker*?

'Na-tasha, please sit down. Please. Let me explain. I know you came to talk about my past, and about Franz, but you see, things are a little more complicated, I'm afraid, and perhaps I should have been more . . . open with you.'

She was silent. Ludwig Hoffmann was not.

'You know, of course, about your mother's involvement in my wife's trial?'

'Your *wife's* . . . Annmarie Goetz is your wife?'

He nodded. 'My . . . estranged wife, to be correct. We . . . but perhaps you don't care to know . . .'

'When did you know my mother?' Natasha said, quietly. Then she screamed, 'Who the hell are you?'

She wanted to apologize, but it wasn't necessary: Hoffmann was smiling, and said, 'I understand your anguish. But there is no mystery, really. Not when you know the truth. And you'll be pleased to hear,' he added almost cheerfully, 'that I knew your mother and Franz in the same place, and at the same time, of course. So we can discuss everything that is of interest to you in one go, so to speak . . .'

'And where was that?' Natasha asked, almost calmly.

'In Theresienstadt.'

'But that's a concentration camp . . . my mother was never . . . and you're not Jewish, you said!'

'No, I'm not.' He stared at her for a moment, without saying a word. 'I . . . It's a long story. But I promise you your mother was in Theresienstadt, and so was Held. That was how we all met . . .' He sounded as casual as if he were describing a pleasant social occasion – a dance or a dinner.

'All?!' I can do one of two things, she thought, quickly. I can walk out of here and forget this conversation ever happened, or I can stay and listen to what this man has to say and deal with it. Somehow.

'Yes, Na-tasha. Your mother was there as a young girl. About sixteen, I think. Her parents were still outside. She was a Mischling. You are familiar with the term?'

Natasha nodded. She had not known that either. Which one of Alice's parents had not been Jewish? she wondered. And how many secrets could one mother have up her sleeve?

'So she had been called up to come to Theresienstadt on her own. At first. And I – we were not all beasts, you know . . . At least, I tried not to be . . . I was still young . . . I offered to post a letter to her parents for her. Twice.'

He poured a drop of water from the heavy crystal carafe into his own glass, but did not drink it. Two massive clocks were ticking in the room, entirely out of sync.

'And Held?'

'Ah, Franz . . . He found out, and asked me to do the same for him. Not to his parents, of course – they were in the camp with him – but to a young woman in Prague. He even offered to pay me. I still don't know how he managed to have money. Real money, I mean.'

'And did you?'

'I did not take his money, no. And the letter, well—'

'What happened?'

He sighed, heavily. 'He was caught, Natasha. Someone denounced him, without implicating me.'

'So – what happened?'

'Well . . . Franz was sent to the Small Fortress . . .'

'What's that?'

'It was a Gestapo prison, a small distance from the Theresienstadt ghetto. It was . . . very bad . . . But Franz . . . he surprised me.'

Natasha waited.

'I did not think he would make it. But you know what? Somehow, he achieved the impossible. After a while, I heard that he was transferred back to the camp. To Theresienstadt. This was quite unheard of. Franz was a very unusual person. Even half-naked, lice-ridden, starved, he had charisma. He . . . how can I put this . . . he shone. This may sound – corny, is that the word you use? Yes. Kitschig. But he was a star. A leader. His name – Held – suited him well. Among all those poor creatures, he was definitely a leader. Leader of the pack,' he chuckled.

Natasha was anxious to go on talking, but Dr Hoffmann suddenly informed her that he was tired. Very, very tired. Perhaps they could meet another time? But Natasha was now desperate to hear more. What about his wife, the trial, her mother's testimony . . . what was *that* all about? But he shook his head.

'Just one more thing, please, Dr Hoffmann.' She could no longer force herself to call him Ludwig. 'That photograph you gave me . . . when and where was it taken? And . . . why?'

'Let me remember . . . in the camp, of course. In Theresienstadt. You know about the film that was made there? "Hitler's Gift to the Jews" we called it. It was supposed to make the ghetto look beautiful for the outside world . . . and if you ask me, it did.'

'Yes.' Natasha knew about it, but not enough. But that wasn't the point.

'And the photo?' she asked, impatiently.

'Well, Franz Held had been chosen to star in the film, so to speak.' He paused, evidently suppressing another dry chuckle. 'As a photographer, and cameraman, I had been asked to take portraits of several inmates. We made them look good . . . healthy, you know . . . happy . . . The film crew was selecting the most suitable faces to show in the film. Franz had that face. Wouldn't you agree? But in the end, you know, he was edited out, I never knew why. And now, my dear, I really must stop.'

As he walked her to the door, Natasha turned to him.

'Dr Hoffmann, please help me decide. Should we or shouldn't we accept your money?'

He smiled. 'You mean, am I a good German or a bad German? Na-ta-sha, I did my best. Under the circumstances. Ask your mother.'

I sure will, she thought, going home. And that's not all I'm going to ask her. We have some catching up to do. Mega, as Erica would say.

The jerky rhythm of the moving train brought back the amazing things she'd just heard. Her adolescent mother, alone in Theresienstadt . . . Held, starring in a Holocaust production . . . Held, the charismatic leader . . . Leader of the pack . . . Leader of the pack! Wasn't that the title of that song from the early 1960s? The Shangri-las, a girl band with a tough image, sang it and brought a real motorcycle into the studio. The sound of its revving engine was part of the song, as was a motorcycle crash at the end . . . Now she couldn't get the chorus out of her head.

How strange: with a sixties hit reverberating in her head, she was doing that history thing again. Once again, she had been allowed to listen to stories from the past, and then imagine it. As if that was possible . . . But this time, she realized, and sat up in her seat as she did so, this time it was something a little different. This wasn't only about Held. Or Hoffmann. Or *The Nose* . . . This was about her own mother!

Jesus, thought Natasha, this is about my *own* history. *I* have a history . . . how very, very weird. Which means that Philip has that history, too . . . She couldn't wait to tell him.

She completely forgot to check her reflection in the opposite window. If she had, she would have become aware that she was smiling.

13 The Obituary

'Natasha, you're an idiot.'

Later that day, Philip had listened, long-distance, to Natasha's breathless report on her conversation with Hoffmann and immediately discovered a major flaw in her response to the old man's account of their mother's past.

'Even if he did what he says he did, i.e. delivered some letters for a young female inmate in Theresienstadt, how on earth could he have guessed or assumed that this girl was *your* mother? Just because of the trial? That's insane. And how could you let him get away with that? Why didn't you probe a little more? About his wife, for instance?'

'Shit. It never occurred to me. You're right. But he kind of cut me short at a crucial moment. And he seemed so sure . . . I just couldn't . . .'

'Natasha, I'm telling you, this guy is a dubious character. Did you ever ask him how he made his money? What sort of business is he in?'

'Don't know. He says he's a photographer or something.'

Philip was furious.

'How dare he barge into your life like that – *our* lives – and spread crazy stories. Let me have his full name and address, I'll do some checking from my end.'

'But what if it's true? Shouldn't we at least ask Mom, see what she says?'

'Don't even think about it. Not now. Maybe later. And certainly not before she boards that plane for London. You know how she hates talking about any private stuff that's more than a day old. I bet she's only doing it because they forced her. Well, if they did, I'm glad – at least we'll hear some *facts*, for once . . . Am I contradicting myself? Fuck, I hate it when I don't know what to think. But I'm still convinced your German sugar daddy is a fraud. By the way, Mom is leaving this Friday night, it's all arranged. Good luck, to all of you!'

So, as far as Philip was concerned, that was that. No more probing into their mother's past, no more excitement at the thought that there had been more to their lives than a crazy childhood in New York. Excitement was the wrong word, of course: how could she be thrilled by the fact that her mother had lived through something Natasha could not even begin to imagine . . . But, she couldn't help it – excitement was what she felt. Well, Philip had to be right, Hoffmann had to be some sort of disturbed character. Like the people who wrote her those weird e-mails (NettySurvivor!), only from the other side . . . For all she knew, that cheque wasn't even real.

But when she looked at it again, just out of curiosity, it looked real enough. A bona fide Coutts & Co. cheque. You didn't fool around with *those* . . . And why should Philip *always* be right? Her intuition, and her unshakeable belief in the power of coincidences, told her otherwise. She decided to pursue the matter, and talk to her mother, and to Hoffmann, until the entire story became crystal clear.

There were a few key questions she could, and would, ask Hoffmann in order to determine whether he was playing some sort of game. Philip had a point: Hoffmann would have to explain to her how he'd made the connection between the girl in the camp and herself. And, at the same time, she could check up on the story he told her about Held in Theresienstadt. It should be easy enough to determine whether he had, in fact, been there.

Erica was at Amy's, thank God, so she had time to extend her working hours into the early evening. But tonight, she would forget all about it and at least try to be a normal human being . . . Tim deserved a surprise . . .

Looking at the list of trustees, Natasha tried to remember which of them had a long enough connection with the magazine and was therefore likely to have known anything about its founder's past.

Zygmunt Levy-Newman came to mind; didn't he also tell her he would help with anything to do with Hoffmann? But she didn't like the idea of approaching him. She'd wait until she had explored all other options. Then there was Joel Hirsch, who was a survivor himself, apparently. But he was too close to Sussman and she didn't want Sidney to know anything about her new interest in Held.

That left two people: Karl Spitzer and Charles Sugarman. In fact, between them, these two were likely to tell her everything there was to know about Held. Suddenly, it occurred to her that she could begin by reading Sugarman's obituary of Franz Held. Now, where the hell was it?

Natasha began leafing through some older issues of *The Nose*; surely, they would have run the obituary in the first issue not under Held's editorship. That would be about two years ago.

And here it was, mixed in with the rest, without any chronological order. She was surprised to see that the magazine itself was like all the others – filled with the usual assortment of good, bad and mediocre articles on the pros and cons of left or right-wing Zionism, a debate on circumcision, an interview with a Jewish-Catholic convert, some fiction and poetry by authors whose names were familiar to her from her rejection tray. The obituary was placed on the very last page, like an awkward afterthought, and it was clear that Held himself had edited this issue of *The Nose* and had died, presumably, after it had gone to the printers.

Natasha read:

Franz Zvi Held
(1918–93)

Franz Held, who *died* recently, was the visionary founder and editor of this journal from its *birth* in 1955 to the day he *passed away*. Like all great men, he was profoundly simple, yet acutely complex.

While he was admired and, indeed, worshipped by many, he was an intensely private man, giving his all to the magazine he cherished and kept *alive*, at a great cost to his emotional strength, his finances, and even, some would claim, his private *life*. In fact, Franz Held *died*, unexpectedly, while putting the finishing touches on this very issue of *The Nose*, which was to be his *last*, as he *died* before it saw the *light of day*.

Held was a *native* of Prague, where the year of his *birth* coincided with two moments of great historical significance – the *end* of World War I and the *founding* of independent Czechoslovakia. Events of enormous historical import – Hitler's domination of Europe, the Berlin Olympic games, the Shoa, the *birth* of Israel, the birth of state Communism – continued to shape young Held's biography. He took part in them all and re-emerged scarred but very much *alive* and ready to begin a new *life* in post-war Britain, where he found a permanent and happy home somewhere in London. He *lived* there until he *died*.

His contribution to Anglo-Jewish cultural *life* has been as monumental and, indeed, momentous as Anglo-Jewish cultural and literary *life* itself. In the pages of this journal he erected, single-handedly, an extraordinary and unique monument to our rich spiritual tradition, and a chronicle and symbol of our contemporary cultural history. No other publication in this country – nor, indeed anywhere in the Diaspora, including Canada – could ever claim to compete with Held's achievement, and none would be foolish enough to try; not even the esteemed *Jewish Quarterly*, founded by the illustrious Jacob Sonntag.

It is unlikely that this journal will find a successor worthy of Held's creative power and vision. Indeed, it is the current (still unofficial) opinion of the trust that without Franz Held's leadership, *The Nose* must be allowed to *perish*.

Franz Held leaves no survivors. A memorial service may be announced.

Natasha couldn't shake the odd feeling that Sugarman's obituary seemed, well, *abridged*. As if he had left out important chunks of it.

In fact, when she thought about it, she had to conclude that the obituary contained hardly any real information at all. All it demonstrated was Sugarman's obsession with juxtaposing 'birth' and 'death' as often as possible, and in as many variations as he could come up with. Had this truncated necrology been the result of Spitzer's copy-editing? But this text did not look as if it had been edited at all, certainly not by the meticulous Karl Spitzer. It was time for a conversation with Charles Sugarman.

But her phone rang, loudly and insistently. Sometimes she thought of it as an animated thing, which could respond to the vibes of the people using it . . .

'Nata-sha. This is Ludwig.'

Speak of the devil! But this was a great opportunity to—

'I am afraid I was too tired this morning to give you a fuller explanation of my connection with your predecessor . . . and with your mother. I realize you left my house somewhat . . . dissatisfied.'

'Yes, and—'

'So. Unfortunately, as you know, I have to leave for Hamburg tomorrow – my medical condition calls for some further treatment – and we will not be able to meet again until I return, in a few months' time.'

'But could you—'

'So. I have left all the papers, all the *relevant* papers, in a special drawer of my desk, and I have instructed my housekeeper, Mrs Matthews, to direct you to it in my absence. She is here every day from ten until five, so do call any time it will suit you during those hours. Please, Na-ta-sha, do come and leaf through all that . . . material. I am certain that with your analytical acumen, it will tell you more than I could . . . I tire so easily, as you know. I would have to talk to you for *years* to explain all those . . . circumstances.'

'But, just about my mother—'

Again that annoying dry chuckle . . .

'It's all there, my dear.'

Natasha had to swallow her impatience and, thinking of Philip, say as calmly as she could, 'Thank you very much. I will come and read your files. But please tell me one thing now: what sort of business are you – or were you – in?'

'Photography, and film. I am not unknown in my area of expertise, Na-tasha. Well, I look forward to our next conversation. Goodbye now. Mrs Matthews is a very nice lady.'

Well, on to Charles Sugarman, thought Natasha. And she also thought, I am not telling this to Philip. *None* of this. She was suddenly weary of his scepticism, and his lack of enthusiasm. If he wasn't interested, she couldn't force him.

'Charles. It's Natasha. I know you must be busy with your show, but I really need to ask you something.'

Sugarman owned a well-known art gallery in Highgate village. He had begun, many years ago, by exhibiting the work of dissident Soviet and other East European artists, sometimes without their knowledge. After all the velvet revolutions in the east, he broadened his spectrum and was currently hosting an international travelling show entitled *Aimez-Vous Marx*?, which consisted of art installations based on 'Marxist, post-Marxist and neo-Marxist concepts', according to a brochure he once gave Natasha. The most popular of these exhibits, by a young Swiss artist, began with an organized walk to Marx's grave in nearby Highgate cemetery, where each visitor was photographed with a Polaroid camera; the photos then became a part of the installation when the artist's assistant placed them on a miniature conveyor belt, to be circulated once and then deposited in special black plastic containers, which in turn formed the sentence 'Proletarians of the World, Unite'. They were then dropped out of the containers at the push of an automatic button and returned to the conveyor belt, ad infinitum.

'Natasha, of course, anything. You know I'm always happy to help – is it an editorial matter? I'm far better qualified than Sidney to—'

'Not really. Actually, it's about your obituary of Held.'

Sugarman's voice positively beamed with excitement. He was clearly elated.

'Natasha, you've just made me very happy. Nothing excites me more than when people go back and reread my old work, and appreciate it for its inherent literary quality, as it were. Not for its informative value, so to speak, but for its contribution to the *genre*. Do you agree with me that an obituary has to be a well-constructed textual edifice, built on a carefully executed rhythm of white alternating with black, birth with death, in order to tell and explain a person's life, from beginning to end?'

'Yes, Charles, I do. I just have a few questions about this particular one. First of all, did you write it the way it was printed, or had there been a longer version, which had been edited? And: why did you write that Held lived "somewhere" in London. You must admit that's a little unusual.'

'That was some sort of typo,' laughed Sugarman. 'I remember being very puzzled when I saw it in print – but you are the first person to really notice, thank God. Originally, I had written . . . wait a minute . . . I think I'd just written "in London". Yes, I'm sure about that.'

'OK. And the editing?'

'By Spitzer? Well, Natasha, here I have to confess something.'

She waited. Sugarman was damn long-winded and slow. Too bad you couldn't edit people's conversations, she thought viciously.

'You see . . . Well . . . as you know, I have quite a number of *potential* obituaries on file, as it were . . .'

'Yes, Charles, I know.'

'Well, at some point, quite a long time ago, Franz had asked me to show him what I had written about him. The reason being . . . the reason being that I had published – I mean, *The Nose* had published – my portrait of one of our loyal readers and supporters, Max Brass, and both Brass and Held were of the opinion that my piece read a little too much like an obituary.'

He exhaled loudly into the phone. Natasha would have moved hers further away from her ear, if she weren't anxious to catch every word he was saying.

'And in a way, they were right. I do, occasionally, adapt my unused obituaries when I need to write a little profile about someone. In fact, I always do this, but as I don't publish that much, no one has noticed . . . But Max and Franz did, and they weren't happy. So that's why Franz decided to take a look at what I had stored in my files about him.'

'Was he pleased with it? Or did he make any changes?'

'I have no idea, Natasha. He never told me. In fact, he never returned it to me.'

'Oh. So the obituary that appeared in *The Nose* had not, in the end, been approved by him?'

'Well, it's a little more complicated than that.'

This time, Sugarman exhaled and inhaled and said nothing, and Natasha thought that if he didn't finish his explanation now, this minute, she would simply explode and hang up and forget the whole business. But his next sentence floored her.

'Natasha, that obituary of mine was published before I even knew that Held had died. Or at least, pretty much at the same time. One day, I received a phone call from Sidney telling me that our editor was dead, and while I was polishing my obituary in order to send it to Karl and elsewhere, *The Nose* had already appeared, with my obituary in it. Apparently, Franz had given it to Karl some time ago, and so there was no need to contact me about it . . . That's what Karl told me.'

Wise man, that Held, thought Natasha – what a brilliant move on his part, to prevent Sugarman from publishing some nonsense about him, after his death . . . The guy must have been a real control freak. Not unlike herself . . .

'But, Natasha, the odd thing was that the obituary Held gave to Spitzer, or at least the one Spitzer allowed to go to print, was not very different from the one I had written myself. I mean, he left in all the words of praise and all my little stylistic devices which I am so proud of . . . Of course, Spitzer himself must have added the bit about how he died while working on that issue of the magazine . . . and I don't know what else. I don't really remember my original obituary, but I could look it up.'

Natasha had a thought.

'Charles, what about your obituaries of Held that appeared in the daily press?'

'What about them?'

'Well, were they different from the one in our magazine?'

'I don't remember. Maybe. I'll try to find some in my files.'

'Thank you, Charles.'

'It's been a pleasure, Natasha. By the way, how is Tim?'

'Very well, thank you.'

'How is he taking his momentous decision?'

'What momentous decision?' Natasha was baffled. Sugarman's ability to come up with gossip based on invented facts and misunderstandings never ceased to amaze her.

'His decision to convert to Judaism.'

'Where did you get that idea?' Natasha burst out laughing. 'My husband is not planning on converting! At least not that I know of . . .'

'Oh, well, we had a little chat while he was waiting for you outside Sidney's shop after the meeting, and when I asked him how he was, he said that you had both decided that a conversion was definitely a good idea.'

'A co—' Suddenly, she understood. She laughed even harder. 'Charles, Tim was talking about a loft conversion. About extending our house a little, to give us more space . . .'

Sugarman didn't laugh.

'I see. I will have to adjust my . . . well, my understanding of things. Sorry about that.'

Natasha knew what he meant: he would have to update his most recent update of her own obituary, which must, by now, contain the juicy information on Natasha Kaplan's husband's active interest in Judaism. Maybe she should follow Held's example and grab that obituary from Sugarman before it was too late . . .

Her conversation with Karl Spitzer was, as always, short and to the point. Yes, he had printed the obituary Held had given him some time before his death, when he heard (from Sidney) that Held had passed away. Yes, the issue of the magazine was already at the printers and he did not have time to look at it properly, so he is aware of its poor quality and that little mistake ('*somewhere* in London! My God! Well, it's too late now') and quite upset about it.

Would he talk to Natasha about Held? Sure, but what was there to talk about? He could tell her all he knew in a couple of sentences: Held was a very interesting and intelligent editor. A difficult man. Sometimes, he disappeared for days, even weeks, because he got tired of people and needed to be on his own, as he used to say. But, Natasha asked, wasn't he alone all the time anyway? Didn't he live alone?

Spitzer became impatient with her. Held's private life wasn't his business. And why was she so curious all of a sudden?

'I will tell you a secret, Karl, but you must keep it to yourself. I am thinking of writing his biography. I need to find out everything I can.' Would Spitzer warm to this? Would he help her *now*? she wondered.

'Natasha, that's not a good idea. You can't possibly write about a man like that. You are too . . . young.'

'But I can try. Will you help me if I need to know some details? Like, for example, his life during the war. Was he in Theresien—'

'He was a soldier, Natasha. That's all I know, because that's all he ever told me.'

'A *soldier*? Wasn't he in—'

'That is all I know. I'm sorry. Goodbye. By the way, this issue on Jews and crime – congratulations. *Chapeau*, as we used to say. Very, very good stuff.'

Natasha was pleased. A compliment from Karl Spitzer meant a lot to her, she really valued his opinion. 'Thank you, Karl, I will pass it on to the editorial board. But – are you sure you don't know which army he was a soldier in?'

She heard him laugh, heartily, which was rare for Spitzer.

'Natasha, figure it out. There aren't that many possibilities! If you can't do that, how on earth do you plan on being his biographer? I told you, you are too young. You have hardly lived yourself.'

OK, that's enough *Nose* business for the day, she decided after hanging up the phone. She had just enough time to take a shower before picking up Erica. She would have a long, secret talk with her daughter about what she should do with her hair, she decided. Tomorrow was a big day – she was finally getting that haircut.

14 Hair

Erica's rational advice had been to 'please just have a trim, Mum' but Natasha had no intention of obeying her daughter's – and presumably also Tim's – wishes. In any case, Tim had not been consulted – he had been assigned an unexpected double shift last night to fill in for a colleague – and had no idea that the next time he would see his wife, he would, in all probability, get a bit of a shock.

So here she was, at Cutting it Fine in busy North Finchley, leafing through some torn women's magazines, awaiting her turn. She had decided on a free-flowing, shoulder-length, wavy look without any colour change, and while it was being produced – a complicated, fragrant procedure – she chatted to her hairdresser, Monique, about nothing in particular and enjoyed the very loud music they played in this salon. What bliss. She would not let any serious thoughts enter her mind.

She was so absorbed in *feeling good* that she completely forgot to pay attention to what Monique's hands were doing to her hair, so that when she saw the final result, it was too late to protest or beg for mercy. The haircut was a disaster: boring, uninspired, it made her look like a provincial beauty pageant contestant. She managed a smile, paid, and walked out of Cutting it Fine with tears in her eyes.

Natasha was not the kind of person who could live with a bad haircut. Years ago, in New York, she had celebrated the publication of her mystery novel by making an appointment with one of the most expensive hairdressers in town. Massimo Andreotti was his name, and she had paid him two hundred bucks for the most disastrous experiment her hair had ever been subjected to. The idea had sounded great – short and asymmetric, a classic eighties look. But the actual result was so sad she had considered living in total seclusion. That cut, Natasha now realized, had been the reason why she'd let her hair grow so long . . . Some people were scared of dentists – she had developed a phobia about those deceptively friendly men and women who attacked your hair with scissors and a pack of lies.

So, what now? She scanned the high street and noticed a few other salons which looked more or less promising, and fairly empty. Natasha took a deep breath, and began an odyssey she would remember till the end of her days.

In the first one, Peter, Paul and Mary's Hair and Beauty, she was told that both Peter and Mary were busy, but Paul, a very attractive, deeply tanned young man with a red ponytail, happened to be free. Natasha was about to confess that she had just had a cut and needed some sort of improvement, when Paul exclaimed, 'You poor darling, you haven't had a cut in *ages* . . . What, two, three months? Thought so.' As he washed her hair, he suggested a little colour and Natasha agreed. After a few hours, she emerged from salon no. 2 with interesting highlights and a straighter, more geometric version of her original cut. But still deeply unhappy.

Salon no. 3 (Uncle Simon's) was a men's barber shop, as Natasha realized after she had entered it and closed the door behind her. The decor was actually quite stylish – fifties-style chrome and red leather. Soft Sinatra and Dean Martin tunes emanated from somewhere. The clientele were probably middle-aged to elderly men, probably Jewish. If the shop weren't so empty, Natasha imagined she would have felt as if she had entered a room full of trustees . . .

But before she could attempt a dignified exit, she was greeted, very warmly, by Simon, the fast-talking elderly owner.

'Hello my dear please don't worry we do ladies too if only we could get them to come!'

He was a friendly, round man with a broad smile and a huge gap between his two, very yellow front teeth, one of which was chipped. The roundness was accentuated by his polished bald scalp, a vast, open expanse.

'Let me guess my dear you've just had a bad cut and you need Uncle Simon to set it straight so to speak?'

Natasha was so impressed by his powers of perception – the last hairdresser had not guessed that she had just been mutilated by one of his colleagues – that she actually allowed herself to be led to an empty leather chair, like a lamb to slaughter.

'Well,' continued Simon merrily, 'well well well. Oh *well.* This perm is *all wrong* . . . And oh my God who let their scissors loose in this beautiful hair of yours . . . But my dear I think we can help you. Let's have a wash first, and then – just leave it to me. Uncle Simon is *very* experienced. I used to be hairdresser to the stars, bet you didn't know that. Actors, sportsmen, politicians – and their wives, too. I could name names . . . Well, we all have our ups and downs . . .'

Natasha was, by now, so exhausted and traumatized by her multiple haircut operation that she was happy to close her eyes and hope for the best. And Simon's hands were swift and, yes, he did inspire confidence, even in this unreal set-up . . . And he never stopped talking, like a muzak machine that produces automatic speech instead of music.

'Right,' he said, gently drying her hair, 'please sit up, move over here . . . lovely. And now let me tell you that because it's such a pleasure for me to do a lady's hair for a change – no offence, gentlemen,' he apologized to the invisible crowd, 'I am about to give you the time of your life you will thank me forever and come back for more. And just to show you what a connoisseur I am when it comes to appreciating the female sex and the human race in general – I will guess your age, your job and whether you are married or have a boyfriend. Uncle Simon is a bit of a fortune-teller, too . . .'

Natasha caught herself smiling. She was actually having fun!

'Well now you are obviously American but that's not hard to guess is it. But I will also say that you were born and raised in Brooklyn. I used to work there, you see – I have quite a past . . . Right? OK, so far so good. Now for the harder part.'

He stopped cutting for a minute, and bent over her head to take a close look at her scalp. Oh my God, thought Natasha, what if he finds any nits I might have caught from my sweet daughter. But Simon declared, 'I can tell from the condition of your scalp and the roots of your hair that you are around thirty, give or take a year?'

Natasha nodded. The music became a barely audible background noise.

Simon grinned and continued, 'And you are definitely married, with at least one child. Would you like me to tell you how I know that? Your roots are healthy, but the hair itself is neglected. So that means there is a life, there is a spirit under there, but you ignore it, don't pay any attention to it. You have other things to do. Now as for your job . . .'

He fell silent for a long moment, then resumed in an earnest tone of voice, 'You are like me my dear your job is your vocation. Your life. It takes everything out of us doesn't it, we kill ourselves and no one appreciates it.'

Again, Natasha nodded. She felt hypnotized by this peculiar Uncle Simon.

'So, won't you tell us if I've guessed it right?'

She confirmed that he had, and even revealed the nature of her work. Simon became visibly animated when she mentioned the magazine.

'Now that is the most amazing coincidence. I used to cut the hair of your Mr Held!'

Natasha whirled her chair around to face him. Now she had a million questions for Uncle Simon . . .

'A very regular customer he was, our Mr Held. Every fortnight on the dot. Except sometimes, he would come and I would notice that his hair had been done recently – just like yours . . . And not well at all . . . So perhaps he wasn't as loyal as I thought! A lovely gentleman, though . . . Very interesting to talk to . . . Tried to get me to read his magazine, but it was too highbrow for me, if you know what I mean . . . I bet it still is!'

Natasha smiled.

'You must have been sorry to lose him when he died,' she said.

'Well I was very sorry to read in the *Weekly* that he had passed away – and one of our clients who knew him well had mentioned it too. A Mr Sussman.'

Of course, thought Natasha. The barber shop was just around the corner from Sussman's Pets . . .

'But he had stopped coming here long before that. His hair had thinned out quite a lot, you see, there was little left for me to do. Though some gentlemen make the mistake of neglecting their few remaining hairs . . . and even a hairless scalp, like mine, can use a nice, healthy massage, to keep us in shape! There my dear now what do you think?'

He had finished blow-drying her hair, and they both looked at her reflection in the mirror. Natasha was amazed. The result was a triumph for Simon, and in the eyes of his grateful female customer, for his entire profession. He had managed to create a logical synthesis of all the experiments she had undergone that day: the highlights made her natural light colour come alive in a new cut that now framed her face as naturally as if it had been designed just for her. And yet it was, she knew, incredibly trendy. Was Simon a genius? And was she cured of her phobia?

Two older men walked in and she was happy to leave before they started paying much attention to her. She promised 'Uncle Simon' she would definitely come again, and maybe even send her husband to him. A very contented Natasha then floated down Finchley High Street towards her bus.

When she got home, much, much later than she had promised, she rang the bell instead of using her key because she wanted to see Tim's immediate reaction to her new look, before he had a chance to hide his true feelings. She wasn't disappointed: his eyes widened, he made a step backward to take in the full vision of his radically altered wife and then, smiling, articulated his opinion, in its full complexity:

'Very nice.'

Erica came out of the kitchen, subjected her mother to several difficult moments of heavy observation and declared, 'That's Amy's sister's haircut. But, OK, whatever.' And disappeared again.

Neither of them could have guessed that she had just had three haircuts, which had cost her a total of £150. Almost exactly as much as that designer New York cut that had so bruised her self-confidence. Well, this one had made a huge dent in her budget, but had managed to put her on a high. With a little bit of attention from Uncle Simon, her mood had been restored from gloomy and distracted to positive and focused. Now she felt ready to tackle that other business . . . She had to tell Tim what she'd been up to. If only because she had no intention of going to Hoffmann's flat all by herself.

'Natasha, I wish I could help you,' said Tim thoughtfully, after she'd explained everything she'd found out so far, which wasn't that much. 'But I really can't take any time off this week, nor next week. And I guess you want to go there soon?'

Natasha was annoyed. She really didn't like the idea of facing a Mrs Matthews in that spooky flat . . .

'Tim, can't you work in that area one day this week? Like Ian?'

'What do you mean, "like Ian"?'

'Yesterday, when I went there, I bumped into Ian, patrolling Gloucester Road tube station.'

Tim looked puzzled.

'That doesn't seem right. As far as I knew – as far as we *all* knew – he had the whole day off sick. A toothache. That's why I had to take a part of his shift, remember?'

'Well, Tim, I didn't see Ian's ghost, I'm telling you. I guess he told a fib – but why would he parade around in full uniform, if all he wanted was a secret day off?'

'That's what I don't get.'

'Are you going to ask him?'

Tim sighed. Confronting Ian, confronting *anybody*, was not his cup of tea.

'I knew it,' said Natasha. 'Well if you won't, I will.'

'No.' He actually sounded adamant.

'Why the hell not? Look, I know he's your mate, and all that . . . But . . . are you sure about that guy? Sometimes I don't like the way he talks to me. You wouldn't be too pleased to hear some of the stuff he dishes out—'

'What stuff? Has he been coming on to you? Natasha, that's just Ian. I don't want to disappoint you, but he talks that way to every woman he meets . . .'

'OK but I still want to know about yesterday. I saw him sort of harassing a poor old drunk.'

'Really?'

'Yes, Tim, really. Well?'

She could almost see him thinking about it, could see him stretching his mind, very slowly and carefully, this way and that, until he reached a conclusion.

'No. Let's leave him alone. If he has something to tell me – us – I know he will. Are you hungry? Erica and I have eaten, we were starving, but we left you some of that chicken.'

That was the end of the discussion, Natasha knew that. But she couldn't help feeling furious with her calm, methodical, reliable and so incredibly patient husband. We're definitely a mismatch, she thought to herself and almost screamed it out loud.

But then it occurred to her that she certainly wouldn't prefer a hothead like Ian to Tim. Tim's slow, deliberate manner of relating to the world had a lot going for it. She felt safer with a man like that – not because she could read him better but because he didn't care how long it took her to figure him out. So if she made any mistakes along the way, she also had plenty of time to correct them – no rush. Maybe *that* was the reason why they were still together . . .

To change the subject, she told Tim about Sugarman's mistaken belief that he was about to undergo a conversion. Tim laughed.

Erica, who had silently rejoined them, asked, 'Mum, do I have to have a conversion?'

'No, darling, you don't. You're Jewish because I'm Jewish.'

'But Daddy isn't!'

'Doesn't matter. Jewish law says a person is Jewish if their mother is Jewish. And anyway, it doesn't matter.'

'So Daddy doesn't count?'

'Of course he counts . . . But not for . . .' Suddenly, Natasha noticed that Tim's face was red. 'Tim, didn't you know this? I'm so sorry . . .'

He really was upset. Without knowing it, both Natasha and Tim had the same thought which they kept to themselves: 'All this Jewish stuff is so fucking complicated. Who the fuck needs it.'

'Isn't all that Jewish stuff really complicated?' asked Erica. 'Do I have to worry? I mean, is there a Jewish police?'

'What do you mean?' asked Natasha.

'Well, you said there was this Jewish law, so I thought if there's a law, there is probably a police, to make sure Jewish people do everything right . . .'

Tim laughed, finally.

'No, Erica, of course there is no such thing. Jewish law is something different. It's . . . help me out here, Natasha!' he begged.

'Actually,' said Natasha, 'she's not so wrong. We do have various Rabbinates telling people what to do – as Jews, that is – and if some fanatics had their way, the Jewish state would be a kind of . . . religious dictatorship.'

Erica and Tim looked at her in surprise but didn't ask any more questions.

'Natasha, you can be very serious sometimes. You've been too serious lately. It doesn't suit your – your haircut. Is something . . . wrong?'

'Oh-oh, this is where it gets bo-ring. Bye, guys, the TV calls!' said Erica and carefully moved away from her parents. Being an only child, she was well skilled in guessing when her parents' conversations changed from being a family discussion to a private exchange.

'I think I told you.'

'Yeah, and I'm sorry I can't go there with you. But – didn't you say your mother was coming this weekend? Why don't you take her along?'

'Hey, Tim . . . that's not a bad idea. No, wait, that's a *very* bad idea. Philip and I have decided not to tell her anything about what Hoffmann said until, or only if, we're a hundred per cent sure he's not some sort of maniac. Which, by the way, is also a very good reason for me not to go there alone. But, if you insist . . . I can be brave, you know . . .'

'OK,' said Tim, and it was clear that this last argument had finally persuaded him. 'I'll come along. But I'll have to tell my superiors some sort of truth – you know I can't lie . . .'

'Tell them your wife is involved in a life-threatening situation and you have to protect her.'

'Try another one, darling.'

'Tell them . . . I know: tell them I threatened you with divorce unless we spend that day – say, Monday? – together. All of it. Which is true, by the way.'

'You'll laugh, but they might buy it. Apparently, I'm one of the last Mohicans at the BTP . . .'

'Meaning?'

'One of the few not-divorced or not-separated men. Or women.'

They noticed Erica eyeing them anxiously from her bedroom door. Natasha ran to her and hugged her, hard.

'We said *not*-divorced, you silly girl, didn't you hear? Now go to bed. It's almost *our* bedtime!'

But the new haircut had given Natasha so much fresh energy that she stayed awake, again, late into night, surfing the net and e-mailing. Philip had written several consecutive notes, minutes apart:

Natasha

Ludwig Hoffmann, if it's the same guy, would seem to be a German-born film-maker with an international reputation. Especially in the documentary field. Am trying to find out more. Any news your end? Sorry I was a sourpuss. Let's not give up yet, but go slow. Definitely no word to Mom!

P

N:

Am collecting info re Mom in Theresienstadt. Not that hard, there are archives, etc. She was definitely there (as Alice Weiss, of course). Have material on the Nazi propaganda film, but the actual footage survived only in fragments. Well, anyway, it's the OTHER ONE, the GOETZ one, that we want.

P

Natasha

Fuck, can't find anything AT ALL on this Annmarie Goetz and Mom. Goetz had some sort of major film career in Germany before and during the war. But Mom didn't get into film till after she met Dad, so what's that all about? The Nazi film, the one that the trial is about, is not mentioned in any of my sources. Will keep digging.

P

Natasha!!!

Too bad our grandfather Max is not alive . . . He could have told us about pre-war German cinema – I mean, he was IT!!! Remember his famous silent feature? Hey, maybe I'll talk to Dad about that. Yeah, I DEFINITELY will.

Later,
P

John White had sent another dozen messages celebrating the superiority of the white race and predicting the naturally predetermined obliteration of all other races. All of his notes were identical, but, as she was saving them in her gradually expanding FILTH folder, she noticed that one message contained a website ID. Let's see what else this guy has to show for himself, she decided and double-clicked on the vibrant blue line.

Within minutes, she was in a world of interlinking websites which all had a few things in common: a rich display of interesting if repetitive graphics based on S&M images intermingled with swastikas, language clearly derived or borrowed from *Mein Kampf*, though neatly couched in English, and some technical mumbo jumbo she did not understand. One of them played a German song she decided to download: a low, monotonous male voice droned, '*Du kannst mein Bestrafer sein / Du bist groß / Du bist stark / Bestrafe mich / Bestrafe mich.*' ('You can be my master / you are big / you are strong / punish me / punish me.') For some reason, the same site listed the names of some

London tube stations transliterated into German, presenting King's Cross as Kink's Kross. Natasha giggled, and, hoping that she may have uncovered some dirty sex connection in her city, copied down the name of the site. Tim will have a laugh. And King's Cross was definitely *his* domain.

15 Alice in London

Whenever Natasha observed her mother from a distance, as she did now in the Heathrow waiting lounge, she felt both lucky and embarrassed to be this woman's daughter. Alice's solid beauty seemed to intensify rather than wane with years. She radiated complete indifference to her soft wrinkles and her cloud of white hair as she walked, erect, carrying her tall graceful body like a goddess, her full breasts still pointing the way and her hips still swaying with each light step. She was dressed in faded blue jeans and a black leather jacket, wore absolutely no make-up and beamed a huge, generous smile at Natasha, Tim and Erica when she spotted them in the crowd.

Erica ran towards her grandmother, screaming something incomprehensible but unmistakably joyous. Alice held her tight and whispered in Erica's ear, making her explode in a series of giggles. Then they were all one big, laughing bundle, Alice hugging first Natasha, then Tim, without letting go of Erica.

'Excellent,' said Alice. Natasha knew she meant her new haircut. Now, up close, she began to feel that usual, familiar sense of tiredness invariably brought on by her mother's exuberant presence. She could never keep up with her – she used to want to try, desperately, but now she noticed an imperceptible change in herself – a new willingness to let her mother's dramatic high spirits reign supreme, without letting them affect her.

In the car, Alice informed them that the flat she had found through the *London Review of Books* was 'almost ready'.

'What does that mean?' asked Natasha, a little nervously.

'Well, darling, it means that I will have to stay with you children for the weekend, and maybe longer. I can move in by the end of the week, they said. The owners are late leaving for their sabbatical.'

'Where is it, by the way?' asked Tim. 'Natasha told me it would be near us.'

'Yes, very near. Let me see . . . the nearest underground station would be . . . Clapham Common.'

'Mom!!!' screamed Natasha, while Tim tried to concentrate on negotiating a complex roundabout. 'That's the other end of London! You might as well have stayed in New York!'

Alice laughed, a deep throaty laugh. 'Gotcha!' she sang out. 'I was only testing you. You seemed so worried when I said that my place was not quite ready I thought you didn't want me staying with you at all.'

Natasha was not amused. Her mother was the only person in the world who could make her feel like a humourless, rigid, ungenerous person. But wasn't it rational to worry a little that her mother, or maybe even both her parents, might end up living with them for quite some time? Their house was tiny, no extra bedroom for guests, only a spare sofa in the living room.

'OK, joke over,' said Alice, yawning. 'My flat is actually somewhere in a place called Whetstone. Definitely not far from where you are, I've been told, and nice and quiet – you know how I adore a bit of suburbia. And if Sam hates it,' she added, with a wink at Natasha, 'well, he can stay somewhere else when he comes!'

When they arrived at the house in Southgate, Alice declared she was terribly jet-lagged. All she wanted to do was unload the presents and go to sleep.

Her gifts consisted of one large suitcase full of clothes for all three of them, plus a microscope for Erica. It turned out that this was the whispered secret that had made her giggle so hard in the airport: 'Grandma said we would look at my lice together, if we find any!'

Tim gave Natasha a puzzled look, and said: 'Why am I never told about these things? I had no idea Erica had nits.'

'Not any more,' answered Natasha. 'Anyway, you have nothing to worry about – with your mini-crop . . .'

'Lice are not so easy to exterminate,' declared Alice matter-of-factly, 'don't be surprised if they come back. Where am I sleeping?'

'My room!!' shouted Erica. 'PLEASE!!'

Natasha's protests that there was no extra bed there were ignored by Alice, who asked only for a pillow and a blanket and was soon asleep on an old futon on the floor in Erica's room.

Erica was in heaven and announced that she was going to sleep as well, even though it was only one in the afternoon. 'I *really* need a nap,' she said gravely and joined her grandmother in her room.

That left Tim and Natasha with nothing to do for the rest of the afternoon. They had expected a whirlwind of activity which Alice usually managed to produce simply by being there, and her temporary retreat left them stunned and unprepared.

'Well, I could do with a nap, myself,' said Tim slowly.

'Me too,' said Natasha.

But instead, they lay on their bed and gossiped.

'Well, what do you think? Has she changed? My brother doesn't agree with me, but I'm convinced she's going through some sort of transformation. But maybe I'm imagining it.'

'He's probably right. I don't see any change. Your mother is as . . . well, as lively as ever. I love those shirts she brought me! How does she always know what I like?'

'That's not hard, Tim. You like pretty much anything.'

'I do *not*! I have pretty good taste. I like you . . .'

'*Like*?!'

'All right, love.'

'You mean you love me?'

'Yeah.'

'Say it!!'

'I – love you.'

'Even though you have to put up with my mother for quite a while?'

'But I told you, I think she's great. Yeah, I still love you.'

'See, was that so hard?'

It was, actually. For Tim, verbal declarations of love were an unnecessarily demonstrative way of expressing something he preferred to show in other, more physical ways. But Natasha was not being receptive to those, with her mother napping in the room next door.

'Are you nuts?!? They could both be up any second.'

'You're a bit of a prude, you know, considering your . . . origins,' whispered Tim.

Natasha blew up:

'What the fuck is that supposed to mean? Are you saying that because I'm Jewish you expect me to be some sort of sexual dynamo?'

Tim looked at her quizzically; that thought had never entered his mind.

'No, darling,' he laughed quietly, 'I was thinking more of your parents' work . . . you know, the films they used to make. Didn't you tell me it was some sort of mild pornography? So I would expect them to be kind of open about these things.'

'Ah,' said Natasha. 'Now you've made me feel pretty ridiculous. By the way, my dad is still into all that. He is planning a new one.'

Tim was thoroughly amused.

'What's he into, erotica for pensioners? Would that be called – sclerotica?'

They laughed so hard they finally did wake up Natasha's mother, who gently knocked on their door but came in before they were quite ready for her.

'What's so funny?' she asked. 'I want to know.'

Natasha told her, and Tim's rugged cheeks turned red under his stubble. He was pleased with his own joke, but also embarrassed by it.

'He still blushes like a Victorian virgin,' said Alice, smiling at Tim.

'That's why they call him Rosy Parker at work!' said Natasha, smiling as well. 'Or Timid Tim.'

'How *is* your work, Tim? Are you still doing those dangerous things? I've been telling all my friends in New York about my son-in-law the London Underground cop. We all think it's very glamorous!'

'But it's not,' said Tim, simply, getting up from the bed. 'It's just a . . . job.'

Alice turned to her daughter. 'And how's *your* work, Natashka?

You told me your phone never stopped ringing, but it's been pretty quiet today!'

'Well, I'll leave you two alone,' said Tim happily, and quietly closed the door behind him.

'It's Saturday,' said Natasha. 'That's the only day they kind of let me live. But it'll start all over again in the evening, you'll see.'

Alice wanted to know everything about Natasha's routine, and offered to help by spending time with Erica. But she had some other ideas as well: she could be Natasha's secretary, helping her sort through her correspondence and other administrative tasks. And she could assist in evaluating the manuscripts that came in, answer the phone, maybe even deal with the trustees . . .

'Mom! Why don't you just take over my job? Sounds like you'd love to do that.'

Natasha knew that her mother would be excellent at all those things, but she also knew that, no matter how much she complained about her work overload, she could never delegate any of that burden to someone else. They agreed that Alice would help with Erica and maybe with some of the manuscripts and review copies – it would be good to have another reader.

But what Natasha really wanted to say was, Can we talk about why you're here for that trial? She glanced at her mother, who looked happy and animated by the idea of taking a break from her own routine in New York and having some fun in her daughter's London home, and could not bring herself to talk about what was really on her mind. Not yet. Maybe after her visit to Hoffmann's flat, when she'd have more facts at her disposal . . . She would have to remind Tim about their 'date' for Monday she decided, and went to look for him.

The real reason for Alice's animated mood was not something Natasha could have guessed. After a life-long silence on the subject of her past, Alice had decided that enough was enough. Well, it had, in fact, been decided *for* her . . . She was in London in order to open, publicly, some very old chapters of her life; however, in order to do that, she had to reopen them to herself. That would take some time, and quite a bit of work. This was why she had planned a longer stay.

Not that she didn't feel the urge to spend time with Erica and Natasha and Tim; but, if she was honest with herself – and Alice generally was – she would have to admit that without a more serious incentive she might have come only for a short family visit.

Of course, she would share everything with Philip as well, in due time. But her first instinct had been to talk to Natasha, if only because of that funny little magazine of hers. Alice was amused by Natasha's protective attitude towards her work. She had expected her daughter to be ecstatically happy with her offer of help. It would have made things a little easier if Natasha had accepted her volunteer services; she didn't feel like snooping around in Natasha's paperwork and files, like a spy, but now she would have no other choice, thought Alice as she unpacked her suitcase, while her granddaughter watched her from her bed.

'I wish you could stay in my room the whole time,' said Erica. 'Why do you need a flat?'

'I won't be far, honey, and it's better that way – you need your space. For your homework, and your friends . . .'

'I *hate* homework. It's *so* boring!'

'Really? I used to love it when I was your age!'

'Yuk! My grandmother was a geek!'

Alice laughed. 'You're right, I was a bit of a geek. But I just loved learning!'

'I bet your parents never told you off.'

'Sure they did. But . . . not a lot, you're right.'

'My parents are pretty pathetic. No offence, I mean I know my mother is your daughter, but – she can be such a nag.'

'Erica, I don't believe the way you're talking.'

'Do you think I'm rude?'

'No, I mean, you're so grown up.'

Erica sighed a big sigh.

'What's wrong?' asked Alice.

'Well, I know you think I'm so mature and all, but, actually, I get pretty confused sometimes. Last week, I cried because Dad told me that clouds were just air.'

'What did you think they were?' asked Alice, smiling.

'Fluff. Like . . . cotton balls. And I always thought that one day, I could touch a cloud, and take some of that fluff if I put my hand out the window of an airplane. How *dumb* can you get?'

'Sweetheart, that's *beautiful*, not dumb. And if you have any questions about anything, and I mean anything at all, you know you can always ask me.'

'Really? That's great. OK, I have this question . . . I wanted to ask Daddy or Mummy but I think they'd get upset. Is Jesus the son of God or a god? I can't figure it out.'

'Well,' said Alice, trying to keep a straight face, 'he is . . . he is . . . sort of both.'

'What?!!' exclaimed Erica, wrinkling her nose as if she had smelt or tasted something bad. 'You mean he is his own father? That's *disgusting*!!'

'Not exactly. It's complicated. You don't really have to figure it out, do you? It can wait.'

'That's just it, Grandma, it can't. I need to make up my mind now if I want to be Jewish or Christian, so I'm trying to get both and see what I like better.'

'Who told you you need to make up your mind now?' asked Alice, earnestly.

'No one. I just decided.'

Alice looked at Erica and suddenly felt that thing she remembered feeling when she first became acutely aware of what it meant to be a mother: a kind of bubble burst somewhere deep inside her, spreading warmth and joy – no, *ecstasy* – caused directly by the thought that here was a brand new human being, a child – *her* child – who was a real kindred spirit and a friend.

'Darling, when I was a little girl, I had the same problem.'

'But you are Jewish!'

'I am, but only half. My father was Jewish, my mother wasn't.'

'Wow, Grandma, I didn't know!'

'Well, now you know. Anyway, I was also confused, like you. So one day I decided to test myself.'

'How?' Erica was barely breathing.

'One Sunday morning, I was playing in the park near my house, and there was this huge church. A very impressive church. I had always admired it, but my parents never allowed me to go inside. But on that day, I don't know why, I just walked in there with all the people. I remember the organ playing, and the singing, it was so beautiful. But I had no idea what to do next. So I looked around and saw that everyone was kneeling down and praying. I did the same thing: I walked all the way to the front, where the service was going on, and, in the empty space between the two main rows of seats, where all the people could see me, I fell on my knees, just like everybody else.'

'Were you praying?'

'Not really. I was just mimicking what the others were doing, like a parrot. I mumbled something, moving my lips like they did. I didn't really feel anything. And then, suddenly, that huge church became very silent, the wonderful music stopped, and I heard heavy steps behind me, coming closer and closer, and I thought, That's my sign: God is coming to kick me out of here because He must know I don't really belong here.'

'But who was it?' whispered Erica.

'My father. He had come to the park to call me home for lunch, and couldn't find me. So he asked all my friends and they told him I had gone into the church. He marched in there, furious, lifted me up into his arms and carried me out. The whole church was staring at us, I still remember that. When we were outside, he put me down, raised his hand – I thought he was going to slap me – but he only stroked my head and said, very firmly: "Don't *ever* go to a church again. You are Jewish, remember that."'

Erica looked pensive. Then she said, 'You're so lucky! That was your sign. Your father told you what to do.' But then she added, 'Grandma. We have a problem. Mummy told me that you're Jewish if your mother is Jewish – that's what the Jewish law says. So I thought I was because she was, but now you tell me that you are not, so she's not and so I'm not. And I don't think she knows!'

'Don't be so serious,' said Alice. 'All those laws are not so important. What really matters is what you feel. And you can worry about that later.'

Natasha, who had overheard – no, eavesdropped on their conversation behind a half-closed door, thought, Well, that's 1–0 in Hoffmann's favour. He hadn't lied about her mother's parents. Now she really couldn't wait for Monday, and her second visit to Gloucester Road.

16 Secret Identity

'What's so spooky about this place?' said Tim, as soon as they were left alone in Hoffmann's study. He said it in a low voice, but not low enough to conceal how furious he was with Natasha for having dragged him along. The housekeeper, Mrs Matthews, turned out to be a friendly and extremely chatty Welsh lady who was very happy to receive them. 'Oh yes, Dr Hoffmann told me to expect you,' she had trilled into the intercom, and when she opened the door to them, they saw a short woman in her fifties, wearing a pink plastic apron and pink rubber gloves. She was just in the middle of cleaning the bathroom, she had explained, and would have to finish it before she could make them a cup of tea – she hoped they didn't mind. She then pointed to the drawer of the desk they were meant to look in, declared them to be 'a lovely young couple' and left, promising to return with some drinks and snacks later.

Natasha had to agree with Tim: the flat seemed positively cheerful today, but that could be due to Hoffmann's absence and Tim's, and the housekeeper's, presence. She hadn't seen her the last time she visited the flat, but perhaps it had been her day off. Natasha was a bit embarrassed to have begged so hard for Tim to come with her; she knew how guilty he felt about skipping work. Unlike his friend Ian . . . But she couldn't worry about that now.

'Why don't you just relax while I look through these papers here . . . it won't take long.'

Tim scanned the room and, realizing that there was no armchair or sofa to sink into, nodded and made do with one of the hard chairs. He was bored by this little outing, and couldn't wait to get out of there.

Natasha soon became so absorbed in the contents of Hoffmann's desk drawer that she forgot all about Tim and didn't even hear Mrs Matthews come in, some time later, with a tray full of goodies, didn't notice her leaving after talking to Tim for a while.

Some of the papers were handwritten, some were typed. All were worn and tattered, though a few seemed significantly older than others. The only piece of writing in English was an untitled short newspaper clipping, dated 18 April 1955, announcing that

> . . . yet another new Jewish cultural periodical, to be called *The Nose*, was launched this month in London, under the editorship of Franz Held, who has declined to comment on his choice of name for the magazine and has stated that, in spite of the existence of a number of similar journals, there is always room for one more. He compared the recent spread of new Jewish magazines to a healthy competition among neighbouring barber shops in the high street: 'We try to attract the same heads, but it is natural for their owners to have their preferences.'

Natasha smiled, remembering her recent brush with the barber trade in Finchley, and, picturing a young Held saying this to a nosy journalist, gave him a thumbs up.

Underneath this clipping was an untidy bundle of old papers, loosely held together with a thin piece of string. Natasha leafed through them gently, without untying the paper-thin thread. Most were written in Czech, some in German. Natasha didn't speak Czech (except for a simple, baby version she had picked up as a child from her mother) but could easily identify the language. Looking at these sheets, she realized that she would need to consult Alice, tell her everything, ask for her help. At this moment, Natasha no longer cared whether or not her mother would be hurt by her need to talk to her about her past. It simply had to be done.

She would have no other choice, she decided, looking again at the first page of the brittle package as she replaced it in the box. At the top of it, she read the word 'NOS', written, framed and underlined by hand in blue, almost faded ink. If it was Czech, and she was pretty sure it had to be, she knew it meant 'nose'. And underneath this title was a typed poem, also in Czech. She could not read it but she could read the author's name: 'Alice Weiss'.

For a moment, Natasha mistook 'NOS' for the title of the poem, but then realized that what she was holding in her hand was a magazine of that name. It looked like a children's magazine, judging by most of the drawings – of adults and children, farm animals, flowers, houses – and by some of the handwritten contributions it contained. But there were also sophisticated, well-executed pencil sketches. One showed an overcrowded cobbled street so full of haggard people that you could almost *smell* the friction. But the most impressive drawing was a portrait, of a lean-faced, youngish man, smiling warmly behind round spectacles. His smile seemed to be reflecting the smiles of others, as if he were surrounded by an audience, invisible in the picture but present at his sitting with the artist.

She studied the few loose pages of a typewritten German text. This, Natasha now saw, was the same story she had finally succeeded in finding among her files at home: 'Das Phantom von Theresienstadt' – The Phantom of Theresienstadt. The name of the author was missing. Natasha had learned German and knew enough to be able to translate these texts, with some effort, but she would need time.

And this was all. Natasha looked up and saw that Tim, who had finished all the tea and biscuits provided by Mrs Matthews, had nodded off in his hard chair.

'Tim,' she said quietly, 'wake up.'

He opened his eyes instantly. 'Finished? Thank God. Can we go home now?'

He's bored to death, and I'm on the verge of bursting into tears, she thought. Then she said it.

'Why's that?' He was genuinely puzzled by Natasha's emotional response to some old papers.

'Because, how can I explain this . . . well, truth is, I can't. Not right now. I need to get this stuff out of here. Take it home with me.'

'Did the old guy give you permission to do that?'

'No, he didn't.'

'Then you can't.'

'Oh yes I can. I'll leave him a note, and I'll be very careful. I have to show this to my mother. I'm sure that old devil has copies of all this, otherwise he wouldn't have shown it to me. And anyway, I don't care. This is about my mother. Among other things.'

'Natasha, you're shouting.'

'Am I? Sorry. Damn. This is really getting to me.'

Tim looked shocked. But he sensed Natasha's determination, and decided not to argue with her. They placed the box under his heavy coat and told Mrs Matthews they were leaving, thanking her for her help. They didn't mention they were taking Hoffmann's papers with them.

Outside, Tim insisted they have a proper lunch before going home.

'But this stuff . . . what if we lose it or something.'

'Don't worry,' said Tim firmly and led her to a nice little Italian place around the corner. They were both silent over their minestrone, each lost in a separate train of thought. Natasha's centred on the contents of Hoffmann's box file; Tim was thinking about his conversation with Mrs Matthews.

'Let's,' they said simultaneously, inhaling the slightly sour aroma of the hot soup.

They both laughed.

'You first,' said Tim.

'No, you.'

'OK. I wanted to tell you – let's be friends. I hate it when we hate each other.'

To his immense surprise, Natasha's eyes suddenly filled with enormous tears which made their way, slowly, into her bowl of soup.

'I don't know what's going on with me,' she sobbed. 'I've been crying a lot lately. I feel like a baby.'

Tim was hugely grateful for this opportunity to comfort this normally so self-sufficient woman, his wife. But before he could say something soothing, she seemed her usual self again.

'Look,' she said. 'We really have to talk about all this. I think I need your help. In a big way.'

Then, over their pasta, she tried to explain the source of her confusion: Hoffmann's story about her mother, about Held; the material in the box; her mother's maiden name under the Czech poem; her dread of asking her mother anything at all about what her life was like before she was anybody's mother . . .

'Is that all?' asked Tim, when she paused to swallow another spoonful of spaghetti.

Natasha nodded.

'OK. Now. I know you think I don't *get* all this kind of stuff –' he shook his head when she tried to protest – 'but, actually, you're wrong. See, my parents are not that different, when it comes to that. My mum has been silent for years about why she's unhappy with Dad—'

Now it was Natasha's turn to be stunned.

'—but I've been talking to her lately. I'll tell you about it another time. It's kind of sweet, suddenly being able to talk to your own parents, like an adult.'

I must be witnessing the effect of confessional TV on the British public, thought Natasha, incredulously. This isn't my restrained husband talking.

'So anyway. What I wanted to say was that I bet it will be the same with you and Alice. You'll be amazed: she might even be dying to talk to you about all that.'

'Wait, let me finish,' he added, before she could interject her objection. 'Your main problem isn't talking to your mother. Your main problem is what you're both going to find out once you *do* start talking. Because I suspect you're about to unravel a . . . well, something pretty big.'

'How would you know?'

'I'm a cop – well, sort of,' he laughed, but his eyes remained serious. 'I look at the evidence.'

'And . . . what do you see?'

'I see a man called Hoffmann who is playing games with you. He's a tout. Some of what he says is probably true, but he's keeping the full picture very nicely hidden. He wants you to get involved, we don't yet know how or in what precisely. I suspect that a lot of what he says is a lie. And, who knows, maybe some of it isn't.'

'You're probably right, but how do you know?'

'I talked to his housekeeper. She's only been his housekeeper for a day or so.'

'You mean—'

'She told me that Dr Hoffmann found her through some agency only a few days ago and employed her practically sight unseen, without an interview.'

'That's a bit weird, but so what? Maybe his previous housekeeper quit unexpectedly, he was in a hurry . . .'

'There was no previous housekeeper. According to Mrs Matthews, the flat was very dirty, in all the places that matter – kitchen, bathrooms . . .'

'Don't cleaning ladies always say that when they start in a new place?'

'Maybe they do. But I had a good look around while you were going through the contents of that desk, Natasha. She took me on a quick tour of the place. She was definitely right – it was filthy. Mrs Matthews said elderly gentlemen just don't know how to look after themselves, but my feeling was the place had not been lived in.'

'How could you tell?'

'Little details. Empty wardrobe. Empty fridge and bathroom cabinet. No message recorded on the answering machine.'

'Wow! Tim, I'm impressed. You managed to check all that without me noticing you were gone from the room? You're *good*. What else?'

'Isn't that enough for now?'

'God, no. This is only the beginning. Now I'm *really* into it. What do you think I should do next?'

'Natasha, am I to understand you're putting this investigation into my professional hands?'

They smiled at each other. I think we're having fun, thought Natasha, and that can't be bad for a marriage . . .

'Yes, Tim. You're in charge. Technically speaking. I'll just do the dirty work, and report back to you. You'll be the cool head of the investigation. So, what should be our next step?' She was laughing, but neither was sure how much of a joke it really was.

'Think like a cop,' said Tim, like a patient teacher. 'What do we have to find?'

'I don't know. A dead body?' laughed Natasha.

'How can you cry one minute and laugh your head off the next? This is *real*, darling. I mean, it could be. And dangerous. From now on, please don't make any more visits to strange men's homes without telling me what you're up to.'

'Hey, this is pretty rich coming from someone who didn't even want to be here today!' said Natasha, outraged.

'Yeah, I know. I was wrong, though, and I've changed my mind. I don't trust this guy, and we really don't know what's behind his sudden interest in you. But, to come back to my question,' Tim continued when he saw Natasha's silent response to his words of caution, 'a dead body is not what we need now. But we do need a motive. Actually, we need several of them. To begin with, we need to figure out what Hoffmann's spiel is all about.'

'What else?'

'Your mother. She has a motive, too – but I guess the trial will shed light on all that.'

'I agree. And – and Held?'

'Now you've lost me.'

'Ha!' exclaimed Natasha triumphantly. 'The great detective is lost! I am absolutely convinced that without understanding Held's motive we'll never be able to tie all this together.'

'But he's dead,' smiled Tim, patiently.

'Well, great,' said Natasha. 'So there's your dead body. And we still need to know his motive!'

'Why? What's he done that's so important?'

'I don't know. Maybe nothing . . . But my feeling is that this whole thing is about him.'

'Natasha, you can't have feelings. You need facts.'

'You sound like my brother. And you're wrong! We need both. Hey, don't cops always say they've got "a hunch"?'

Tim thought that was *very* funny. 'Yes, but what that means is they've got a lead, some evidence pointing in a certain direction . . .'

'I don't agree with you. I think it means just having an intuition about something.'

'Based on a fact or two.'

'Well, in that case, what's your hunch about Ian?'

'Ian? What's my mate Ian got to do with any of this?' Tim had always been amazed at Natasha's peculiar tendency to jump from one subject to another.

'Nothing. I just remembered seeing him in this neighbourhood that day, on his supposed day off . . .'

'Natasha,' said Tim firmly, 'that's none of your business. And, if you must know, I think he was probably putting in overtime and didn't want me and the others to know about it. Maybe he's got gambling debts . . . I don't even *want* to know.'

'You're amazing. I always want to know everything. But, OK. Let's stick to the Hoffmann case.'

Going home by tube, she reminded him about fifteen times to hold on to the box file, to make sure he had it, not to drop it. When they reached Russell Square, she finally relaxed and cuddled up to him. They smiled at each other, both remembering that this was *their* station, the one that had brought them together.

'Tim,' said Natasha loudly to make herself heard against the cacophony of metallic noises generated by the moving train, 'if it hadn't been for that flasher, we would never have met! Remember that penis you made me describe?' But the train had stopped while she was in mid-sentence, and most of what she had just announced had been received with much interest by a lively group of teenage schoolchildren and their teachers returning from an outing to the British Museum, and a few other lone passengers.

Her husband's face turned a peachy red, as always in these situations. Natasha was suddenly full of tenderness for her shy husband. But when she looked again, he was no longer blushing, he was actually angry: the train had stopped between stations and they were likely to be stuck there for an indeterminate amount of time, according to the official announcement. Fucking signal failure again.

Tim took the poor performance of the London Underground personally. Its constant state of disarray upset him, as if it were up to him, as a transport policeman, to make sure that trains functioned properly. None of his colleagues shared his exaggerated sense of responsibility, and would have laughed if they had known about it. But they didn't. It was Tim's awkward little secret.

Natasha did know and found it very cute – it made her think of Tim as a kind of working-class superman who revealed his secret identity by donning the uniform of a British Transport policeman; and when he was prevented from doing so, like now, he felt inadequate, unable to come to the rescue of all the trapped passengers . . .

Natasha felt like teasing him a little, but did not want another uncomfortable moment of exposure in the now almost silent train. So she kept quiet, thinking about the contents of Hoffmann's box file, waiting for the train to move . . .

She sensed the tension in his body as she let her head drop on his shoulder. It felt almost like being in bed together, alone. They were so very rarely alone . . .

17 Perishables

NATASHKA. I'VE GONE BACK TO SLEEP. JET-LAGGED. I'VE ORGANIZED YOUR DESK. DON'T BE MAD! WAKE ME UP WHEN IT'S TIME TO PICK UP ERICA. YOUR PHONE RANG A FEW TIMES, I WILL GIVE YOU THE MESSAGES. THESE MEN YOU WORK FOR SOUND DELIGHTFUL!

The yellow note lay, barely visible, on the kitchen table, weighted down by a heavy cobalt-blue ceramic bowl full of oranges – not all of them fresh. Natasha had a terrible habit of using perishable foods to help her keep track of time; the 'best before' dates on her milk cartons, yoghurt jars, on the cellophane wrappers covering the slowly decaying cheese, meat, fruit and vegetables in her fridge told her, approximately, the current date – by being either in the (hopefully not too distant) past or in the near future. She wasn't exactly disorganized – her work and her research had always been meticulously exact – but she lived in a bit of a dream-world: dates didn't really matter. It was lucky, actually, that *The Nose* was published with the leisurely frequency of four times a year. And it was of no consequence if an issue happened to be late – as long as it coincided roughly with one of the four seasons . . .

Natasha glanced, again, at her mother's note, at the huge capital letters she remembered so well from her childhood. For some reason, Alice had always scribbled short notes to her children in caps, as if they hadn't graduated – light years ago! – to cursive script. The messages she left for her husband were different – in busy, fast handwriting, they were long, detailed – and all over the place. She wrote so many that it was hard to distinguish new notes from old ones – but it was important to try, because Alice would become furious if her instructions were ignored. She wouldn't step out of the house or take a nap or even a shower without leaving a full set of written instructions for Natasha and Philip and Sam about what to do, or *not* to do, in her absence, however brief:

NATASHA. DON'T TOUCH THE STRUDEL. IT'S FOR TONIGHT.

PHILIP. YOUR DOSTOYEVSKY VOLUMES NEED DUSTING. TODAY.

And:

Darling Sam

There is absolutely no reason for you to rewrite the script now but if you really DO believe we need to rethink the opening shot of me coming out of the butcher shop, then by all means let's do it but bear in mind that the carcass dangling behind my head will obscure the back lighting and then what will happen to all the drama we need in the opening sequence? And are we thinking close up or long shot? We'll discuss when I get back from shopping, in an hour or so.

Well, now, it was Natasha's turn to be furious. What right did her mother have to organize her desk? She saw that her papers had been arranged in tidy, perfectly aligned heaps, the desk cleared of stray notes – where on earth did she put them?? – pens and pencils collected in a small antique crystal holder . . . where had *that* come from? And the box files she always kept tucked away under her desk were no longer there, but sitting neatly on a bookshelf which had been miraculously emptied of a messy pile of review copies. Held's file was now the most prominent one, because, unlike all the others, it had been placed horizontally rather than vertically, his name facing upwards. And now she had another box to add to these: Hoffmann's file. It actually fitted neatly right on top of Held's.

It was almost time to wake up her mother, but when she saw her sleeping face, on Erica's bed, she didn't have the heart. Like most youthful-looking women her age, Alice looked simply old in her sleep, as if she could now relax from the strain of wearing the mask of a much younger woman and allow her face to settle, comfortably, into all her natural lines and wrinkles. She seemed so . . . at peace, like someone who had never known a tortured moment. Natasha saw some of her own features in her mother's face – her strong mouth, chin, cheekbones – but saw also that what added up to real beauty in Alice was, in her own face, no more than a touch of pleasant symmetry. Well, at least she didn't look like her father . . . And at least she had inherited her mother's full, high breasts. She cringed a little, recalling Ian's annoying comments about 'her lovely tits'.

She smiled at her lovely sleeping old mother; looking her age had somehow made her even lovelier. Natasha quickly forgave her for touching her precious desk, and almost turned to leave the room, when Alice suddenly opened her eyes and sat up. The light blanket slipped off her shoulders and revealed that she was fully dressed, in jeans and a T-shirt, like on the day she arrived. There was never any sleepiness in Alice's expression when she awoke: she just seemed to have made a conscious decision simply to stop sleeping and become instantly alert; and, as soon as she did so, her blue-grey eyes became the bright focus of her face and made her look young again. Or, at the very least, ageless.

'Is it time?' asked Alice.

'Soon.'

'Good. I would really love a cup of coffee.'

'Coffee' was one of the few words Alice never learned to pronounce without a foreign accent. The vowels came out slightly wrong – long and open instead of long and sharp. But most of the time, unless she was tired, Alice sounded very American. Her speech betrayed no trace of her immigrant background, of her very un-American roots. Only rarely did New Yorkers ask whether she was British, or Canadian, recognizing a non-native elegance in her voice.

'Nice coffee, Natashka. Strong. Tastes a bit like . . . Czech coffee.'

'It's Greek. I get it from Christina's café, around the corner. We'll take you there for dinner one night.'

'Oh, good.'

Natasha was fed up. Suddenly, trying to communicate with her naturally chatty mother seemed a more difficult exercise than talking to her taciturn husband. She looked at Alice without a smile and said, 'I need to know something. Do you know a German guy called Ludwig Hoffmann?'

'Sure,' said Alice, without losing her composure even for a second, at least not outwardly. 'He's a well-known photographer and documentary film-maker.'

'But do you know him . . . personally?'

Alice fell silent. Then: 'There was a time, yes . . . a long time ago . . . but why do you ask?'

There were several ways Natasha could have answered that question. She could have said, because he told me he knew you as a young girl in a Nazi camp. And because he gave me some old papers with a poem written by you, in Czech. And also because he was the husband of the woman whose trial you are here for.

But instead, she said, 'He has just made a huge donation to the magazine, and I knew he was in the film business or something, so I thought you may have heard of him . . .'

'Oh,' said Alice, looking a little bored. It wasn't easy, but she managed it. Then she became more animated. 'That reminds me, I have to give you some messages. Some people called on your office line, and while I was tidying your desk . . .'

'Mom, I wish you wouldn't.'

'Wouldn't what, Natasha?'

'Wouldn't touch my desk and wouldn't answer my business phone.'

Alice looked hurt. 'But I was only trying to help . . . you have so much to do . . .'

Natasha softened. 'That's OK, Mom, I can handle it. I always do. Anyway, what were those messages?'

Alice sat up straight, like a schoolgirl, and began a detailed recital of her conversations with several trustees who had, for some reason, all decided to ring that morning.

'OK. First you had a call from a Mr Sussman. *So* charming! He invited me to come to your next meeting, said his wife would send extra-special cookies or something. He asked me whether you were good with money when you were a child, because he didn't think you had the knack of it now! We had a good laugh. He really likes you.'

'Mom,' said Natasha, 'you're a . . . traitor.'

'Why do you say that?' Alice was taken aback and seemed really upset.

'Because Sussman doesn't like me at all. He gives me a really hard time at each meeting. It's almost . . . abuse. So he's just sucking up to you as a way of getting back at me.'

Alice stared at her daughter for one brief moment and then burst out laughing. 'Natasha, you make it sound so dramatic. I'm sure you're exaggerating, or maybe you misunderstand the man. You *know* I'm a very good judge of character and I could tell that Sussman is a decent person.'

'Yeah, because he was flirting with you. You always like the guys who do that.'

'Natasha,' said Alice, emphatically, 'that's not fair. I *do* flirt with men – and I wish you would too, by the way, haven't I always told you, it's an important skill – but that would never cloud my judgement. Anyway, do you want to hear the actual message?'

'Yes,' said Natasha, with a grudging smile.

'He said his research is going well and he would like to discuss some preliminary findings with you, as well as the possibility of devoting an entire issue to his project. I don't know what he means but I'm sure you . . .'

'Yes, Mom. Next message?'

'Charles Sugarman. Now *there's* a gentleman. He was *so* interested in you, asked so many interesting questions. He invited me, too – to his gallery. Something to do with Marx? Of course I said yes. If there's anything I don't know about Marx, I want to find out. Really, Natasha, these are lovely people.'

'Yes, Mom. And the message?'

'Ah, the message. What was it . . . Ah yes. Something about an obituary. I *think* he said he found another copy of an obituary you were looking for. He'll explain. And then there was one more . . . heavy German accent . . . I asked him if he would prefer to speak to me in German but he said, Of course not!, and sounded upset . . . what was his name . . . I know, Spitzer.'

'Really?' Natasha was surprised. Spitzer phoned her very rarely, and they had spoken not too long ago. 'What did he say?'

'He asked me to be sure to tell you that he was very sorry for sounding so discouraging last time you talked, and that he would help you, of course.'

OK, this is it, Natasha decided. No more manoeuvring around the real issue. Thank you, Karl Spitzer, she thought gratefully, for providing me with the cue I needed.

Calmly, she said, 'Well, that's a relief. Now I can tackle that biography.'

'What biography?'

'Of Franz Held. You know, the founding editor. I haven't told anyone yet, except Spitzer, but I've been thinking about researching the man's life and writing a book about him.'

'And why did you tell Spitzer, of all people? Who is he, by the way?'

'He's the sub-editor, and he's been with the magazine almost from the beginning, so I was hoping he could tell me a lot about the man. It's a funny thing – they all revere the guy, but nobody seems to have known Held that well.'

They looked at each other in brief silence.

'Except you, Mom.'

Alice's face suddenly turned white, and stone-hard. She looks like an old angel, thought Natasha, and I really want to hug her. But I need to break this silence of hers first . . .

'You knew him, Mom, I know you did. Look . . . I'm a grown-up. Just like you. A mother. Just like you. Please tell me . . . those things. I just can't take it any more. I'm your daughter, for God's sake. I have the right to know everything about you!'

The sudden hardness in Alice's face somehow managed to slide into her voice and colour it with an unfamiliar, harsh tinge. And, strangely, her accent was less, rather than more, pronounced when she said, 'I *will* tell you. Not everything. Only some things. And not because you have the *right* to know, Natasha. You have no such right. My life belongs to me, not to you. Yes, we are mother and daughter. But we are also two completely separate human beings. And remember this: even if I did tell you everything, as you say, you would understand . . . nothing. What's in the past is in the past and can't be brought into the present. It's gone. Memories are nothing. They're just a lot of empty talk about things that have perished.' She paused, took a sip of her now cold coffee and continued, without softening her voice:

'But I will tell you some things, yes. Not because I want to, but because I have been . . . well, summoned. I am an important witness at this trial, and will have to tell a great deal, I am sure. And so, some of my past will now become public knowledge. There is nothing I can do about it. But it's not my choice, Natasha. If it were up to me, you and Philip would *never* be burdened with your mother's past.'

In spite of the unusually sharp delivery, Alice hadn't actually said anything new so far. Suddenly, this moment didn't feel like such a major breakthrough . . .

'Will you at least tell me what I need to know, now, in order to put together Held's biography? I mean, that's not really all about you, is it?'

Alice looked at Natasha a little quizzically and said nothing. Then she nodded. 'What do you need to know?' she asked, and now she had her own warm, luminous voice back. 'I'll try.'

'This man, the German guy, Ludwig Hoffmann, told me he knew both you and Held in Theresienstadt. And he gave me this. Wait.' She ran out of the kitchen and quickly came back with Hoffmann's file. 'Look, Mom. This is . . . by you, isn't it?' she asked, carefully picking up the brownish-yellow sheet of paper with the Czech poem signed 'Alice Weiss'.

Alice was an actress. An accomplished and very experienced actress. But now she stripped her face and her body of all layers of artifice or pretence or simulated strength or hardness, and simply exposed her naked soul. It was as if a hard-boiled egg had lost its thin shell and suddenly turned out to be soft, liquid inside. Natasha held her crying mother – her mother, who never ever cried – the way she would hold and comfort Erica if she had had a nightmare. But there was nothing she could say to soothe her mother's pain: she still had no idea what it was about, and it seemed more abstract to her, less tangible even than her daughter's bad dreams.

'Oh my God,' said Natasha, suddenly realizing what time it was. 'Erica! We forgot to pick her up! I'll be right back, Mom. You just stay here and . . . try to calm down. Sorry!'

Running down the street, she saw parents with their children, walking away from the school. She was late, but not too late. She felt terrible about leaving her mother sitting there like that, in a state of shock, but what could she have done . . .

Erica was angry, and disappointed. 'You're late,' she said. 'And you promised you'd pick me up with Grandma Al. Did you know that's my new nickname for her? She said it was OK to call her that.' Natasha explained that her mother was tired, and would see Erica at home. In two minutes exactly.

But when they got there, Alice was gone. She had taken Hoffmann's file with her, and left no note.

18 Bliss

Alice needed to be alone somewhere, in a far-removed mental space of her own. But she hadn't put much of a physical distance between herself and Natasha's home: she had only gone to the nearest café, Christina's, where she sat down at a corner table, asked for a glass of hot water with lemon, and sat immobile, staring at the closed file. She couldn't have known that this particular table was reserved for Christina herself, hadn't noticed the full ashtray and the half-drunk, still hot cup of coffee, its edges smeared with crimson lipstick. Christina would normally inform, affectionately but firmly, any customer who mistook her table for a free one to please choose another place to sit. This is where she smoked her endless cigarettes, drank her coffee, read her cookery books and held long, serious discussions with members of her large family, who arrived at all hours, from morning till night, in search of her soothing wise words, her food and drink, and sometimes her money. But Alice looked so . . . absent, so distant, so unaware of her surroundings that Christina simply left her alone, without saying a word, except to take her unusual order. But she was intrigued by this elegant older woman who didn't seem to have noticed that the café was full of a noisy crowd of people, talking and laughing and, above all, digging with gusto into Christina's idiosyncratic mix of Greek and English dishes, stuffed vine leaves next to fish and chips, chicken souvlakia next to bacon and eggs, a bowl of garlicky olives next to a basket of crisps.

The file lay on the table like a heavy, black magnet, forcing Alice to look at it and repelling her at the same time. But finally she opened it and made herself go through its contents, touching the brittle papers inside as if they were live butterflies struggling to fly away, or dead moths about to disintegrate into a powder. She stared at them without being able to read a word. Then she did read them, page after page, lifting them close to her face, almost breathing through them as if they were made of thin gauze. Looking at her, no one could have guessed that at that moment Alice felt close to disintegrating herself.

But Christina sensed it and finally sat down in her usual place, opposite Alice.

'What is it, love?' she asked Alice with irresistible kindness in her warm, gruff voice, 'What's wrong? Tell Christina. You'll feel better, I promise.'

Alice looked up from the sheet of paper she was reading. And suddenly, she felt an overpowering need to talk to this complete stranger. She said, slowly, softly, as if she were untying the words in her mind as she spoke them, 'I – can't – do it . . .' And then she finally felt that hotness in her eyes which meant she might soon be actually able to let go.

But Christina stopped her by asking, matter-of-factly, 'Are you American? Lovely accent. I have another American customer, a young woman, a neighbour, lovely girl, married to a local boy . . . he's a policeman, but you wouldn't have guessed, he's such a gentle man . . . they love my Greek food, both of them . . .'

'That's my daughter,' said Alice, and smiled.

Christina was overjoyed to hear that, and would have continued singing Natasha's young family's praises, if other customers hadn't demanded her attention. 'Will you have something nice to eat?' she asked Alice, who was making a visible effort to appear collected – and, at least outwardly, succeeding.

'No, not today, thank you,' said Alice. 'But I'll definitely be back soon, with my daughter.'

'Yes, please come! Natasha told me you are an actress – I can tell you my life story, you'll make ten films out of it, I promise you!'

'Thank you,' smiled Alice, with her usual poise, and left, clutching Hoffmann's file, carefully, under her coat, the way Tim had carried it on the way home from Hoffmann's flat.

During the short walk back to Natasha's, Alice thought of the time when she had written that poem. She thought of it with defiance, and her step was light. Hoffmann wouldn't succeed in demoralizing her again, as his wife had done, many years ago, with his help. For *that*, in Alice's eyes, had been their real crime: their ability to reduce live human beings to . . . nothing, without actually killing them. They did it by zeroing in on one's greatest strength, or weakness, it didn't really matter which – both would serve their purpose equally well. Then they would *extract* it from you, like a healthy tooth with a pair of large, rusty pliers, without allowing you the pleasure of dying in the process. No: they would *force* you to live, if that was their plan, but only for as long as it suited them. For so many years Alice had banished all memories of the people that had made her live against her will, but their faces were coming back to her now, floating towards her out of the semi-darkness of this suburban London street.

The young German woman, Annmarie Goetz, was pretty, with delicate, small features, shiny brown hair cut in a sleek bob and a neat fringe that covered only one half of her very high forehead. She was petite and graceful, like a fairy, but when she spoke, she had everyone's instant and permanent attention, without raising her voice. It wasn't a harsh, or strident voice; but it was uttered in an icy monotone, like a blast of cold wind hitting the vocal cords. The result was an almost metallic sound which was terribly at odds with her feminine appearance, and had been the original reason why Annmarie Goetz turned to directing films rather than acting in them.

Hoffmann's face was and remained a foggy blur, a slow-moving, heavy, blond shape in his wife's shadow. And then, Held. When she saw the photo in Natasha's box file that morning, while she was looking through her papers under the pretext of organizing her messy desk, she had not recognized him at first. Or, perhaps, had *tried* not to recognize him. But then she saw that it was Franz, unmistakably so, and the old picture triggered in her a stream of such conflicting emotions that she had turned it face down, closed the box and, after scribbling a quick note to Natasha, collapsed on Erica's bed, exhausted.

Now, as she re-entered her daughter's house, Alice registered the enormous relief in everyone's eyes. Tim had come home in the meantime, and, responding to his wife's almost hysterical concern about her mother, had already offered his professional resources to track Alice down.

'Mom, where did you go? I was so worried about you,' said Natasha, weakly.

'Why should you worry? I just needed to be by myself for a while, so I had a drink at Christina's. Nice woman. Nice place.'

She handed the file back to Natasha, and added, 'All this . . . this Terezìn file . . . is . . . meant to be a mighty weapon against me. Hoffmann knew what he was doing when he made sure it landed in your hands. But I'm working on a defence system. I'll tell you later. I'll also tell you how all those papers ended up in his hands. Now I want to spend time with my granddaughter. Did you hear that I'm Grandma Al from now on? Erica, do you know how to play chess? *No*? Well come on, let me teach you,' and they both disappeared into Erica's room.

Tim looked at Natasha in disbelief. A few minutes ago, she was telling him that her mother was in a deep state of shock, but here was Alice, unchanged, lively as ever.

Natasha shrugged her shoulders and said, helplessly, 'What should we do about dinner?'

'No idea. Pasta? Even though we had it for lunch?'

'OK.'

'Do you want me to make it?'

'Yes, Tim, please. I have to make some calls, while Erica is busy with Mom.'

I love the way she says 'Mom', thought Tim as he searched for a clean pot in which to boil the water. Natasha says 'Mom' and Erica says 'Mum', as if they were speaking two different languages. He felt surrounded by women in his house – three generations of them, at the moment – and didn't mind it at all. After the rough male camaraderie at work, which had recently become a bit of a strain because of Ian's erratic behaviour and unpredictable outbursts, he loved his all-female cocoon at home. It was comfortable, and fun; easy to ignore when he wanted to be left alone – he had the right, he wasn't one of them – and equally easy to join when he felt like it.

Ian was no longer Tim's most reliable pal at work. He had always been temperamental, but now he was almost unpleasantly so, like a frequently and violently erupting geyser. Tim didn't know what his problem was, and Ian wouldn't tell him. The tension between them had, imperceptibly, begun to rise, ever since that joke Ian orchestrated against Tim in the pub. He would think of Ian as having some private problems, and push him out of his mind, Tim decided. But if things didn't improve, he'd need another partner, and soon. While working in the kitchen, he heard Erica's and Alice's voices from one room, and Natasha talking on the phone in another. And suddenly, for no reason at all, he had to stop rinsing the lettuce for the salad, take a deep breath and face the incredible fact that he had just been overcome by a profound sense of bliss. *This*, thought Tim, was happiness, all of it. The good with the bad, the straightforward with the peculiar and the strange. Unlike his wife, he didn't believe in mysteries. That morning's trip to the German man's flat had made him think that there might be a case here, maybe; a case to be solved, rationally, not a mystery to be intimidated by. And now it occurred to him that it would be helpful to think of Ian in the same way . . . Yes, Ian was definitely a case, he thought, and smiled to himself.

Natasha had to return the three calls she had received that morning. They were all important, and soon it would be too late.

'Sidney,' she said to Sussman, 'I hear you have made a breakthrough on your project.'

'Well, Natasha, there's so much more here than I originally thought that I would propose this: a special issue of the magazine on the subject, plus a symposium. Or rather, a symposium, consisting of a lecture by myself and a discussion among highly ranked experts, which could then be published as a special issue of *The Nose*.'

'Experts on what, Sidney?'

'Well . . . historians, I suppose. Psychologists. Sociologists. Yes, definitely sociologists. Computer experts. People who could talk about the implications of my truly astonishing findings.'

'Which are? You haven't told me, you know.'

'I'm sorry. I should have explained at the beginning. Natasha, the results of my research – although it is still far from complete – so let us say the preliminary results of my research would seem to suggest that, amazingly, most people *would* buy life insurance from Hitler.'

'Really? That's interesting. And do you know why?'

'What do you mean, Natasha?'

'I mean, in your questionnaire, did you specify what they were getting if they were buying life insurance from Hitler, as opposed to, say, Scottish Widows?'

'Funny you should mention this . . . because yes, as a matter of fact, people did ask me that question. This happened so frequently that I had to build it in as a sort of follow-up detail.'

'And what was that detail, Sidney?'

'Well, purely hypothetically of course, I suggested that it was cheaper than Scottish Widows, or whatever they were buying at the moment.'

'So, in effect, you told your research subjects that Hitler would offer them a better deal on their life insurance, as compared with their current one?'

'Well, yes . . .'

'Sidney, I think you need to restructure your questionnaire. I'm not an expert on this sort of thing, and, as you told my mother, I'm not very good with money—'

'Natasha, I never—'

'— but it seems to me that you will only get a clear-cut, objective response if Hitler's life insurance isn't presented as being cheaper than what's generally out there. So why don't we wait till you get those results, and only *then* discuss a symposium?'

'Fine,' said Sussman.

Natasha would have been vaguely pleased with this conversation, if she hadn't been so bored by it. But Sidney wasn't finished yet.

'Natasha, one more thing, please. How about that German cheque? Any news?'

'Not . . . really,' she answered, 'I'm still working on it. It's not that simple.'

'Well, let me know as soon as you can,' he said, almost gently.

Maybe her mother was right, Natasha thought, maybe he *was* really a nice man. And why didn't he – or anyone else, for that matter – ever flirt with her? Well, Ian tried, but that was another matter . . .

Charles Sugarman was in a hurry, and could only tell her, quickly, that he had looked up Held's obituaries in other publications, and that they were all identical, including that funny description of him living 'somewhere in London'.

Karl Spitzer, on the other hand, was in an uncharacteristically chatty mood, and very happy to hear her voice.

'Natasha,' he said with a German accent that was heavier than Hoffmann's, 'I have changed my mind completely. I will help you with your endeavour, as much as I can.'

'What made you . . . reconsider?' asked Natasha, with some glee.

To her great surprise, he began to laugh, a light, bubbly laugh. Almost a giggle.

'You will not believe it . . . and you will find it odd . . . but it was a . . . coincidence, really . . . I had a haircut this morning, you see.'

Had Spitzer lost his very lucid mind?

'And I hear you had yours at the same barber's, Uncle Simon's, and not too long ago?'

Natasha, who never ever blushed, now turned a deep red. Shit. She knew it was their kind of place . . .

'And Uncle Simon, as we all so affectionately call him, told me all about your visit there. And how interested you were in talking about your predecessor. So I simply decided, there and then, that rather than let you pick up arbitrary bits and pieces which may not add up to anything in the end, I would simply tell you what I know. Perhaps it isn't much, but I don't feel I have the right to withhold that information.'

'Thank you, Karl,' said Natasha, simply, and thought, maybe that haircut was worth it after all. 'Would you like me to visit you one day and we'll talk?'

'Yes,' said Spitzer, 'and let's make it sooner rather than later.'

Natasha was happy. This was major progress. First her mother, then Spitzer: she was finally beginning to get somewhere.

Tim was still busy preparing the salad to go with the pasta, and so she had time to check her e-mail quickly. There was a note from Philip:

How is it going? Is Mom behaving OK? I can't find out anything more about Hoffmann. Very strange. Am thinking of coming to London for the trial. Nothing to hold me here anyway . . . What do you think? Don't tell Mom yet.
love
your bro

Natasha wrote back an enthusiastic note, filling in the details about her visit to Hoffmann's flat, and Alice's reaction to the papers she found there. She also begged him to come to London. What a difference that would make!

Then she read this:

YOU FILTHY KIKES MAY YOU ROT IN HELL AS YOU DID IN THE HOLOCAUST WHICH NEVER HAPPENED!!!

And this:

USE YOUR DIRECT KIKE LINE TO SATAN TO FIND OUT WHAT'S IN STORE FOR YOU

Natasha sat there, frozen, staring at the capitals which looked like burning crosses. Her impulse was to delete the two e-mails, which had arrived under the innocent headline 'hello!' from a complicated return address. But that would be too easy. So, with a slightly trembling hand, she saved them in her FILTH folder, and, after forwarding the messages to her brother, decided also to show them to Tim. Later, after dinner.

He was calling everyone to eat now, and, when she saw the steaming plates on the kitchen table, Tim looking flushed and pleased with himself, and her mother and Erica sitting down without interrupting their passionate debate about kings and queens in chess, Natasha was suddenly hit with an overwhelming sense of . . . happiness. Bliss. This was what she wanted, and nothing else: this closeness, these stories, these people, this . . . safety. And all that mystery. It would all fall into place, and soon, she thought, pouring water into Erica's glass, ignoring her pleas for Pepsi.

19 History in Motion

As it turned out, Alice's flat became available the following day, and, except for Erica, everyone was happy about her moving there. Natasha and Tim needed their privacy back – the presence of a visitor always made them realize how tiny their house was – and so did Alice. The flat was only a short bus ride away, a comfortable ground-floor studio with its own little garden. 'It will be a good place to work,' Alice had said to Natasha when she left her there, with her one suitcase. They both knew what she meant: she had promised to translate all the Czech and German texts in Hoffmann's file into English. 'I will be fine,' she had added, in answer to Natasha's gently phrased question. In fact, she was sure that the translation would help her 'restore her equilibrium', as she put it. And there was no point in trying to talk about anything until she had done that.

And in the meantime, while Alice submerged herself in what seemed to be a written documentation of her youth (though she didn't forget to spend a little time every day with Erica), Natasha had a twofold task: to continue with her daily duties for *The Nose*, and to pursue her research into Held's life. And there was Hoffmann, of course; the trustees were waiting for her verdict on his 'acceptability as a sponsor', and one or another of them would phone her, daily, to ask her what she had found out about the man. She kept them in the dark by using his temporary absence from London as an excuse. The truth was more complicated: she already knew enough to be able to inform them that they should, really, kiss that lovely cream-coloured Coutts & Co. cheque goodbye. And yet, something was stopping her. It was something about the man himself, a certain appealing quality in his manner that she had liked, before she knew who he really was, and even after. Actually, Natasha had to correct herself: she still didn't know who he really was. In fact, she knew as little about Hoffmann as she did about Held. And, strangely, in both cases, it was her own mother who held the key to the mystery of their past . . .

The past had, somehow, lost its aura of a hidden tableau with a huge meaning, and become, more than ever, just a collection of real people's real-life stories, a sort of 'history in motion'. Hoffmann, Held, her mother, and now this Annmarie Goetz: it was true that history had shaped their lives, but what she really needed to know was how all these people had, themselves, shaped history. Yes, they had all played a part in the events of the past; Natasha's question was, what part? She felt, suddenly, warm admiration for Max Brass, with his endearingly self-important, amateurish memoir. At least he had nothing to hide.

Franz Held, on the other hand, if Spitzer's account was correct, had had plenty to hide. She had gone to his flat in Finchley, not far from Sussman's pet shop, immediately after dropping Alice off at her new place, arriving a few minutes later than the agreed time. Spitzer wasn't pleased, and said so. But when she began apologizing, he told her to stop being silly and motioned her inside, with an impatient wave of the hand: 'We have too much to talk about tonight, let us not waste any time,' he said, with a curt smile.

It was a peculiar flat, cavernous yet overstuffed, in chaotic disarray, with books, papers, paintings and an oddly disjointed assortment of furniture from different time periods. Natasha had always assumed that Spitzer was a bachelor, like Held; but she had been wrong, for there, in a dark corner of the living room, was his wife, a tiny, grey-haired woman, asleep in a large armchair.

'We'll disturb her, won't we?' whispered Natasha.

'Oh no,' he said, in a loud and cheerful voice. 'My wife paints all day and then sleeps like a log, she can't hear a thing. Don't worry. Tea?'

'No, thank you,' said Natasha, and looked at Karl Spitzer with new curiosity. He was definitely in the 'sprightly old man' category, as her mother would put it, and the new haircut from Uncle Simon made him look fairly attractive: a tidy head of straight white hair framing a strongly lined, masculine face. Natasha wondered what happened to old men's penises: could they, too, be described as sprightly?

'Let me know if you change your mind. Well, shall we begin at the beginning?'

'1955?'

'Around then, yes.'

'But you knew him before?'

'Well . . . long before.'

Oh God, thought Natasha, not another Theresienstadt story!

But Spitzer continued: 'I met him . . . at the Berlin Olympics. In 1936. He was with the Czechoslovak team. Runner. Superb athlete. Just missed winning a bronze.'

'I thought Jewish sportsmen were not exactly allowed there at the time,' said Natasha.

'You are right. Certainly not on the German team . . . But some countries managed to sneak in some Jews . . . especially if their names didn't sound overtly Jewish . . . Held, for example! By the way, you do know it means "hero" in German, don't you? Anyway, I myself was not a sportsman, of course. I was a young sports reporter, covering the Olympics for a British newspaper. In fact, I left Germany immediately after. The Games crystallized the future for me, if you understand what I mean. I could see it coming, as clearly as Speer's searchlight spectacle illuminated the arena. In fact, the interview with Franz was my last German assignment.'

Spitzer didn't want to tell Natasha more than she needed to know. His own life story was irrelevant to her project, he decided, and so said nothing about his defection from his parents' palatial villa in Hamburg, on the Elbe. His father was a wealthy shipbuilder and Karl, his only son, had been meant to follow in his footsteps. But he fell in love with sport, not the sea, and books, not ships. And also with the English language: as a boy, he had frequently travelled to England and America with his parents, and had been provided with a private tutor to teach him English as soon as he started school. Karl's talented teacher was an earnest, love-stricken young Irish woman who had come to Germany to marry a famous composer, only to discover that he had emigrated without leaving a forwarding address. The boy adored her and demanded English lessons two or three times a week; his parents were happy to pay for them, and finally asked Kathleen to move into the family villa so she could converse with young Karl in English on a daily basis. She stayed for many years, until Karl reached his teens, when she returned to Dublin.

For the boy's father, Kathleen's presence in the house was an ever-present, exquisite torture, though he never touched her. Karl had always felt their attraction for each other, and had been deeply jealous. This emotional pattern remained with him throughout his life: he would always combine jealousy with love and friendship, as if he could only feel close to people who made him miserable. Like his wife, Claire. Or, in a different way, Franz Held . . . But, he thought, why burden Natasha with any of that.

'What did he talk about?'

Spitzer smiled: 'Only his achievements.'

'No . . . political comments? About Germany, or Czechoslovakia?'

'Oh, no,' said Spitzer, emphatically. 'In fact, Franz hardly ever expressed political opinions, even later, when we met again, quite by chance, in London. After the war. Long after the war. It was in one of those cafés in Swiss Cottage where central European émigrés used to meet over the right kind of tea and coffee and pastries . . . Like most Czech Jews at the time, he spoke native German. I noticed him first, in conversation with two older Viennese writers. Both dead now. As is Franz. Alas.'

He paused, but only to rearrange his thoughts. It was clear to Natasha that she wasn't expected to interrupt with any questions.

'I came up to him and introduced myself, but, miraculously, there was no need: Franz remembered me. We shared a drink, talked for a while and he told me about his magazine. And also about the fact that he needed help, because his English was not really good enough to edit the articles properly. In fact, I remember he said there had been some criticism. Well, I offered my services, thinking of it as a favour to an old acquaintance, but to my surprise, he offered to pay me, and quite a decent wage, too.

'And so I added *The Nose* to the rest of my freelance editorial workload, even though, at the time, I had already begun earning most of my living as an antiques dealer. Still, I thought, working with Franz would be interesting, and I wasn't wrong.

'The quality of the submissions varied wildly, but most of the time it was well worth polishing them into publishable pieces. We used to joke that we had to polish Polish into English . . . And again, I was impressed that, in spite of the fact that the magazine was such a shoestring operation, Franz always managed to set aside enough money to pay his contributors.'

'Held paid his contributors?' broke in Natasha. 'I'm astonished to hear that. I was told he didn't.'

'He certainly did in those days. Perhaps the trustees changed the rules later on, I don't know. But back then, you certainly got a fee. I know this for a fact, because I once got paid myself, for a small piece of my own original writing. A love poem, actually,' he said, looking slightly embarrassed.

'In any case,' Spitzer continued, 'Franz Held and I soon established a very good working relationship. He would deliver those manuscripts to me, we'd have a long talk about them, and then he would just leave them with me. My job was to edit them, of course, and give him back material that could go straight into the magazine. And while I was doing my editing, he would vanish.'

'What do you mean, vanish?' asked Natasha.

'Just that: disappear. From London I mean. It used to exasperate me, because if I had any questions, I could not reach him.'

'Where did he go?'

'I have absolutely no idea, my dear Natasha. We could sit here and speculate ad infinitum, and perhaps you would like to do just that. But I won't, it would be a waste of time. I hate wasting my time, as you know. This was the pattern throughout those years, though occasionally, he would stick around and not go away. But on the whole, I would say that he probably divided his time between London and some other place.'

Natasha wasn't sure how to go on. She was *dying* to speculate – did Held have a family somewhere? Was there a woman, maybe? Or, hell, a *man*? But she knew that Spitzer couldn't be forced into that sort of conversation.

So she asked, 'But what about the war years? What did he tell you about that? You once said he was in the army and I don't really understand how that fits in with—'

'Natasha, I don't know what else you may have heard about his life during the war,' interrupted Spitzer, 'but I can tell you with some certainty that Franz Held was a soldier in the Czech unit of the Russian army, under General Svoboda. In fact, it was the first thing we talked about when we met by chance, after the war. I told him I had left for England immediately after the Berlin Olympics, and stayed here ever since. And he told me he happened to be in Russia for some sports events when the Nazis occupied Czechoslovakia in 1939. Ended up in a Soviet camp, and then in Svoboda's army. I know this not only because he spoke of it, but also because he once wrote a brief account of his experience there, for *The Nose.* Alas, it was never published.'

'Why not?'

'I'm not sure . . . It was, in fact, meant to be included in his last issue – of course he had no idea it would be his last – and I did edit it, and return it to him with all the rest. But when the magazine came back from the printers, Held's autobiographical piece was missing.'

'Do you have a copy of it?'

'I think I must. I always make and keep copies of everything, that's why this place is such a mess,' he sighed. 'But I will find it for you, just give me a few days.'

'While you're looking for that one, could you also try and collect as many of the old papers as you can? You know, all the old material, whether it was published or not? For some reason, the files I inherited were quite slim, and now that I'm interested in writing Held's biography, I'd like to see everything, of course.'

'Of course,' said Spitzer, and gave her a curious look.

'Is something wrong?' Natasha asked him.

'No, my dear. It's just that . . . I suspect you haven't really thought about why you want to write his biography.'

'Well,' said Natasha, 'out of curiosity, really. I'm intrigued by the fact that no one seems to have really known him. Not even . . . you, Karl.'

'And you think a biographer can fill in all those gaps? Explain who a person is?'

'I can at least try,' said Natasha, a little defiantly. 'And I love mysteries. Franz Held is a mystery to me, and to everybody else.'

'I wish you luck, Natasha, I really do. But . . . you've chosen an almost impossible subject. However, I will do what I can to help you, as I said. Franz was a difficult man, a charming man, and, yes, a mysterious man, but I was very fond of him. Who knows, maybe your fresh perspective is the right one.'

'He was also a very devious man,' said a very elegant English voice, startling Natasha, but not Karl.

His wife had woken up – had she ever been really asleep? Natasha wondered – and was now sitting up in her armchair, peering at them, bleary-eyed, a messy, shapeless bundle. Everything seemed incongruous here: the woman's voice clashed with her physical appearance, none of the furniture matched, the dusty books and papers everywhere did not go with the bleach-like odour of sanitized cleanliness in the flat, and the contrast between the neat, trim, German-sounding Spitzer and his slovenly, upper-class English wife could not have been more stark.

'This is my wife, Claire. Claire, this is Natasha, our young editor.'

Natasha wanted to say something pleasant, but Claire was not interested in politeness: 'I know. Did you hear what I just said?'

'Yes,' nodded Natasha, and suddenly felt that Spitzer was probably right: if appearances told you nothing about people, what could she possibly hope to accomplish by researching the past of a person who seemed to have left nothing behind except a lifetime of misleading impressions?

'Held wasn't mysterious. He was devious. Deceptive. He *thrrrived* on deception,' she said, trilling the 'r' like a Shakespearean actress. 'I should know, darling,' she continued, without a glance at her husband, 'I had an affair with him. A brief one, but still . . .'

Spitzer didn't look uncomfortable at all. He merely smiled and offered both ladies some sherry.

'There was a time – when we were all very young, about your age, maybe – when Franz would come to this flat to deliver manuscripts for Karl. He would arrive a little early, knowing that Karl was at a lecture. And in the mere fifteen minutes before my husband's imminent arrival, he would rrravish me right here, in this armchair, then clean himself up and be ready for Karl when he arrived for their talk. No sign of any . . . activity.'

'Don't worry, my dear,' said Spitzer, glancing at Natasha, 'I am a seasoned . . . listener to my wife's adventures. And the episode with Franz didn't last too long. Still, I suppose it serves to illustrate a point. My wife is quite right about his ability to deceive. He certainly succeeded in deceiving me . . .'

'*And* me,' said Claire, with surprising emotion. 'He had told me he would marry me, begged me to leave Karl. That was on a Monday. A week later, he had changed his mind.'

'What happened in between?'

'We think,' said Karl as if *he* had been the jilted lover, 'it was something to do with one of his trips. He went away, and came back a somewhat changed man.'

'Changed, how?'

'Apathetic, slow . . . a shell of his previous self.'

'When was this?'

'In 1957,' said Karl and Claire, in perfect unison, in spite of their very different accents. 'We have no idea,' continued Karl, now without his wife's vocal support, 'what had caused the sudden transformation in him. He seemed . . . broken, somehow. Even frightened.'

So 1957 was a significant date in Held's life, thought Natasha, and she would have asked many more questions if Claire hadn't yawned, demonstratively, looking at her watch.

'God, it's very late, I must go.'

'I'll drive you home,' said Karl, unexpectedly. 'It's not far, and there are a few more things I'd like to tell you.'

His wife said a perfunctory goodbye without changing her position.

In the car – dark, small and compact, Natasha noticed – Spitzer said nothing at all. Neither did Natasha, except for a few directions. They would talk properly another time, she thought.

Then, almost in front of her house, he blurted out, 'I'm not unhappy. I love her. She's my . . . England, the bitch. Goodbye, Natasha. I hope *you* are happy. I'll be in touch.'

What's all this got to do with *me* being happy, thought Natasha, as she unlocked her door. The house was quiet. She saw that Tim was asleep in front of the television. 'Hey,' she said. 'Wake up. I'm home.'

He opened his eyes, and smiled. He had enjoyed having Alice, but now he was pleased to have their little house back to themselves.

'Is your Mum happy in her flat?'

She nodded.

'You look like . . . you're finally getting somewhere. True?'

'How did you know?'

'I know that look . . . The guys at work get it, especially the CID guys . . . Do you want to tell me?'

'Not yet,' said Natasha. 'I really, really want to go to sleep now. We'll talk tomorrow, OK?'

'OK,' said Tim. 'By the way, about Ian? It's all sorted. Turns out he's been on some secret assignment. He can't talk about it, but he seems to be acting normal again, which is a relief.'

'Yes,' said Natasha, and fell, exhausted, into bed, without checking her e-mail, or the day's post, or her messages. Which was just as well, because there was a letter on her desk which would have kept her awake, for hours.

20 Designer Phantoms

Tim knew more about Ian's secret task than he had led Natasha to believe. In fact, as of today, he had been assigned to work together with Ian on tracking some suspicious signs of criminal activity which seemed to be connected with a number of abandoned stations in London's underground system. The old man Natasha had seen Ian talking to on the platform of Gloucester Road tube station was not just any drunk. He was a valuable, and very resourceful, informant. Known, for some reason, as Charlie Darwin, he had contacts among what was beginning to emerge as a cohesive group of people he had observed moving in and out of entrances to the sites of disused tube stops.

It had, originally, been Ian's idea to follow up on Charlie's casual reference to 'them phantoms from Brompton Road'. He had a solid working relationship with the old man, who practically lived on the trains and the platforms and sometimes even in the tunnels of the Piccadilly Line, always drinking but never too drunk to be spoken to – and so Ian often did. Charlie had the ragged, properly shabby look of a Parisian *clochard*, but in fact was never without a valid travel card in his pocket, and actually resided in a small but fairly decent room in a Quaker guesthouse in Bloomsbury. His accent would alternate between slightly muffled, lispy Oxbridge tones and a curiously inauthentic, almost archaic-sounding version of Cockney; either way, he sounded a bit theatrical, but not too much so. No one knew what his original speech would have been like.

'Tell you what,' Ian had said to Charlie a few months ago, when he'd found him, seemingly very drunk, on a crowded platform at King's Cross, 'I'll help you get home. Where's home, young man?'

At this, Charlie had burst out laughing, bearing a surprisingly pristine-looking set of sparkling-white dentures behind his filthy grey beard, and responded in his most elegant, posh voice: 'Don't you worry about me and my home, officer. But perhaps you'd like to talk about yours?'

Ian was used to dealing with all sorts of nutcases in his line of duty, and, unlike Tim, he did not believe in coddling them. But there was something appealing about this eccentric character, a kind of warmth, and so he found himself saying, without his usual aggressive smirk, 'Better not.'

And yet, only a few minutes later, they were sitting in the tube going towards Russell Square, the old man's stop, and Ian was so anxious to tell him his life story that they missed it and just stayed on the train until they reached Heathrow Airport. He told, or rather shouted it, in short, almost monosyllabic sentences, as if he had no doubt that Charlie could fill in the gaps and complete the picture from the condensed highlights, barely audible over the racket produced by the moving train: 'Tiny farm. Muddy. South Wales. Hills, yes, hills. Green. Loved them. But . . . Same faces. Year after year. After year. Same fucking . . . cunts! Shagged them. *All* of them. Not the girls. The *women*. Had me panting like . . . my sheep dogs. Everybody had to be in a fucking choir. Guess what, Charlie: PC Jones can't sing! Got teased a lot, but . . . they shut up when I shagged them. Funny, you know? They were so quiet back home. In London, they're screamers. English girls, I mean. And the foreign ones . . . they talk, and moan of course. Love it.'

Here Charlie interrupted him, for the first time: 'Sorry, who loves what here? Do you love the foreign girls' love talk and moaning, or do *they* love you shagging them? One has to be specific, you know. Clarity is important.'

'Oh I don't know . . .' sighed Ian. 'Guess what I mean is . . . I love London. Yes. I love shagging women in London. English, foreign – any sort. It just feels better here than—'

'Back home?' asked Charlie. 'And why is that?'

Ian was not accustomed to this much analysis of his thoughts and feelings. But it didn't feel bad at all. He risked a longer sentence.

'This city makes me feel like I'm something special. Like a . . .'

'Hero?' suggested Charlie Darwin, helpfully.

'Yes. A hero. That's it.'

They got out at Heathrow Airport and, instead of taking the next train back towards the city centre, walked (slowly, because Charlie shuffled his feet like a very old man), to Terminal 2 and had a coffee and sandwich at one of the cafés. And there, in the midst of the noise and the buzz and the Babylonian multitude of voices, over a comfortingly fragrant cup of very hot, milky coffee, Charlie suddenly began to tell Ian about 'them phantoms', changing his accent, momentarily, to his peculiar Cockney dialect, but then reverting to his no less peculiar plummy voice.

Ian was very interested. Not intrigued, as Tim would have been, but definitely interested.

'Are you sure?' he asked. 'Brompton Road station? But it's been closed for ages.'

'Exactly,' Charlie nodded. 'Since 1934, actually. I was there.'

'When they closed it?'

'Before, and after.'

'I don't get you,' said Ian.

'Well it used to be a regular tube station, of course, but later, just before the Second World War started, it was sold to the War Office. For the anti-aircraft division.'

'What, the whole station?'

'The street-level building – have you ever noticed it? I must show it to you. Plus some passageways and liftshafts. That's where I spent some time during the war. In the operations room of the air defence command, for example . . .' Charlie's eyes cleared as he said this, his voice sounded younger, more vigorous.

Ian was impressed: 'Wow. What were you in the army?'

'Nothing. I was a pacifist. Conscientious objector. Spent some time in jail, as a matter of fact. I'm a Quaker, you know. '

'But – the air defence office underground?'

Charlie sighed, a heavy, violent sigh which ruffled the surface of his drink, like a muddy lake under a sudden gust of wind.

'There was a girl . . . in the army . . . in that office . . . she despised me, for being a pacifist, as you do, I'm sure . . .'

Ian said nothing. It was true.

'But she was crazy about me. Used to smuggle me in there, occasionally. It was almost impossible but we loved the risk. We . . . how do you call it these days? Shagged?

'Silly word, PC Jones. Very silly word. Violet and I, we didn't shag. We *fucked*. Right there, underground. In one of those shafts. Against a tiled wall. On some table. On a platform. What *used* to be a platform, of course. I would meet her by that rusty-red terracotta-tiled entrance – it's still there, you can see for yourself – we'd sneak in and it was instantly erotic, like entering a huge cunt. We'd walk down those winding stairs, slowly, carefully, and there'd be a platform. I liked a spot right under the tiled name panel, BROMPTON ROAD. Near the tunnel. Sometimes *in* the tunnel. That's where we fucked, PC Jones, and do you know what I mean by fucking? Let me explain this to you, because, as I told you before, clarity is important. Fucking is fearless. Fucking is this: you and the woman, alone in the whole wide world. Nothing else matters. You could die the next second and it would have been worth it. Worth being together, fucking, rather than, say, sitting at home, saying goodbye to your sweet old mother. But most of all, fucking isn't selfish, it's not about having a good time, it's not about satisfaction, and it's not about the consequences. Fucking is about, to borrow Churchill's phrase, blood, sweat and tears. Do you understand me, PC Jones, or do I have to get clinical and explain about my prick, her cunt, and how they made each other weep when we fucked?'

PC Jones understood. Or said he did. What he really thought was, shit, I don't think I've *ever* fucked a woman. Not like this. Had never even met a woman like that . . . a Violet . . . Except . . . Natasha. He could easily imagine himself with her, *fucking* her. Natasha would be a definite . . . challenge. And a danger. He was a bit obsessed with her already . . . Maybe that was all it took – a bit of danger. But her husband was his partner, and so annoyingly *nice* . . . Nothing to be done . . .

' . . . anyway, about those phantoms,' Charlie was saying, forcing

Ian to concentrate again. 'I visit my old haunts sometimes . . . nostalgia, I guess . . . memories . . . and it's a refuge . . . not just Brompton Road, you know . . . there is also Down Street in Mayfair . . . and others . . . lovely, dark vaults . . . full of ghosts . . . I like being alone with them . . .'

Ah, thought Ian, disappointed, so he's only talking about his past, the phantoms from his past, how boring . . .

'And then I started noticing them, PC Jones. Several men and one or two women. Sometimes on their own, sometimes in a group. Saw them go in, come out. Stay a while, just like me.'

'So?'

'So I decided to befriend one of them, because I didn't want any trouble. People can be quite territorial about forbidden spaces, you know . . . I thought, if I make myself visible but inoffensive, they'll leave me alone.'

'And? Did it work?'

'Yes . . . at least, I hope so. Because these are dangerous people, PC Jones. They are planning something. My hunch is, it may be a robbery. I have seen them huddled over maps and drawings. Visiting the same spots, again and again. Observing the underground areas as well as the street above, very closely. Taking photographs. They have video cameras, tiny digital ones, the works.'

'*Very* interesting,' said Ian, slowly. 'Have you told anyone else?'

Charlie grinned: 'No; who would I tell? Besides, I have no evidence . . . none whatsoever . . . they really are like phantoms . . . very well-dressed, clean . . . I call them designer phantoms . . .'

On the train back to Russell Square both men were silent: everything had been said, for the moment. They had agreed to stay in touch. Charlie would go on observing his 'phantoms', and report, periodically, to Ian, who couldn't wait to tell his superior officers about his amazing lead. He could already smell a nice promotion – finally! – and maybe even a special reward . . .

He wasn't mistaken: the information provided by Charlie caused a real stir among the higher echelons of British Transport Police. Not immediately, though. At first, due to Ian's bad reputation as a volatile adventurer, his breathlessly delivered, incoherent report – 'old drunk . . . not what he seems . . . abandoned underground stations . . . Brompton Road . . . phantoms . . . criminals . . . robbery in progress . . .' – was received with suspicion. But Ian calmed down, and persevered, explaining, more convincingly each time, the facts he had learned from Charlie Darwin, in detail. And suddenly, there was a great deal of interest in the story, which eventually became 'a case', officially nicknamed 'Underground Phantoms'. Ian was given the task of monitoring Charlie's contacts with the mysterious criminals. His assignment was to be kept secret from his colleagues, and he was, in fact, the only transport policeman involved, as most of the work had been transferred to a special criminal investigation unit of the Metropolitan Police.

The reasoning behind pursuing Ian's – or rather Charlie Darwin's – leads on such a large scale was based on a theory, first suggested by Charlie himself, that the mysterious criminals were after the priceless contents of the British Museum. Some of its art treasures had, in fact, been stored in the safety of the underground vaults of several of the closed stations during the war, which also served as air-raid shelters. Charlie assumed that the high-class art robbers he was watching were in the process of reopening and reconnecting old underground passageways, using the dormant tube stations as an invisible subterranean escape route, originating under the museum itself and leading away from it, into one or possibly all of the abandoned stops. Perhaps they even formed a kind of network, out of everyone's sight . . . a phantom underworld . . . It was a nearly plausible idea and Ian was told to keep talking to Charlie, while the rest of the investigation was going on, separately.

They would meet, once or twice a week, somewhere along the Piccadilly Line, and it was easy to camouflage their encounters as 'BT policeman evicts / reprimands / accompanies inebriated elderly citizen'. They would then find a quiet spot to talk and Charlie would tell Ian about his latest discoveries. Occasionally, Ian would be undercover, and they would go to one of the abandoned stations and Charlie would give him a tour of it, like a guide, complete with its history and a knowledgeable analysis of its architecture and design. Once or twice, they bumped into one of the 'phantoms', but, as Ian was wearing filthy old clothes, looking like a younger version of Charlie, he did not arouse their interest. They were exactly as the old man had described them: well-dressed, efficient-looking people, youngish, polite and friendly. A few words were exchanged, nothing of any importance. Ian kept his eyes open for any significant details, and felt happy: finally, finally!, he was doing something truly exciting, and it had been his own discovery, and he was allowed to work on it alone and in secrecy – a special privilege.

And then, one day, he found that Tim Parker – Tim, of all people! – had suddenly been assigned to share the job with him. Not only that, but the direction of the investigation seemed to have been changed, and, according to Tim, he had had something to do with that.

'How?' asked Ian, as they walked, together, into King's Cross station, looking for Charlie Darwin.

'Natasha showed me some strange stuff she found on the internet, websites, you know, Nazi material. And one of them listed the names of some London tube stations, spelled in a funny way. German, I guess.'

'Like what?'

'Kink's Kross, for example, this station.'

'So what?' Ian was genuinely puzzled. How could this ridiculous detail have any meaning at all?

'Well, I went and showed it to Palmer, because I thought it might be some vice-related stuff. Something dirty . . . A porn ring, maybe. But . . .'

They were almost at the appointed meeting place.

' . . . then they did some research and discovered it might have something to do with terrorism. Right wing. That's all I know, honest.'

However, the truth was that, for once, Tim was *not* being honest: he knew more than that, a lot more than that. Still, he was deceiving

Ian on orders from above, so the dishonesty was entirely in the line of duty, so to speak, and it wasn't his fault that the case was being handled cautiously, with emphasis on preventing leaks. That didn't make him feel any better about it. Ian was a friend. But Tim couldn't tell him that the usually laid-back, monosyllabic Inspector Palmer had become very excited and talkative when he saw those 'kinky e-mails' involving London Underground stations. He explained to Tim that those messages had – unfortunately! – nothing to do with pornography.

It turned out that Natasha had, inadvertently, provided British Transport Police, and its counterparts in other countries, with a missing clue to an investigation which had been going on for some time. It involved a small but apparently very affluent international sect which called itself, simply, 'The Group of '33'.

'They're nutters,' Palmer had said to Tim. 'Love to cause havoc in the underground train system. *Deadly* havoc. Remember the big explosion in the Moscow underground last summer? Three hundred dead? And the one in New York, a week after that? Two hundred? That was them. The Russians blamed it on Chechen rebels, and the Yanks on Arab terrorists, of course. But it was these guys. They're terrorists all right, but they're, you know, *white*. Never seen racists like 'em. They're looking for "brothers of Satan", I heard. That's your Jews, your blacks, your Gypsies, your Pakistanis. Those characters think the white race is threatened by non-whites. Especially by the Jews. For my money, they're a branch of neo-Nazi geezers, *proper* racists. But, 'cause they're a sect, we give them special treatment. We found this statement of theirs on the net. Take a look. They don't just blow up underground trains, they've got a major Hitler fixation, too.'

He'd shown Tim a computer printout, an attractively styled but incoherent little paragraph about 'The Group of '33'.

Tim read, with growing incredulity, about the founding principles of the sect. The number referred to 1933, 'the glorious year when our Führer Adolf Hitler became the sanctified Chancellor of Germany, and began the holy war against the satanic Jews', and, astonishingly, also the year when an authority known as London Transport was set up in charge of the London Underground. According to the authors of the leaflet, a conflict, of sorts, developed between Hitler and London Transport. The Führer's war (1939–45) actually managed to interfere with the plans of the authority to expand existing tube lines; instead, a tunnel of an uncompleted Central Line was used as an underground aircraft component factory, 'in order to attack The Fatherland', and many tube stations became air-raid shelters.

The Group perceived all this as a significant historical link, and therefore selected London as its 'defiant headquarters', and the city's underground system, which had been used against the Führer, as its 'ultimate means of attack'. 'Our final act will turn back the clock of history,' the leaflet declared, 'and 1933 will, once again, be the beginning of all beginnings. In one stroke, we shall destroy an old arch-enemy and his pitiful infrastructure, and also the masses of non-white races who have chosen London as their favoured metropolis.'

'So they want to bomb the tube,' Tim had said to Palmer, summing up the puzzling contents of the 'manifesto' he'd just read. 'Yep,' Palmer had nodded. 'Well, they're right about the pitiful infrastructure,' said Tim. 'Still, not a good enough reason to bomb it.' They had laughed, fairly heartily, relieved to be able to joke, when in fact both were worried about a mass disaster they may not be able to prevent. Tim was then briefed on his task – 'to observe events from the point of view of preventing an act of terrorism'; Ian could be told of this new version of events, but not in any detail. 'We're not sure about your partner, or his source,' Palmer had said to Tim, apologetically. 'Some of us think PC Jones is a dark horse. Or at least a pretty crazy one.'

Tim had not defended Ian. He'd said nothing. Maybe he should have put in a few words in his mate's favour; but he happened to agree with Palmer: Ian was unpredictable, to say the least. And now he was actually relieved not to have to go into detail about what the terrorism angle was all about.

*

Ian was flabbergasted. *Terrorism*? What the hell did that mean?

'And, by the way,' said Tim quickly, 'not a word about any of this to your informant. Official orders. They want us to talk to him as before.'

Charlie was waiting for them on a bench, at the end of a long platform. Piccadilly Line, of course, northbound. He seemed drunk, as usual, but perfectly lucid – as usual.

'This is my colleague, PC Parker,' said Ian.

'Charles Darwin, but you can call me Charlie,' mumbled the old man, without getting up.

Tim joined him on the bench. 'Call me Tim,' he said. 'You can tell me everything you tell PC Jones.'

'I don't think so,' said Charlie, with a mischievously sly smile.

'Oh? And why's that?' said Tim.

Charlie glanced at Ian, who was busy eyeing a cheerfully noisy group of attractive Norwegian students, in their late teens. He leaned towards Tim and whispered in his ear, his breath surprisingly unpolluted: 'Because, PC Parker, you are smarter than your colleague. And you have something to lose.'

'What's that?' asked Tim, incredulously.

'Your wife,' said Charlie Darwin, and finally stood up.

21 What is a *Jewish* Magazine?

Miss Natasha Kaplan
Editor, The Jewish Nose

Dear Miss Kaplan,

I am writing to you at the suggestion of Mr Nigel Pearce, who is the treasurer of our association, 'The Royal Society for the Protection of Natural Victims of Cruel Prejudice'. As you may have guessed, we are interested in members of all colours. Every August, RSPNVCP organizes a conference on a relevant theme. This summer, our topic will be 'Have Jews Invented Victimhood?' You have been chosen to deliver the keynote address, and we would be delighted if you would agree to do so.

Please let me know as soon as possible whether you are interested in being our main speaker. (I should perhaps tell you that we have already approached Mr Elie Wiesel in the United States, and your Chief Rabbi here in Britain; unfortunately, both have sent their regrets.)

I look forward to hearing from you.

Yours very truly,

Miss Margaret Kronick
Chairman, RSPNVCP

~

Natasha Kaplan,
Editor,
NOSES *Magazine*

Dear Madam,

I am a politically daring, because spiritually astute Jewish (albeit only on my grandfather's side, alas!), conceptual artist and sculptor. Your magazine, NOSES, *appeals to me because, unlike most literary journals, you show an interest in visual arts, as demonstrated by your interesting covers. It is also impressive that your magazine's fearlessly visual name –* NOSES *– rhymes, fearlessly, with the name of that great Jewish leader,* MOSES. *And this is, in fact, my main reason for writing to you: I have created a Jewishly inspired modern sculpture, entitled* BUYING TIME, *which I believe would not only be an appropriate adornment for your office, but also a uniquely suitable reproduction for the pages of* NOSES. *I am not in the habit of explaining my own work, but I shall make an exception in this case, as the enclosed photograph of my sculpture does not, perhaps, do full justice to its immense complexity and rewarding richness, not to speak of its size.*

BUYING TIME is a conceptually concrete yet stylistically abstract work of art about the depth of Christian anti-Semitism, which is shown here in the form of a deep cave. The darkness of the cave and its very cave-ness stand for the irrational and 'black' state of mind of those who live in fear of the other, the outsider, THE JEW; *a state of mind which is as old as the human race itself, or should I say the inhuman race? No amount of social change and evolution has had any impact on the primitiveness of the human mind: the ancient cave is unchanged today, as dark as ever, and here to stay.*

You will notice that the cave is shaped like a womb, and that it is giving birth, as it were, to a revolting multi-headed monster: vultures, snakes and swine. I owe this imagery to that infamous sham, the ludicrous anti-Semitic pack of lies known as 'The

Protocols of the Elders of Zion', and am quite pleased with the striking visual result. I have also derived certain obvious elements from that other scam, the blood libel: the tiny Christian boy sandwiched between two pieces of matzo, dripping with ossified blood.

BUYING TIME is, as I have already mentioned, a sculpture about anti-Semitism. But where, you might ask, are the Jews? Well, in my artistic vision, the Jews are but an optical illusion: if you look carefully, and only from a certain angle, you may discern shadows and silhouettes which disappear almost instantly – those are the Jews in my sculpture. The relationship between those fleeting moments of exposure on one hand, and the cave with its poisonous, all-devouring monsters on the other, is precisely the theme here, as expressed in the suggestive title.

I sincerely hope that the size of my sculpture (a little over six feet) will not present a problem for you. It is made of bronze, and weighs about a ton. I would be willing to sell it to you at a reduced price of £750,000, plus delivery charge. I look forward to your speedy response.

Yours sincerely,

Hugh Morton

~

Editor,
The Nose

Dear Sir/Madam,

I would like to submit, for your consideration, two articles of considerable scientific interest on medical issues of Jewish concern. I am a retired freelance reform rabbi and former acupuncturist.

The shorter, less substantial, piece deals with a little-known but serious affliction known as Scrot Rot, an inflammatory skin disorder which occurs when boys' and men's testicles are rubbed against the skin of their legs whilst riding camels in the desert. I trace the origins of Scrot Rot from the time of our Exodus from Egypt and follow its various manifestations and treatments all the way to modern-day Israel. Most of my research is based on fascinating anecdotal evidence from local sources, both written and oral. I might add that, having spent many years in the Sinai desert I have been an intermittent Scrot Rot sufferer myself.

My second article deals with the issue of Jewish identity and what forges us into a nation, from the point of view of orthodox rabbinic views on contemporary fertility treatments. Although I am a reform Jew myself, I believe it is important to engage in an open discussion with our orthodoxy. I have therefore undertaken to examine the ultra-orthodox rabbinic view on artificial insemination; specifically, how it deals with the question of whether artificial insemination with donor sperm constitutes adultery, according to Jewish law. In traditional terms, adultery is defined as sexual intercourse between a married Jewish woman and a Jewish man who is not her husband. A child conceived in this way would be considered a mamzer, *a bastard, and be highly stigmatized. The rabbis have ruled, therefore, that artificial insemination of a married woman's egg with a Jewish donor sperm (where the sperm comes from a man who is not her husband) is forbidden; according to these rabbis, the solution here is to use* non-Jewish sperm. *Gentile sperm, it seems, is ideal for the purpose of avoiding adultery yet still guarantee a fully Jewish conception, since Judaism is passed on through the mother.*

As a non-orthodox Jew, I am both puzzled and fascinated by the ultra-orthodox preference for non-Jewish sperm donors. In my article, I ask the following question (among others): what happens if the non-Jewish sperm is donated by a man who has converted to Judaism (prior to becoming a donor)? I assume that an orthodox conversion would preclude him from being a kosher, sperm-giving candidate, but what if the conversion was a reform or conservative one? What would that signify, in terms of the man's sperm? Another related question I ask is the following: if goyishe *sperm is so kosher, why shouldn't married Jewish women indulge in affairs with non-Jewish men with perfect impunity? (I am indebted to my wife, Avital, for bringing this interpretation of the rabbinic law to my attention.)*

If you are interested in reading these articles, please let me know.

Shalom,

Rabbi Baruch Cohn-Goldsmith

~

Dear N,

They should be knifing you in the back any day now.

Cordially,

C

~

Natasha skimmed through these, thinking that perhaps the sculptor, Hugh Morton, would be the right person to deliver the keynote address to Miss Kronick's society. His speech was practically written: he could just read his letter, perhaps leaning on his majestic work of art . . . Maybe they would even buy it!

She rested her forehead in the palm of her left hand, digging her elbow into the hard surface of her desk. She had done nothing more this morning than look at some of her post; so why was she already exhausted, as if she had hours of hard work behind her? Natasha always found it easier to concentrate late at night and had a tendency to feel a bit tired and groggy in the morning, but this was a new kind of exhaustion: it seemed to have, at its core, a sense of not having done enough, rather than too much. An emptiness, a hollow feeling of being off-target. She craved clarity and sharp focus, and had to accept murky vagueness instead. It suddenly occurred to her that she had received very few interesting submissions recently, and worse, that she had not commissioned any decent contributions for quite some time now. Why was that?

Natasha glanced at the neat stack of the four most recent issues of *The Nose* – her work. She loved to look at each new number when it came back from the printers, examining every page, searching for mistakes, things that did not come out the way she had planned them to. And, mysteriously, there would always be *something* out of order – a wrong word or letter here, a missing caption under a photograph there . . . But she knew that most readers would probably never notice, and quickly learned to live with the imperfections and enjoy the overall impression the magazine made, which she knew was a good one. Held's *Nose* had been an ugly duckling: sheets of reading matter joined together by an authoritative yet aesthetically blind editorial hand. Natasha's *Nose*, on the other hand, had evolved into an elegant swan: the redesign she had introduced, with the trustees' reluctant blessing, created airy, attractive pages, easy to read and easy to look at.

She had worked with the designer on creating this image, going through endless possibilities, rejecting one after another, until this stylish – even Yvette Moskowitz thought so – combination of fonts and visual elements emerged as the only right one. But what did 'right' mean? Did it reflect Natasha's own personality, as much as her editorial decisions on what to publish and what to leave out? As much as her editorials? Did she have the right to think of this little publication as something that had a bit of *her* in it? As if it were her own book?

What *was* a magazine, anyway? Or, more precisely, what was *this* magazine? This *Jewish* magazine? Natasha knew, of course, that *The Nose* did not even inhabit the same universe as the mainstream press. She could publish rare masterpieces in it – if she were lucky enough to find them – and they would go completely unnoticed, as if they hadn't been published at all. Jewish culture in this country, unlike in her native America, was a barely visible affair, alive but only just, hidden in a quiet corner, a little too unassuming, a little too modest for Natasha's taste. Perhaps that was the reason why the magazine had almost no financial backing, and therefore no professional safety net

– a team of people who would be employed to guarantee its quality and survival. It had been the brainchild of just one man – Franz Held – who for years had somehow found the money to print issue after issue of what he considered to be relevant material on the subject of being Jewish, in the fifties, sixties, seventies, eighties, and briefly, into the nineties . . . The trustees helped, but they had not been there at the very beginning. How did he manage it, all by himself? Natasha wondered.

It had taken her this long – a full year – to begin to understand just what it really meant to edit Held's magazine. It was a perennial exercise in role-playing: one day she would be the fund-raising whore, attending an elegant tea or dinner, trying to pitch the peculiar idea that a Jewish literary magazine was 'very, very important' to an assortment of robust, vigorous businessmen and their wives, who would all look at her in mild disbelief and respond with kindly, bemused smiles and hardly any cash. Natasha had noticed that even the older wives of these men tended to have excellent legs, and that they all wore almost identical pearl necklaces, as if it were a sign of belonging to a secret club. After giving the perky, unpleasantly enthusiastic editor of some unknown little magazine five minutes of their attention, both the men and the women at these functions would go straight back to discussing golf and opera and recent trips to Israel. Natasha didn't really mind; the food was always fantastic, and occasionally she would meet a nice man or woman who would give her no money but would reward her, instead, with his or her interesting life story. Natasha had a weakness for life stories. Only one time did she become so frustrated by the hopelessness of her impassioned pleas on behalf of her poor little *Nose* that she indulged in another weakness of hers and stole all the gorgeous, plump, wine-red cherries off her neighbour's elegant dessert plate, to everyone's silent surprise, and without an apology.

And then there were her other roles. There was the actual editing of the magazine, of course; translating her own and other people's fleeting ideas into pages of readable, attractive, tangible, hopefully lasting material. There was the strangely non-interactive game she had to play with The Midgets, never really understanding who they were and why they were investing so much time in endless meetings which seemed to serve no visible purpose. Well, perhaps one: the supportive system the trustees had provided for Held seemed to have been replaced by an intricate filigree of obstacles they decided to put in Natasha's way. She couldn't understand why, and wondered how on earth they could have hired her in the first place. Then she remembered: no one else had applied for the job . . .

But all this now seemed like a distant memory, an age of innocence, a mere background to the shifting of gears that had occurred, imperceptibly at first, when she met Hoffmann and was faced with his frank take on her mother's veiled past. And Hoffmann himself, whose bizarrely, incomprehensibly generous donation to the magazine had sparked off her interest in his life story and in Held's, especially as there seemed to have been an unknown connection between the two . . . And that enticingly ambiguous photograph of Held as a young man, a perfect symbol of the perfect enigma he was to become . . . And, finally, the upcoming trial of the old Nazi film-maker, and her mother's role in it – these were parts of a mystery she simply *had* to solve.

There was no doubt in Natasha's mind that she *would* solve all these riddles and tie them together, sooner or later. But what then? It wouldn't be the same as finding the answer to a fun crossword puzzle; it would be more like cracking a code, an important one. This made her think of those typewriter-like contraptions the Germans used to encrypt secret information during the Second World War – only to have them, and the files, decoded by the enemy, thus precipitating their own defeat. Natasha's projected scenario was based on the same premise: she would uncover the truth and, in the process, celebrate a victory over those who had kept it from her. Secret-bearers, deceitful impostors by definition, could only be on the wrong side of the fence; *she* was on the right side of it, and this excited her. All these concealed bits and pieces, waiting for her to bring them out into the light of day . . . It wasn't unlike the excitement she felt when writing her mystery – beginning with a death for which she, the author, had no explanation at the outset. Mrs Cohen, her obese heroine, had had her last supper and was, suddenly, dead. She had been a quiet, shy widow, didn't know many people and spent most of her time watching television and eating. And bit by bit, Natasha had unravelled her past, and shown that old Mrs Cohen had had a great deal to be shy about.

And so it would be with these characters – Hoffmann, Held . . . even her mother. Yes, even Alice. Natasha was quite sure that she had every right to know, and understand, her own mother's past, whatever it had been.

I'm a self-righteous bitch, Natasha thought suddenly. Excited as she was about the prospect of playing detective, it did not escape her inner attention that she may be on the 'wrong' side of the fence herself. She wasn't exactly without secrets, and her concept of right and wrong was pretty much out of whack here. Anyway, people could have 'good' secrets as well as 'bad' ones . . . After a self-chastising moment, Natasha decided to untangle this web of mysteries as best she could, but not to play judge when it came to evaluating the results.

Natasha was pleased with that formulation: she wouldn't evaluate her findings, but she *would* publish them. She could do that, she had a whole magazine at her disposal. Yes, that was it: the next issue of *The Nose,* which had been held up anyway, for financial reasons, could wait even longer, until she had all the information she needed. Then it would come out, and it would contain the full results of her detective work. And, thought Natasha, with unexpected conviction, this next issue would be her last. Her swan song.

The decision made her feel lighter, and lifted the tiredness from her mind and body. She was just about to leave her desk and make herself a cup of strong, bittersweet coffee when she noticed a small blue air-mail envelope that had escaped her attention. Unlike the other letters, it was addressed to her own home address. Natasha was pleased: she rarely received personal letters by post, and this could be from a friend.

But it wasn't even signed. Well, not really. It was a clean page produced on a word processor, a few lines, neatly centred:

NATASHA KAPLAN I WOULDN'T TAKE MY LIFE FOR GRANTED IF I WAS THE JEW BITCH THAT YOU ARE.

A FRIEND OF JOHN WHITE

Natasha let the letter slide out of her hand, as if she had lost her strength. Right, she thought, this is scary. This isn't e-mail. Somebody knows where I *live*. And then she said out loud, 'God, this is a fucking death threat!!'

She was alone in the house, but she didn't feel alone. 'I'm fine,' she said, very loudly, as if she were lecturing her invisible, pathetic enemy. 'My husband is a fucking cop, for God's sake.'

Then it struck her as funny that Tim was, actually, an employee of the British Transport Police. A *transport* cop, then. Did that count? Still, it was better than nothing. She hid the letter in one of the overflowing drawers of her desk, and dialled her mother's number, thinking how nice it was that she didn't have to call her long-distance, at least for a while.

22 Sam Kaplan

Sam couldn't remember the last time he had been alone, without Alice. She never travelled anywhere by herself, knowing that he felt hopeless and helpless without her. But this time, there had been no choice – a trial was a trial and she simply had to attend. He had thought of joining her, but Alice had not encouraged him; in fact, she had made it perfectly clear she didn't want him to be there with her, in that courtroom. Sam was disappointed: the case concerned a film-maker, and he was vaguely interested in the details. But Alice didn't explain what her role would be at the trial – 'a small, insignificant witness; don't know why they're even bothering with me,' she had said, indifferently – and that was that. So Alice had a past he knew nothing about; so what else was new? It didn't *matter*, that past of hers. She had always wanted it that way and he had co-operated. Why change now?

Maybe he was a little sorry about missing out on a trip abroad; but then he remembered how much he had hated London when he was there some years ago for his daughter's wedding – a strangely foreign, strangely mixed affair, at least to him. Sam was used to being the centre of attention in large joyous gatherings, the star, the magnet attracting clusters of emotionally charged admirers, hangers-on, even real friends. But at Natasha's wedding, he had felt superfluous and isolated. And bored. Tim's parents were quietly impressive people: his burly father had towered over small, mercurial Sam, and so, come to think of it, had Tim's very subdued mother. They had smiled a great deal and said many pleasant things in tediously calm, controlled voices ('doesn't our Tim look lovely'; 'doesn't our Natasha look lovely'; 'isn't this a lovely wedding'; 'wasn't your rabbi a lovely lady';

'isn't it lovely you came'; 'what a lovely cake'; 'won't it be lovely when the children move into their own home'; 'isn't it lovely for Natasha to live in such a safe city' . . .). Sam had had no idea how to reply to any of these statements, but eventually found a person he could talk to, sort of – the rabbi who had agreed to marry Natasha and her Gentile boyfriend.

She was a friendly youngish woman with a warm, casual manner, and had handled the sensitive issue of the mixed wedding ceremony with great competence. Ms Rosenberg, Sam had said to her, are you gay? Yes I am, Mr Kaplan, she had replied with an open smile, how did you guess? Oh, because, as you were standing there under that canopy, I imagined you in bed with another lesbian rabbi, sucking each other's tits, what a picture, wish I could film it. Well, why don't you, Mr Kaplan, I am sure my partner and I would be *gay*me. Sam laughed at this, relieved there was at least one person at the wedding he could have an intelligent conversation with. Of course, it had been all in his head. *And* there had been no canopy.

This was the way his films always developed, from a glimpse of something that made his (by now senescent) dick respond, quickly and deliciously, discharging a complex signal to some creative corner of his brain. His imagination began working instantly, casting Alice in the role of the lesbian rabbi (which one?), it would probably be a good idea to start with the wedding, the ceremony performed by *both* female rabbis, shots of the young couple in their tumescent innocence (innocent tumescence? would that make a visual difference?) while the rabbis' nipples *stretch* under their austere suits; desire, desire, desire . . . Then cut to their bedroom, soft lighting on Alice, as always . . . It didn't bother Sam in the least that Alice was now an old woman; she hadn't lost any of her iridescence and could still illuminate every frame, like a bright young star of the silent cinema.

She had no trouble shining everywhere she went, even at that wedding reception. Sam watched, mesmerized, as Alice moved from one person to another – Tim's family, Tim's colleagues, Natasha's friends – chatting, chatting, chatting, so at ease with everyone, as if she had known them forever. The (very understated) Jewishness of the wedding had been a surprise to quite a few people on Tim's side, and on Natasha's as well. It had been her idea and her wish. When Sam asked her why – religion had never been a part of their lives – she had simply said, 'I don't know, Dad. Maybe because I want Tim to know he and I are different people. I don't want to *merge* with him; do you understand that?'

Sam said he did, but in truth was not really interested in his daughter's view on Jewishness. In fact, he wasn't all that interested in anything his children did or didn't do. He was focused on one thing only: making love to his wife, in the flesh and on the screen. Everything else was secondary.

Now, he tried to lighten his solitude by watching some of his old Alice favourites, going all the way back to the first films they did together. The young woman on the screen – younger than their daughter was now – radiated a very physical presence, even when she was fully dressed. But Sam liked to show Alice naked, or very transparently dressed; he wanted the whole world to see her shimmering curves and angles, to see what *he* saw. The result was something between soft porn and refined erotica, a sort of documentary of his own desire. Sam never fantasized about other women, he only fed their images into his fantasies about Alice. The best ones were eventually transformed into his films, always with Alice's advice and support.

In fact, it had been Alice's idea that Sam should start directing these strange films, made for a small (but gradually widening) circle of friends and interested kindred spirits. At first, she had only been the charming nimble waitress – the only woman among all the male waiters – at his favourite jazz club, Café Society in Sheridan Square. Sam always tried to talk to her a little, but she was busy fluttering and disappearing among the tables in the soft semi-darkness, like a graceful wraith, there but untouchable. But gradually, she began lingering near Sam and his buddies, enchanting them all – the men *and* the women – with her warm, vivacious manner and her European accent. And then, almost imperceptibly, something happened, something changed, and suddenly Alice was 'Sam's girl'.

She joined his group of friends as naturally as if she had always known them. They were a noisy bunch, though not at the club, where they sat enraptured, listening to sensual jazz and watching mordant political cabaret, not missing a single beat, whether it was music or words. They were almost all students, but Sam, who was living on his father's generous allowance, had more money than the others, and liked to treat everyone to Scotch and sodas; at seventy-five cents a shot, it didn't even make a dent in his budget. They would all spend half the night at the Café Society, and the remaining half in Sam's dark little apartment, just around the corner. It was like a never-ending party, but with a serious undertone: every issue *mattered* and had to be debated until the original point was completely forgotten, transformed into myriads of others.

Alice was not exactly the heart of those parties, she was too modest for that, but she did, eventually, take on the subtly informal role of hostess. She was naive or ignorant about much of what was being discussed when it dealt with politics, and it often did. She usually listened attentively when others argued, and when Sam saw how she concentrated, how she wrinkled her forehead trying not to lose a word, especially the words she did not yet understand, he was overcome with such tender desire for this unusual creature he decided to marry her, even though he had never wanted to be married to anyone. So one night he asked her, in a low voice and out of the blue, in front of all their friends at the club, just as a particularly good, teasingly syncopated sax solo was winding down on stage: 'Alice I love you. Will you be my wife, for God's sake?' Everyone laughed and applauded, blending their support for Sam's proposal with their appreciation of the music, and Alice simply nodded and said, 'Of course.'

She soon stopped waitressing and began working during the day, in an uptown antique shop, where her knowledge of European languages as well as history was greatly appreciated by the elderly German-Jewish owner. Alice was soon managing the small store, earning a decent, if modest, living. Sam, meanwhile, tried to work up the courage to break the news of his marriage to his father, whom he had not invited to the wedding. It had been celebrated by and among his and Alice's friends only, no family. Well, Alice didn't have any, not in her new country, except a very old aunt who lived in Brooklyn and never left her house, and who had sponsored Alice when she decided to start a new life in America.

But Sam had a father and many other relatives he could have invited, though he had no siblings and his mother was dead. The problem with inviting his father was, as he explained to Alice who seemed very puzzled by it all, that he simply didn't want to *see* him. He didn't hate him exactly, but he despised him. Why was that? Alice wanted to know. As far as she knew, Sam's father supported him generously, never asking for 'results' – he didn't want to know how the money was spent or how his son was doing at university. Maybe he had guessed that Sam had drifted away from his studies a long time ago, and never intended to go back; maybe he didn't want to hear that his money was being squandered on just about anything that caught Sam's fancy. Most recently, it was a fur coat for Alice (which she insisted on returning, finding it deliciously warm but ridiculously extravagant) and a very silly speckled orange, brown and green felt hat, studded with silver fish lures (which she loved and wore every day).

So why the contempt? She was curious to know. And how could it be so strong that there was no place for this man in Sam's life? Who was he? Sam's replies were scant and evasive. But bit by bit, she managed to piece together a picture which contained at least a few explanatory elements.

Max Kaplan was a very busy man. He wrote screenplays in Hollywood, which was no mean feat for a man whose first language was German. A native Berliner, he had been snapped up by Paramount in the 1920s, when Hollywood was in the process of crippling, financially and creatively, its main European competitor, the German UFA. Max, who at the time had written only one major film, *Der Bluthund und das Mädchen*, received an offer from America which only a fool would refuse, and had remained in California ever since. The movie had been a dark, stylized masterpiece based on a fairytale of unknown origin, in which a beautiful, angelic young girl is almost bitten to death by a vicious bloodhound. At the last minute, the girl saves herself by looking, imploringly, into the dog's huge, bloodshot eyes; the beast relents, and its spirit enters the girl, while the girl's spirit enters the hound. It turns into a meek, servile animal, whereas the girl, with her angelic appearance intact, becomes a bloodthirsty devil. Together, they roam the streets of night-time Berlin, looking for unsuspecting victims. Elegant men and women are seduced by the girl who then attacks them like a little vampire, while the bloodhound looks on, tenderly. The film had been a big success in inter-war Germany.

In Hollywood, Max was asked to write lighter films, dramas involving awkward love affairs which could be resolved quickly enough for the audiences not to lose interest, and to go home satisfied. It turned out that he had a real knack for this sort of thing, and became one of those magic formula screenwriters, turning out perfect and perfectly forgettable entertainment with amazing speed and ease.

Still, Alice didn't get it: was *that* the reason Sam despised his father? Surely not.

Sam lost his usual manic cheerfulness for a moment and explained that no, the reason had to do with his mother. Max had brought a young wife with him from Germany, a secretary who used to work for UFA. She had been happy in California, very happy, Sam remembered that . . . She used to take him swimming a lot, she loved the sun and the free lifestyle and how easy everything was. And then she committed suicide, drowned herself in a friend's pool, when Sam was only ten years old. He still remembers her body, fully clothed in a red dress with big white dots, white shoes, floating by the edge of the pool. By the edge! She could have pulled herself up, she could have pulled herself *together* . . . He has always blamed his father for this, but he wouldn't tell Alice why exactly. Was it a love affair? Maybe, he said darkly. And that was all he would tell her.

After that, she never probed again, and Sam was grateful. But she did insist on meeting his father – she *was* his daughter-in-law, she had said, it was only right. And she did meet him, in New York, when Max came to visit, and in California, where they sometimes travelled before the children were born. Sam was amazed to see how well she got along with his father; he would often leave them alone together, because their long, heavy conversations bored him. Max was clearly charmed by his European daughter-in-law, and the sensitive subject – the mother's story – never came up. Yet even Sam, who was not very good at perceiving people's secret thoughts and feelings, could sense that Max's sentiments were not really reciprocated: Alice didn't like him, in spite of all their long chats.

But something good did come of their relationship. Alice was so inspired by all that talk about movies that she suggested to Sam he should try his hand at them, too. She said this knowing full well that he loathed the idea of being in the same business as his father. But Alice didn't let him talk; instead, she had said: 'Sam, I don't mean *his* kind of movies. I mean *our* kind. A whole new . . . genre. You know I've always wanted to act, but I'd be too shy to try it with someone else. You'd direct me and film me like a . . . God!' Then she proceeded to explain how one could take an uncomplicated plot and, simply by showing it from an erotic angle, transform it into a thing of beauty. 'We won't do it for money, of course. Nothing commercial, not at all like your father's ridiculous material. It'll be our joint creation.' She was glowing, and Sam soon caught the bug, and they began producing their 'things of beauty', one after another, year after year.

Alice's freedom in front of the camera was breathtaking. Even when it came time to give birth to Philip, she insisted on being filmed, and managed to fill the screen with every exposed, vulnerable part of herself. She was not ashamed to cry and scream, and when it was over, she wept, cradling the dark-haired baby against her breast. And then she said, with a smile: 'Was I good, Sam, or do we need another take?'

This was the film Sam was replaying now, alone in the apartment. Again and again. Yes, he decided, he would take it to London, later, for their retrospective. A pivotal one for both of them, he thought. Definitely important. It didn't occur to him that there was no sign of the baby's father showing any interest in the brand new, wet infant. Sam had remained behind the camera, and kept it focused, as lovingly as ever, on his wife. And now he saw a glimpse of pain in her face, a horrible contortion he hadn't noticed before, and he wondered why; the birth was over, and it had gone well.

He was still staring at Alice's unfamiliar expression, and at her cracked lips which seemed to be mouthing some words he couldn't hear, when the phone rang. When he heard Philip's voice, Sam couldn't help laughing.

'What's the matter, Dad?' Philip asked, a little sternly.

'I was just looking at your . . . birth, you were such a tiny thing, and here you are, calling me . . .'

'Oh God, Dad, not *that* one.'

Philip was deeply embarrassed by the film which showed his inaugural moments, first between his mother's legs, then on her stomach and breast.

'It's a masterpiece, Philip, if I do say so myself. I'm taking it to the retrospective in London.'

'You're *not* . . . Oh well, I guess I don't hold the copyright to my own birth.'

'Damn right you don't. It belongs to your mother and me.'

'OK Dad, drop it, will you? I'm calling about something a bit more important. About going to London, as a matter of fact.'

'Yeah, I told you I'm going to show my films. In a couple of months' time.'

'I know. But I think we should both go there for the trial, and that's next week. I mean it, Dad. It's important.'

'Why, all of a sudden? She said it was a minor thing . . .'

'Dad, listen to me. That's what I thought. Well, I've done some digging . . . turns out the woman is a major war criminal.'

'Your mother?!!' Sam grabbed his heart. Was *that* his wife's lifelong secret? Jesus Christ . . .

'No, the Nazi woman. The one who's on trial. Dad, have you lost your mind or something?'

Philip was concerned. Talking to his father was never easy – he tended to use his far more coherent mother as a filter – but this was a bit much. He wished, he *longed*, to have a father he could actually talk to, not this emotionally underdeveloped man who only came alive in his mother's hands (literally, Philip had to concede). If he'd had such a father, he would have told him about everything he had been working on lately, and they would both enjoy that sort of talk . . .

For example, using the crackpot e-mails Natasha had been forwarding to him, Philip had managed to get very close to a bona fide white supremacist, a loner who called himself John White but whose real name was actually Paul Brandt. He was an accountant, lived in a nice suburban split-level house in Pleasantville, New York, had a wife and three young children with whom he played football on the lawn. Friendly man, good-looking, gentle. He had two hobbies – underground trains and the internet. On his website, he featured daily variations on an imaginative graphic depiction of a devil-like creature, in black, red and yellow. The figure was sometimes male, sometimes female, always sporting a large hooked nose and a star of David. John White was flattered when Philip asked to be allowed to talk to him, and readily explained his connection with 'The Group of '33', whose website was interlinked with his own: 'Well, to be honest, there isn't any. They do their own thing and I do my own. I'm not an organized sort of guy, if you know what I mean. I do my own thing. But they got the know-how, so I follow their instructions, sometimes. Easier that way. You a kike? Thought so.' Philip was excited about his scoop and had already got clearance from his paper to pursue the story in a big way. But he couldn't tell his father any of this – his immature father who had the attention span of a goldfish.

'All right, all right. So what about her?'

'It's a very serious trial. And Mom is a *very* important witness.'

'But she said—'

'Never mind what she told you. I know. But it's not the truth. I think she's the key witness, as a matter of fact. Haven't you noticed that she's getting VIP treatment, being flown there, they're paying for her flat?'

Sam's attention picked up, and Philip used this precious moment to explain what was involved in the trial, for Alice and for everyone else. He didn't have all the details, but the gist of it was that Alice was, possibly, the only surviving witness of a mass murder.

'Jesus,' said Sam. 'That's . . . major. OK, I'll come. We'll fly together. But . . . I don't understand something, Philip. I thought this Goetz woman was a film-maker? And a pretty good one, I hear?'

'Yes. That's just it. Have you heard of an old German movie called *The Girl and the Bloodhound*? A 1920s classic. You know, an innocent-looking evil spirit devouring people left and right, while looking like an angel? Doesn't sound familiar? No? Well, Goetz made a remake of that during the war, with some significant changes. She used inmates from a concentration camp and had them die for real, in front of the cameras. To make it more realistic, more convincing . . . Mom was one of those inmates, but she survived. I don't know how. Maybe because she played the lead.'

23 Franz Held, Almost Live

Spitzer had kept his word, as usual: he did, finally, find Held's brief memoir about his time with the Czech unit of the Russian army. When Natasha came out of the shower, she found a message from Spitzer saying that he would like to bring it to her this morning, along with a few other relics she might enjoy ('and I don't mean myself, dear', he'd added with a slight laugh). She hadn't planned on staying at home – Alice had suggested a shopping excursion somewhere nice, to take a break from the heaviness she began to feel now that the day of the trial was so near – but this was important. So Natasha cancelled the shopping and told Spitzer he could come.

She made herself a cup of unsweetened, strong tea, for a change, while she waited for him, and decided to make a quick survey, on the phone, of what all the trustees had to say about Franz Held. This would help her determine which leads to follow when searching for clues as to his mysterious absences from London, and she was now convinced that without understanding these, it would be impossible to piece his life together.

Zygmunt Levy-Newman had, predictably, nothing to say. Natasha's cautious questions – Did he ever visit Held at home? Did his frequent travels interfere with the job of editing *The Nose*? – were met with point-blank refusal to engage in a conversation. His telephone silence was even more oppressive and empowering than his silence at the meetings, but Natasha had expected it, and had a little manoeuvre up her sleeve.

'Zygmunt, you did say I could come to you if I needed help with my investigation of Ludwig Hoffmann.'

Levy-Newman suddenly came alive, with a roar, like a bear who has been forced out of hibernation. 'Of course. Yes. What do you need, Natasha?'

'I would like to know whether, in your opinion, Held would have accepted a donation from a man like Hoffmann. I mean, was there anything in his own past that . . .'

'In *Held*'s past? No, no, no. He was no . . . victim. Of the Nazis, I mean. On the contrary.'

'What do you mean, "on the contrary"?' Natasha was pleased. Her strategy seemed to be working. The clever Zygmunt Levy-yNewman hadn't even noticed how she had deflected his attention from Hoffmann back to Held . . .

'Natasha, what would you say is the opposite of a victim?' He sounded testy.

'I don't know . . . a bully? Oppressor? Fascist? Na—' She stopped but almost added: *You*?

'How about hero?'

Natasha decided to try her opponent's tactic: she remained silent.

'I said,' repeated Zygmunt Levy-Newman, 'have you thought of a hero as the opposite of a victim? Because that's what our Franz was. As his name indicates – by pure coincidence, of course . . .'

'I *know*,' said Natasha, impatiently. How many times did she have to be told about the German meaning of Held's name?

'He was,' continued Zygmunt Levy-Newman, suddenly gathering some speed, 'the kind of hero that *counts*. A soldier, and a very brave one. Unlike some of us who either perished or fled, Franz *fought*. The Germans were his enemy, not his jailers. That's a big difference. And that is why I believe he would not be averse to dealing with someone like Herr Hoffmann . . .'

'And you?' asked Natasha, without specifying what she meant.

'I was one that fled. Early on. *Very* early on. Paid a price. Had to forget about writing Polish poetry and learned to make smart leather handbags for elegant English ladies instead. So what? It saved my life.'

He wasn't silent any longer. Words came pouring out of him. Natasha suddenly saw first a little Polish boy, then a young man called Zygmunt who excelled at reciting Polish poetry and was soon writing it himself, a wunderkind, though not to his half-crazy orthodox mother, who thought she had given birth to a *goyishe* devil in disguise. The approaching war was a great excuse for him to escape, from Poland and from his mother, and while he was being initiated into the leather trade by a kind distant relative in Manchester, his mother and the rest of his family vanished without a trace, in this or that ghetto in Poland. And so his love of Polish poetry vanished too, though not painlessly, not overnight, leaving a bloody imprint in his mind like an ugly bruise. And in his new language, he became a man of few words and no poetry – 'only the essentials, Natasha, just enough to get by' – but the magazine was, nevertheless, a sort of link with his pre-war self, and he was glad to help. Especially when he heard about Franz Held's own wartime past, which he found so admirable.

'You mean the fact that he was fighting under General Svoboda? Did he receive any distinctions?'

'How do you know this?'

'Karl told me.'

'I see.' He sounded surprised and disappointed. Did he think he was the only one who knew?

'Well, then, this call was unnecessary, wasn't it?' Natasha heard in his hard voice how sorry he was to have revealed so much about himself. Now he would retreat into his silence again . . . She didn't have the strength to start again, not with him. She still had the other trustees to call . . .

'No, Zygmunt, it wasn't. Thank you very much.' She put down the phone, pretending not to hear him ask about Hoffmann.

Who next? Sugarman wouldn't have anything new to say; Maurice wouldn't be of much help here, as he hadn't known Held in the past; Yvette was too young . . . God, she really didn't feel like talking to any of the others. How about Joel Hirsch? He was certainly old enough.

Unlike Zygmunt, Joel was chatty and forthcoming. And also, to Natasha's great amazement, very knowledgeable about the early years.

'Oh yes, of course I knew he travelled a lot. In fact, we travelled together at one point.'

'*Really*?' Natasha, excited by this unexpected bit of promising information, sat up abruptly in her chair, knocking down her cup of tea. Its contents, fortunately only a few remaining drops of dark-brown, lukewarm liquid, spilt on to some papers on her desk. Luckily, nothing that important, only an old letter from Nigel Pearce.

'Oh yes, in the early days, you know . . . It was an interesting journey, and very . . . emotional, for both of us. This was quite a few years before Franz started the magazine, by the way. In 1948, if I recall correctly. Yes. I was just starting my dental waste business, and asked Franz to accompany me on my first trip to Czechoslovakia for that purpose. First *and* last, I should add. After the Communists took over there, in 1948, I had to remove that place from my list of client countries, of course . . . Anyway, Franz and I were only casually acquainted at the time, and so I was rather pleasantly surprised when he agreed to help me on that business trip. His help was invaluable, of course, as he is a native of Prague – but you know that . . .'

'Yes,' said Natasha. 'By the way, how did you and Franz meet? Originally, I mean?'

'I don't know if I remember that . . . by chance, somewhere, I believe . . . perhaps Sidney introduced us . . . I really don't remember . . . We were very different. He was a single man, I was married. He was younger than me, of course, and very cultured, and I could not compete with his worldliness – and, by the way, I had no interest in his magazine, none at all, when Sidney told me about it some years later – but they both persuaded me to become involved . . . Well, that's another story. In any case, as I was telling you, we travelled to Prague together, to bring back some dental waste which was very good value in central Europe at the time. Franz knew some dentists in Prague who were interested in selling me the fruits of their labour, if you know what I mean—'

'So was Franz living in London at the time?'

'Of course, Natasha, what do you think?'

'Well I thought . . . I thought he arrived here later, in the fifties. I believe his obituary said something to that effect.'

'Oh, *that* obituary!' The perennially complacent Joel suddenly sounded almost angry.

'What's wrong?' asked Natasha, intrigued.

'What's wrong?! It didn't tell you anything, that's what's wrong. Between you and me, Natasha, it's a good thing you don't publish obituaries any more. Charles should never have been allowed to get away with the nonsense he puts together. What does *he* know? Nothing. Nothing at all.'

'What do you mean specifically, in Held's case? What was wrong or missing in that obituary?'

'Well, for starters, was there any mention of Theresienstadt? No. Or his army service? No and no. His double persecution – first by the Nazis, then by the Communists? No again. That's because our dear Charles hasn't got a clue. Collects facts, at random, and doesn't know how to explain them. What an idiot.'

Natasha smiled. Joel Hirsch was turning into an entertaining character. Who would have known . . . Then she had a thought.

'Joel, what are you saying? That he was *both*? A soldier *and* a concentration camp inmate? How could that be?'

'I have no idea, Natasha, but it's true. You know I was in Auschwitz . . .' This was the first time he had ever mentioned his past to her, though she had heard about it, of course. 'Well, one day, a large transport arrived, from Theresienstadt. I got to know some of them because . . . Never mind why. Anyway, there was a special man among them, a famous writer, all the Czechs revered him. I'm Austrian myself, so his name meant nothing to me. Pavel Miller. But I came into contact with him – never mind how – and I could see why everyone liked him. A really special man, and I don't use the word lightly. I'm not like Charles!

'This Pavel Miller was – how should I explain this – a very sad man, but that wouldn't be surprising, would it. People were drawn to him, he gave them something, some sort of warmth. And humour – yes, humour. Believe it or not, he could make us laugh. He even wrote a couple of humorous skits which the women performed one day. He looked well, by the way, considering . . . Quite well fed, I mean, at least when he first arrived. Someone told me he had enjoyed special privileges in Theresienstadt, better food, even a room of his own – unheard-of luxury. But it was given to him because he was like a folk hero. People tried to lighten his suffering a little.

'I am telling you about Pavel Miller because he mentioned Franz Held to me once.'

'Really?'

'Yes. He told me how Franz arrived in Theresienstadt one day, not with any transport, but by himself. How he quickly became known as a sportsman and as the editor of a magazine – doesn't that sound like our Franz?' he said, with some pride. 'He also told me that they were meant to be in the same transport to Auschwitz, in January 1943, but Franz had somehow managed to avoid it, it wasn't clear how.

'Pavel Miller told me Franz was always trying to convince him to write something for that magazine, but Pavel refused. They had had an argument about this, apparently, a big one. Franz was of the view that one had to do whatever one could to keep one's spirit alive in the camp: write, draw, perform plays, compose music, compete in sports, listen to lectures . . . But Pavel believed that to be too creative would be to somehow play into the hands of the Nazis; didn't they want to present Theresienstadt as the model ghetto where Jews were not even suffering, but only living among themselves, cheerfully and productively? Didn't they even make a film to "prove" that this was so? The right thing to do, Pavel Miller said to me, was *not* to write. To stop composing if you were a composer. You were there to starve and die, and you should do just that. Are you confused, Natasha? So was I. Because this same Pavel Miller *did* make people happy by writing those little skits. And he *did* give some lectures in Theresienstadt, as I'd heard. But that seemed to be a different matter, had a different meaning, at least to him. Natasha, what do *I* know? I'm not a learned man, no matter what Sidney likes to say about me. Shall I tell you what my job was in the camp?' His voice was strong, unbroken, but Natasha felt the undertow of emotion.

'Joel, you don't have to—'

'It's all right. I had to extract the gold from the teeth of those who . . . were dead. You might as well know this. In my real life, Natasha, before the war, I was a chef at a famous Viennese hotel. I fed people, I stuffed their fat mouths with delicious Wiener schnitzels and bouillons with egg floating on top and Sacher Torte, and when they laughed and expressed their appreciation, I could sometimes see their gold fillings sparkle. Now I was forced to extract those precious fillings from people's mouths – I became very skilled at it . . . Sometimes it seemed to me as if those were the very same mouths I had been feeding for years. I managed to keep a bit of that horrible gold to myself: saved my life . . . And after the war, well, who knows why we do what we do? I just couldn't go back to being a chef . . .

'Natasha, I have to go, so I'll be quick now. What I really wanted to tell you was that Pavel Miller did, in the end, write a little something for Held's magazine in the camp. But it wasn't a literary piece, it was more of a political essay. Quite serious. About Zionism. That's what I heard, anyway. I told you, I don't know Czech. He told me himself, Pavel did. By the way, he survived Auschwitz and went back to Prague. When I was there with Franz, I wanted to find him, but Franz discouraged me. Said there wasn't enough time, we had so many business calls to make. Later, I was sorry not to have tried, because I read that Pavel Miller had been sentenced to a lifetime in jail at one of those show-trials in the 1950s. He died in a prison. I guess he was weakened by – you know . . . his other life sentence. The one he *did* survive.'

Natasha thought Joel was finished and was about to thank him, when he suddenly added, 'One more thing. That time, Franz and I brought back more than dental waste. We also brought a bag of ancient Jewish . . . well, bones. From a very old Jewish cemetery somewhere near Prague. It was about to be desecrated by some modern construction or other – a hospital, I believe – and someone had asked Franz to dig out these bones and take them back to England. To rehouse them, so to speak, give them another burial where they would be safe . . . I remember bringing them home in a bag and putting it on the kitchen table. My wife, who always helped me sort through the bags of dental amalgams, saw this one and asked what it was. I told her and she screamed at me to get it off the table, and how could I bring this into the house . . . I said, You don't mind stuff from people's teeth but a little bit of ancient Jewish dust bothers you? I was teasing, of course, she had a point. Anyway, Franz came and took it away, and gave it to some rabbi. I just remembered this because it happened on that same trip. Funny, the things one remembers.' His natural joviality restored, Joel said goodbye, leaving Natasha too perplexed to make any more phone calls.

It would have been too late anyway, because Karl Spitzer arrived at that very moment, carrying a folder of papers.

'I found more material for you, you'll find it interesting, I believe,' he said as he came through the door. He looked even better than the last time she saw him. Really, thought Natasha, he's quite an attractive man. She noticed his sharp blue eyes and quiet, strong features; and how lightly he moved around the room, not like an old man at all. More like an ageless, weightless male. Weightless? Hardly. He seemed so . . . solid. Firm. So rooted in whatever his mind was concentrating on at the moment.

'Natasha, what's wrong? You look like you are about to cry.'

Was she that transparent? Natasha had always thought of herself as inscrutable, if she wanted to be; open, when she felt like it. Accessible, when she chose to be; off limits, when she decided to be. It was always *her* choice, she believed.

But now she realized she was no longer in charge of her emotions, which came and went like trains on a track, sometimes stopping, sometimes only passing through, with deafening noise. She heard herself crying, with relief. She told Karl everything – about her mother, about Held, about the strange death threat, the e-mail – she even told him about Erica's headlice. And about Tim's shy love which was all it was supposed to be but, somehow, wasn't – or was it hers for him? She was confused. She told him what she knew and what she didn't know. And how she longed to know *all*, but was afraid to.

And when she was done, he said, 'Natasha, if I were a younger man believe me I would—'

'Why don't you fuck me anyway,' she said, no longer crying.

So he did. And her mind, numbed by the intense pleasure of yielding to his unfamiliar touch, didn't wander. Except once, when it occurred to her that she was fucking a man whose wife had fucked Held, which put Natasha within, well, fucking distance of her dead predecessor – who was finally beginning to emerge out of the shadows of the past, still a dark figure, but perhaps just a little more tangible. A little more *alive.* History, she thought cheerfully, was not such an abstract thing, after all.

24 **Not Everything is a Joke**

Philip and Sam had arrived in London only a few days before the trial of Annmarie Goetz, and had at first considered not telling Alice until the last moment. But Natasha objected, and insisted they all meet for lunch and talk – a family reunion! Sam wanted to do this at some fun, special place, like the Ivy restaurant in Covent Garden, where he hoped to be noticed and admired, a little taster of the star treatment he was counting on receiving at his upcoming London retrospective. After all these years of being famous among people who knew him anyway, Sam was looking forward to a slice of *real* glamour. He still hated London, but, if he had an audience here, maybe the place could grow on him . . .

But Alice wanted a quiet meal, in private, and so Philip and Sam took the Piccadilly Line train from their hotel in Bloomsbury and joined Alice and Natasha at Christina's. When she saw Alice, Christina smiled a big smile and gave them her own table, to Natasha's amazement. Then she hugged them all, pronounced them to be a 'bootiful family' and disappeared into the kitchen.

Philip cut straight to the point, as he always did: 'Mom, I know you understand why Dad and I just *had* to be here. I know you do. But what I don't get is why you had to be so secretive about all this. You're not a minor witness here, you're a major one. Did you really think we'd never find out? I'm a journalist, for God's sake. A *gossip* journalist! I can find out anything I want. Not that I really have to. I mean, this thing is starting to be all over the papers, anyway.'

It was true. Almost every single one of that morning's broadsheets carried a piece on Annmarie Goetz, the film-maker / Nazi war criminal, and her upcoming trial. The photographs showed a very old woman who looked barely strong enough to appear in court. Already, there had been voices – including letters to the editors of the same papers – questioning the wisdom of trying such a frail old lady: it wasn't fair, it didn't look good. Alice Kaplan's name was mentioned along with a few other witnesses, and so maybe she had been right in downplaying her role.

'Philip,' said Alice, without one of her radiant smiles, 'I'm glad you came. I really am. But please don't flatter yourself. You're not such a hotshot, darling. I mean, you didn't even know your charming girlfriend was a Republican.'

'Ouch,' said Natasha. 'That was vicious, Mom.'

'Was it?' Alice asked innocently, without a trace of apology. 'I don't see why. I'm only making a point here. Which is this: neither Philip, nor you, wizards that you are, know anything at all, for all your expertise at sniffing around and all your brilliance. All you're good at is picking up odd bits and pieces here and there. Smithereens. But you can't put them together to see the whole picture, because that picture has been shattered. For good. So you might as well stop trying. But,' she added, when she saw their hurt looks, 'if there's anything you want to know, just ask *me*. I've decided to "tell all", as they say in celebrity interviews. And I don't mean only in court. I mean here. At *home*.' She winked at Sam, and finally smiled. 'You've waited long enough. All three of you. So have I. Here's my new rule: I don't volunteer any information, but if you ask a good, intelligent question, I'll answer. And no badgering of the witness,' she laughed, looking at her son.

They all fell silent while Christina filled their table with a colourful selection of her best meze dishes. She was fond of this American family, and wanted them all to feel happy under her roof. Looking at their slightly strained faces, she wasn't sure they *were* happy. Except for Natasha, who seemed to be beaming today. Christina hugged her and whispered, very loudly, in her ear: 'You look won-derful today, my love. Bootiful. You are in love, right? And why not. Good for you!' Natasha laughed and wanted to deny it, but Christina had already disappeared in the kitchen.

'OK, Mom, here's my first question,' said Philip, not missing the fact that his little sister did, in fact, look very good today. London, or her job, or her marriage, or motherhood, became her. She seemed to have shed several unnecessary skins and revealed the one she was most comfortable in, the essential one. He felt a little jealous, because the opposite had happened to him over the years: he had piled on layer upon heavy protective layer, until he had lost sight of what lay buried underneath. Did he once have a bright, optimistic core? He didn't even remember. He felt dark, opaque inside. Blunt, and bored. 'Jesus, this tabbouleh is good,' he said. 'Sorry, Mom . . . My question is about the film you are going to talk about at the trial. How come you—'

'No, no, no, Philip. I can't talk about that. And you'll hear it all in courtroom 73, anyway. Sorry, I should have made that clear. Next question?'

'Wait, actually, I'm not finished. I mean, I don't think you know what I was going to ask you. It's this,' he said and took a sip from his glass of mineral water, trying to delay the difficult moment. 'This film Goetz made during the war – the one she is now being prosecuted for – it was a remake of a film our grandfather had made in the twenties, wasn't it? *The Bloodhound and the Girl*, or something like that?'

Everyone, including Alice, looked at Sam. Sam looked at no one in particular.

'You didn't tell me this before we left, son,' he said, quietly.

'I did tell you the title of the film, and I figured, if you knew about it, you'd draw your own conclusions.'

'Don't bother arguing about this,' said Alice, calmly. Natasha felt transported back to the days of her childhood, when Alice cut everyone's fights short by pronouncing those very same words: don't bother arguing about this. It was as if the subject of their argument were of no significance whatsoever unless she sanctified it with her gentle authority.

'Yes, Philip, it was a remake of Max's film. So?'

Philip hesitated, but only long enough to dip his pitta bread in a bowl of hummus.

'So I'm wondering, Mom. When you met Dad, was it an accident? Or was it . . . a plan of some sort?'

It suddenly dawned on Natasha that, while she was doing her best to make some progress on her investigation in London, Philip had been 'covering' the American end of the story: Alice and Sam, and now Max, too. She gave her brother an admiring look, and thought if his research happened to complete hers, they could come up with quite a . . . closure. It would be a wonderful reward for all of this hard work, and pure bliss, to finally have all those questions answered. But the longer she listened to Alice and Philip, the more overwhelmed she felt by the American side of her mother's history.

'It was both. A plan and an accident. The accident was that I fell in love with him, and he with me, the plan was . . . to use him. Don't look so shocked, Sam,' she said, matter-of-factly, even though Sam didn't actually seem in the least perturbed. 'You *know* what your father was like. You know what he has done.'

'Wonderful,' laughed Natasha. 'Dad's got secrets too. *And* granddad. What a family. Are we special or are all families like this?' As far as she knew, Tim's parents had nothing to hide – but now she wasn't so sure.

'Natasha, be serious. Not everything is a joke,' said Philip, sharply. 'I'm still waiting to hear about Max. What on earth could the old man have done?'

'Shall I tell them, or will you?' asked Alice. Sam shrugged his shoulders. He didn't look so much shocked as *shell*-shocked, thought Natasha. Philip was right, this wasn't funny. And she had a feeling it could end badly. Thank God they were at Christina's rather than at home. Christina wouldn't allow for anything too awful to happen to them, she would shield them from disaster – like, for instance, her father having a heart attack.

'All right. I'll explain, and I'll have to be very blunt. You know there is no other way.' She added those last few words for her husband's benefit, even though he wasn't even looking at her. He wasn't looking at anybody. Alice, not Sam, was the one who had spent hours talking to Max; she was the one, the only one, who could 'explain' him.

'Your grandfather was responsible for a couple of suicides. One heart attack. One stroke. Several divorces. That sort of thing. When he came to Hollywood from Germany in the late 1920s, he was just another imported European talent. There were quite a few of them. Some were great, others mediocre. Max was a small, solid talent with a major character flaw: he was a coward. A big coward. A genuine coward. A coward of the old school, the kind that bows to the powers that be, whatever or whoever they may be. He ought to have done well in Germany, but the fact that he was Jewish rendered his brand of cowardice irrelevant. It wouldn't have *helped*, if you know what I mean. Not that he knew this when he left for America; I'm only explaining it so that you'll understand why he did what he did, why he was too frightened to do anything else.

'Max was very helpful during the Congressional witch-hunts, beginning in the thirties and forties, and then again in the fifties, under Senator McCarthy. The word "Un-American" made him afraid and insecure, as if it were a direct personal accusation. It made him feel like a European parvenu, deserving of every suspicion that was pointed at him. So to bury those suspicions, he "co-operated". He informed on every single one of his friends and colleagues who had, in the past – in many cases while they were still living in Europe – had any communist sympathies or had belonged to the Communist Party. Those friends then had to deal with the consequences of his reports – and I've just told you how . . . But Max himself flourished, his writing contracts multiplied like worms after a spring rain, and, as his contribution to both American politics and American culture grew and intensified, he felt more and more American and less insecure. And then his wife, your grandmother, drowned herself.

'As Sam will confirm, Hannah, his mother, was happy living in America, happy in Hollywood, happy as Sam's parent and Max's wife. So why did she jump into a friend's pool, fully dressed and with her best shoes on, as if she were ready for a party? The friend was someone whose husband, a producer, also German-born, had been denounced by Max as a once card-carrying member of the Communist Party, and who had responded by collapsing from heart failure. Hannah knew about the others as well, and now couldn't face living with Max, or rather living with herself for having lived with him all these years. Her love and admiration for him turned into sharp, bitter nausea and hatred and some insanity, too. She felt poisoned. One day, she could think of no other way of cleansing herself except by taking her life. She forgot all about Sam that day, who was only ten years old.'

Natasha imagined Erica, being left alone to cope with the rest of her life if she, her mother, did something like that. Unthinkable. Hannah must have been insane and severely depressed to have forgotten all about her child. And yet, Natasha could also see that there was a firm, self-sufficient core in her daughter which would carry her through and allow her to keep her strength, even if she were left alone in the world.

'And how did Max respond to his wife's suicide? Believe me, I'm telling you the truth when I say, not at all. He did wish she hadn't done it, of course, and did not appreciate the burden of having to raise his son on his own, but he did not miss Hannah in his life. In fact, he had stopped noticing her quite some time ago, and disliked her silent disapproval of his weakness. And so now, without Hannah, there was no reason whatsoever for Max to stop helping the American people by revealing who among his friends and colleagues was siding with the communist enemy.'

Alice's speech had a miraculous effect on her husband. He woke up from his stupor and said loudly, looking directly at Philip and Natasha, 'Very different in our case. Very, very different. Alice means everything to me. If she disapproved of me, I couldn't live. Do you approve of me, Alice baby?'

Philip stared at his father in disgust. His lack of seriousness, his infantile behaviour had always bothered him immensely, but now, after what they had just heard, he really felt like punching the old man. But Alice ignored Sam completely, and continued, with a smile.

'And now comes my part of the story, and you had better start paying attention, because it's about to get complicated.' She kept the smile but her voice suddenly became more businesslike than before. Now she was a delivering a report, not a speech. 'When I came to this country after the war – sorry, *that* country, America – I was a communist. In fact, I came *because* I was a communist. They sent me, from Prague. My job was to get to Max Kaplan, via his son, Sam Kaplan, and to monitor what sort of information he was passing on to the American . . . investigators. The idea was to find out whether he was vulnerable in any way, and turn him into a minor agent or double agent. I'm not sure. I was very young at the time, and had just come out of . . . well you'll hear all about that in the next few days. In courtroom 73.'

It was the second time she had referred to the trial in that way. Natasha suddenly saw a clear sign of strain in her mother's face, the sort she normally had under complete control. She wanted to hug her, hard, but she didn't want to interrupt her.

'So I came to New York City, and a communist friend of the owner of Café Society arranged for a job for me there, as a waitress – even though they didn't actually employ women in that role. All their waiters and bartenders were men, veterans of the Abraham Lincoln Brigade; did you not notice that, Sam?'

'I did, and I liked you all the better for it.' Sam's eyes misted over with an old picture of a very young Alice, serving him drinks at the jazz club in the Village . . .

'I loved that job, you know. It was a wonderful, wonderful place. All that music, and the people . . . it reminded me of a European cabaret sometimes, but only a little. The only thing that bothered me was that ape-like Hitler doll they had hanging on a coat-check from the ceiling. But if I didn't look up too often it was fine.'

'You know,' said Sam, slowly, 'in all those years, I never even noticed it. Are you sure it was there?'

'Oh yes. Definitely.'

Philip sat up in his chair and said, coldly, 'So, Mom, you were a spy for the communists. Just as I thought. Hey, it's no big deal. This is the nineties. The only weird thing is you were initiated through Kaplan *père* and Kaplan *fils*. What an initiation.'

Natasha laughed. So did Sam. Even Philip was now laughing at his own comment.

But Alice interrupted: 'What do you mean, "just as you thought"?' She looked at her eldest with sudden curiosity. His earnestness had receded, for a moment, behind the easy laughter. She loved the solemn meticulousness of his mind as much she loved her daughter's lightness of spirit. Her children: a man, a woman. *All grown up. All hers*.

Philip had taken her question seriously: 'I'm a journalist, Mom, not a great one, but still. We snoop around. Our grandfather's dirty past is not that much of a secret. In fact, his name was mentioned in a couple of recent Hollywood biographies. There was gossip, I interviewed some people, pretending I was doing it for the *Voice* . . . Well, what can I tell you: he got some people blacklisted in his day, but in a lot of people's books, he's the one on a blacklist now. Sorry, Dad.' He glanced at his father, who did not, in fact, seem at all perturbed. Rather pleased, in fact. '. . . And so, remembering your long talks with Grandfather when I was a kid; and how you could never hide that you were angry about the poor Rosenbergs . . . and didn't you used to say Klaus Fuchs was a hero? Little details like that – I put it all together and . . . well, Mom, my next step would have been a trip to Prague, to look at the secret service archives from the 1950s – I bet I would have found your name.'

Alice nodded, and smiled a little guiltily, as if she had been accused of an innocent prank. Philip tried to look triumphant, but couldn't. As always, his mother was the unbeaten one. Victorious. How on earth did she always pull it off? he wondered. Where did her strength come from?

'But wait a minute, Mom,' said Natasha. 'I bet you didn't stop with that. Didn't you go on? Spying, I mean? Grandfather wasn't such a great catch, was he?'

'No,' answered Alice. 'He wasn't. Bored me to death. That's why I came up with the idea of making those films. Kept us busy, didn't it Sam my darling?'

'Oh *yes*.' Within a split second, they were back in that silly world of their own, as if Alice's revelations had not changed a thing.

Well, obviously it hadn't, thought Natasha, gratefully, but persisted: 'Mom? What else did you do, though? In terms of spying, I mean?'

'Oh, nothing special, Natashka. I had a contact in England whom I supplied with fairly irregular information on what was going on in the American show-business world. You could call it gossip, really. Who was doing what, people's private lives, that sort of thing. It was a bit like your column, in fact,' she said to Philip, who did not look at all pleased, 'except it paid better. A *lot* better. How do you think we were able to afford the big apartment? But you know, I didn't do it for the money – I mean, not only. I really *was* a Communist. My heart was in it. I only stopped believing when . . . never mind.'

'Finish that sentence, Alice,' said Sam, with surprising harshness in his voice. 'For God's sake, finish that goddam sentence. For once.'

'During and after the communist witch-hunts in Prague.' Alice sounded like an obedient little girl all of a sudden. How many faces did her mother have? Natasha wondered. And her father? Would she have to go on revising and readjusting her opinion of her parents, for ever?

'The Prague show-trials did it. Against the Jewish communists and intellectuals. I knew some of them. I would have been one of them, if I had stayed in Prague.

'And also the fact that the man who had . . . introduced me to that world – first communism, then my bit of spying – had been involved in the trial of a very special man I admired. A famous Czech Jewish writer. He provided the evidence which was the basis for the writer's life sentence, and I knew it was a fabrication. That was the end, for me. Obviously.'

'Was this your contact in England, Mom?' asked Natasha.

'Yes.' Alice smiled, radiant again, relieved to have told them so much, relieved at least *that* was now over. But there was one more thing she had to say: 'His name was Franz Held.'

25 'Cut!'

Sam, Philip and Natasha chose to sit together in the courtroom, in one of the front benches. There was a struggle to obtain those privileged seats, but Natasha suddenly remembered – how could she have forgotten? – that she was a member of the press, editor of a magazine, for Christ's sake, editor of a *Jewish* magazine. Normally, when representing her small, fringe publication, she knew she was invisible to the big players, the journalists from the mainstream papers and magazines. She quite enjoyed that and felt free rather than ostracized, independent rather than impoverished. An illusion maybe, but, except when it came to arguing with Sidney Sussman about money for postage stamps, and, by extension, trying to manage on the very low salary she was earning for all her efforts, she didn't really mind at all that her magazine was a small one. And today, being its editor – more than being the daughter of the main witness, for this was clearly Alice's role at the trial – helped her get a good seat from which to watch her mother perform.

Yes, perform. Natasha decided to think of the trial as a show, and, of course, it had all the elements of one: there was a stage with its changing cast of actors, there was clever behind-the-scenes directing, there was an audience, and then the daily reviews in the press. The audience, to Natasha's surprise, did not consist of familiar faces; she had expected to see those same people who came to minor Jewish literary events, polite ladies and gentlemen with time to spare and strong views on 'Jewish culture'. Well, their interest did not seem to extend to the most famous trial against a Nazi war criminal in recent history. There seemed to be more young Germans – journalists, students – in the audience than Jews, except for a couple of Holocaust survivors, one man and one woman, and a number of well-known Jewish historians. The historians, she noticed, were taking copious notes; whereas the two survivors – she had a clear view of both of them – sat stone-faced and white-knuckled throughout most of the trial. Natasha knew one of them, and was pleased when the woman nodded in her direction, with a smile. There was an atmosphere of airy friendliness in the courtroom, as if everyone gathered there had come to attend a party of some sort. A good way to spend your day, or days – the trial was to go on for weeks – if you didn't have a job to go to. She noticed an entire row of white-haired, dainty old ladies – probably the same ones that wrote those letters to the press, protesting the cruelty of prosecuting the frail old woman. The judge, a soft-faced, grandfatherly type, smiled a lot and made frequent jokes, good and bad. 'This is so *English*,' whispered Philip to Natasha. 'I can't stand it.'

Annmarie Goetz, the defendant, really was an unlikely war criminal, Natasha had to concede. A tiny, delicate old woman, with a graceful demeanour and controlled little gestures, not a movement out of place. She was, apparently, only about ten years older than Alice, but looked like she could be her grandmother. Natasha was proud, in a funny way. She would have been devastated if the Nazi woman had looked better than her beautiful mother.

And Alice *did* look beautiful today. She was wearing a pale blue suit and no jewellery whatsoever. Her loose white curls gave her a sort of glow, whereas Goetz's trim grey-yellow bob made her shrink even more. Well, at least in Natasha's eyes . . .

The defendant's English was excellent, she did not require an interpreter. But her voice! It had a very peculiar, metallic quality, thought Natasha. It reminded her of the noise their lawnmower made when it hit an aluminium can in the grass – awful. She almost giggled.

Alice's testimony had been supposed to last for a number of consecutive days, maybe a week, and she was to be questioned, at length, by both the prosecution and the defence. But something very unusual happened on the very first day: she gave such a vivid account of all she had to say that further questioning seemed, somehow, unnecessary.

She began by explaining how, as a sixteen-year-old Mischling, she had to join a transport to Terezìn (Alice always refused to call it by its German name, Theresienstadt), alone. Her parents were in Prague (she was an only child); her Jewish father was supposed to arrive later, but managed to hide with friends in the Moravian countryside, where he died towards the end of the war. Their Prague home was a gorgeous big apartment in Månesova Street, number 23, in an elegant art nouveau quarter called Vinohrady, near St Wenceslas Square, and many parks. The day Alice received the notice informing her that her life, as she knew it, was over, she said to her mother: 'I want to be dead. I don't want to go anywhere without the two of you.'

The defence made an attempt to object to the personal nature of Alice's account, but the judge took no notice. So she continued.

'My mother wouldn't even allow me to shed a tear. She simply sat down and quickly began to sew folded bills of paper money into the cloth buttons of my coat. Some years later, they saved my life.

'In Terezìn, I lived in a barracks with girls like myself. I . . . adjusted, to everything. The hunger, the disease, the stench, the lice . . .' she suddenly found Natasha's face in the audience and smiled, imperceptibly. 'The hearse in the streets of the ghetto, transporting the dead and the old. The old people everywhere, rummaging for scraps.

'But I found friends there, too, and things to do. Important, interesting things. I worked in the library. I helped produce – which meant copy by hand and sometimes type – a magazine, in Czech. It looked like a children's magazine, but that was only the façade. In fact, it was a political magazine, with some literary material thrown in, for cover. Poems and the like. Children's drawings. It began as a Zionist publication, under one editor, and then was taken over by another, who made it a communist one. There were fights about things like that . . . I belonged to the communist camp, for . . . private reasons. I should state at this point that the name of the editor who asked for my help with this potentially very dangerous activity was

Franz Held. The so-called children's magazine was called *Nos*, which means 'the nose' in Czech. It was a reference to Pinocchio, and his nose, which was, in effect, a lie detector. Our *Nos* was a clever ruse and, in that sense, a lie. The Nazis never found out.

'I mention this because it was Franz Held who introduced me to the defendant.'

There was a slight murmur in the audience which had, until this moment, been absolutely silent. Not a single whisper or cough had interrupted Alice's speech.

'Franz Held had always been interested in acting, among many other things. He was an attractive, charismatic young man, as everyone who has ever known him will confirm. In Terezìn, Franz was my hero. More than that: he became my lover, and the father of my . . . child.'

Now there should have been a collective gasp, a shriek, or something. But there was total silence. Alice had the uncanny ability to suddenly look like the young girl she must have been then, on the verge of death yet still thinking, living, loving. Passionately so, it seems, thought Natasha and looked at her father. If he had any prior knowledge of this, he didn't show it now.

'Two film crews arrived in Terezìn; the first one to produce a Nazi propaganda film about the "model ghetto", making us all pose for happy shots, forcing us to smile. We were filmed working, playing, enjoying our leisure and the sunshine, we had music, concerts, a band played, the children ate rich sandwiches . . . we were made to look good and healthy, as if we were merely passing the time in a pleasant sanatorium. We *did* in fact have some of that; the concerts, and the lectures. But Terezìn as the place where most of us were either dying or already dead – I once helped empty the ashes of 30,000 dead Jews into the river, to make room for new transports – was nowhere to be seen in that pretty picture. But that is irrelevant here. What matters is that Franz Held was desperate to be in that film, and didn't make it. I don't know whether it was his personal vanity that made him want it so much, or whether he believed that it would save him from a transport to Poland (which meant Auschwitz, though we didn't know it). In any event, he hadn't been filmed for it, though many others had. He was therefore very pleased when a German cameraman, Ludwig Hoffmann, approached him with the request to participate in yet another film.

'Ludwig Hoffmann and Franz Held knew each other from before the war. Franz told me this. I believe they had met in Berlin, during the 1936 Olympics. They were about the same age and quite fond of each other. The war made forced enemies of many people who were not necessarily inclined to feel that way about one another . . .

'In any case, Ludwig had been a photographer and cameraman before the war, and would have been sent as a cameraman to the Eastern Front, if he had not met and married Annmarie Goetz, the brilliant star-director of Nazi cinema.'

Everyone looked at Annmarie Goetz, who betrayed absolutely no emotion. If anything, she looked flattered by Alice's description.

'It is not my role to give you this woman's resumé. Before the Nazis came to power, she had made a number of interesting films. Slightly derivative of Leni Riefenstahl, but with less art and more feeling, perhaps.

'During the war, Annmarie Goetz decided to create an innovative remake of an old silent hit, *The Bloodhound and the Girl*. She was ambitious and wanted this film to surpass absolutely everything that had ever been done before. She was no longer happy with the dramatic interplay between light and darkness, shadow and blinding flares. She wasn't satisfied with the possibilities of clever editing, and perspective, and speed, and that new toy – close-ups. Of course she needed all those elements; but above all, she wanted to achieve supreme realism. Blood was to be blood, just like a tear was a real tear. She wanted real life on the screen. And she also wanted real death.

'And she was lucky, because she was making films at a time when human life, if it happened to be Jewish, or Gypsy, was hers to be used for special effects. Annmarie Goetz was close to some very high Nazi officials, who liked the idea of UFA-Film GmbH producing highly effective material which, unlike most of their propaganda films, would *not* flop at the box office. She was given a green light to locate, carefully select and "employ" a number of Jewish inmates for her film. Given that she was shooting on location in the shadowy streets of old Prague, Terezìn was the closest concentration camp from which to "borrow" her "extras". The fact that her husband knew one of the inmates was a lucky coincidence. And so this was how Franz Held became involved in Annmarie Goetz's film. As a casting agent, so to speak.

'Of course, he had no idea that participation in the film meant a virtual death sentence. Well, maybe he guessed this, to some extent, when he discovered that the names of the "extras" he selected were automatically placed on the lists of those who were to be sent east – even though he was well aware they were only going to Prague. Franz selected me to play the lead, because my looks and my age were right for the role, and also because I was pregnant at the time. The role I played did not, actually, call for my own death. But it did involve the death of my baby, at birth. The script called for a very young mother to push a child out into the world, and then, in order to save the infant from deadly attack by the crazed bloodhound, she . . . had to strangle the baby with her own hands. I did this. My only thought and prayer was that this child had no wish to live. Annmarie Goetz said "Schnitt!" That's "cut".'

Now there was a gasp in the audience. Annmarie Goetz made a peculiar grimace, wrinkling her nose and pursing her lips. But Alice remained perfectly composed. She had promised herself she would never give in to them this time. She would keep that promise.

'I understand,' Alice continued, 'that the final film – which, by the way, never made it into the theatres and turned out to be another Nazi flop – will be presented here as evidence. I would like to be excused from this screening. In fact, I have nothing further to say, except to repeat that I have personally seen how Annmarie Goetz directed Jewish inmates from Terezìn to be murdered in front of her cameras, saying only "cut" when the victim was dead. My baby was such an inmate and I begged to be allowed to die with . . . him. But they forced me to live, because my death was not in the script. Not in *that* script, anyway.

'I should add that after the film was finished, both Franz and myself would have found ourselves on a transport to Auschwitz. But, using his underground communist connections and the money my mother had sewn into the buttons of my coat, we managed to stay in Prague and hide – separately, not together – until the end of the war, which was not too far away at the time.'

A lunch-break was announced but it was made clear to Alice that her testimony was considered complete, and that the film would, indeed, be shown after the break. She could now leave.

Journalists began to surround her, like vultures, but Natasha, using her own press card, pushed forward and prised her mother away from the sweaty crowd. All four of them moved, as quickly as possible, through the long, echoing corridors of the Royal Courts of Justice, and, as soon as they reached the Strand, jumped in the first black taxi and went home, to Natasha's house.

Mom, I love you, Natasha wanted to say a million times as the cab jerked forward, in never-ending London traffic. But for some reason, she couldn't.

26 Last Issue

Strangely, neither Alice nor Natasha, nor Sam or Philip for that matter, were all that interested in the outcome of the trial. They glanced at the papers in the following days and weeks, were a little concerned when they read that Alice's testimony was being dismissed as 'hearsay' when it transpired that the film was very badly preserved and several crucial details were hard to discern. But eventually, Annmarie Goetz was sentenced to – something, they didn't even know what exactly. She had been living in England all these years, a quiet little old lady in a quiet little village in Oxfordshire. She and Hoffmann had been divorced for years, but he continued to support her. It made no difference to Alice whether Goetz died at home or in a jail. It should have, but it didn't. She could not explain to Natasha why. Perhaps it was for the same reason that her mother wouldn't let her cry when she had been summoned to Theresienstadt.

One thing became clear in courtroom 73, though: the fact that Ludwig Hoffmann should have been on trial, too. He was more than 'just' Goetz's husband and assistant; he had been fully aware of the nature of the film had knowingly helped select suitable extras / victims, and filmed some of the scenes himself. In fact, it had been Hoffmann's idea to produce a remake of the original silent version of the film – which, by sheer coincidence, had been written by Max Kaplan. Like his wife, Hoffmann had become a respectable citizen after the war, without leaving his profession.

It also transpired in the course of the trial that Alice had been a little naive about the reason why the film had not been shown in wartime cinemas: it wasn't only because of its poor artistic quality, as she had assumed, but also because, by the time all the footage had been edited, the war was near its end, and the film had become a liability, as evidence of a major war crime. To hide all traces of their co-operation, Hoffmann and Goetz divorced, but in truth, their marriage continued, like an undercover, clandestine love affair. Ludwig Hoffmann foresaw, shrewdly, that the time would yet arrive when *The Bloodhound* would come into unwelcome focus. He prepared himself by 'cultivating' his friendship with Franz Held; even before the war ended, he offered to look after the manuscripts Franz had accumulated for his Theresienstadt magazine, and return them at some point in the future.

In fact, as Alice now understood, Hoffmann had kept the papers as potential blackmail material – moral rather than financial, against both Franz and herself. It was in fact Hoffmann who had helped them hide and escape when the film was finished, at a price: they were never to disclose how the film was made. If they did, he would have 'exposed' Held as a Nazi collaborator, using the magazine as evidence, claiming some of its contributors had been selected by him as extras for the film (which they were, in fact). But Alice knew the truth, knew that Franz had no idea what Goetz had in mind; and, even if he had known, he would have had no choice but to do as he was told. She would have testified against Hoffmann, of course.

'I'm on a roll,' she said to her family, the day after the trial, at breakfast. 'No more secrets.' She seemed to be intoxicated with her new freedom, could hardly contain her exuberance. 'I can go on and on and on . . . I'll tell them everything now.' However, the man was nowhere to be found; Natasha gave the authorities all the information she had on him – the flat, the housekeeper, the papers she had been given – and the cheque for £50,000. Her task of 'investigating' the man had been brought to quite a finale.

The trial turned a kind of celebrity spotlight on Alice and Sam; their ICA retrospective became a much-publicised event, and was moved forward by a few weeks, due to a great deal of popular and critical interest. Natasha and Philip were suddenly proud of their silly, infantile parents; proud that, in spite of everything they had been through, they remained silly and infantile, and made wonderful dirty movies, and celebrated their love for each other that way.

And then, quite suddenly, it was time for things to go back to normal. Philip and Sam, who had bought their return tickets together, left first. Alice wanted to stay just a little longer. She had a wish: to take Natasha to Prague and to Terezìn, just a quick trip, only three days or so. It was so near. Why not?

So they went. Alice was devastated to find that Månesova 23, the house she had grown up in, had been replaced by a modernistic, angular fifties construction. It turned out that her building had been one of the very, very few sites in Prague that had been destroyed by a bomb. In the 1950s, the new building, with its spacious flats, was reserved mainly for Communist Party apparatchiks.

They took the bus from Prague to Terezìn; it was a quick journey, under one hour. Suddenly, they were walking on cobbled pavements among low, uniform houses painted a dreary mustard colour. Children were playing ball games, riding bikes and little scooters. Alice came alive, and began remembering: this had been her first barrack, then she moved over there. Here was a secret synagogue (they found terracotta-coloured Hebrew lettering on the ceiling), and this was a sort of loft room where she and Franz (and others) made love. She laughed: 'It was a boys' room, and they had a sign: if you were told "go wash your feet", it meant, get lost, someone needs to be alone here.'

Alice told Natasha how she had once invented a mythical figure called the Phantom of Theresienstadt, a real man who lived in the cellars; not an inmate, someone who simply stayed where he was when the Germans evacuated the original population to make room for the future inhabitants of the ghetto. This 'phantom' was real but invisible, could move around freely among both Jews and Germans, confusing them all . . . In fact, she had written this down as a sort of tale for Held's magazine. 'And now, I've found it again. I hated Hoffmann for trying to manipulate my feelings through all those old papers, but in the end, I was almost grateful to him for preserving all that stuff. It's my life, Natashka, all that debris is my life. I've changed my mind about something in the last few days. I used to think I was all broken up, that there were only pieces of me left, pieces, and those didn't matter. And now I think . . . Those pieces, dead or alive, those fragments, that's me.'

She pulled Natasha into one of the buildings and, without thinking about it for a second, walked straight down into a dark, damp cellar. 'This is where we rehearsed our concerts, and here is where I copied all those pages. And here,' she said, inserting the nail of her little finger inside a tiny crack in the wall, and carefully removing a stone, 'here is where I hid something. Let's see if it's still there, after all these years.'

She extracted a tiny silver locket. Her hands were shaking, so she gave it to Natasha to open. There was a photo inside, of a young man.

Alice finally broke down and cried, though very quietly. 'I loved him so much,' she said, 'I have never known such love before, or since . . . Sorry Natashka . . . this has all been a bit . . . much.

'He never let me down. Franz did, but Pavel – never. Do you understand the difference, Natasha? Franz was my lover, but not my love. I felt . . . *chosen* by him . . . like a fool. I was so young, a child, almost . . . Of course it wasn't true. He had many, many women. You have no idea how many slept with him, for a little extra food which he knew how to get, for a bit of warmth, even to get published in his magazine! And because he made us feel *human*. Desirable, even. You'd look at me in Terezìn and see a dirty rag hiding a walking skeleton, but Franz made me feel like a *woman*. I would have done anything for him. That was his talent. Later, I understood that the only woman he ever loved was his mother. He was a . . . cripple. Our great charismatic Franz, our charming hero, was just a heartless little boy. With a huge appetite for survival. And Pavel . . . he knew I loved him. But even though I saw he had feelings for me, he tried to hide them. Said I was too young! As if it mattered, *there*!! But he was right. And, you know, I think Pavel really *wanted* to die. In fact, when he heard that he had been selected for the next transport to Auschwitz, he could have stayed behind. People offered to help him, he was so loved. But he said, no no no, this is my fate. I have to go. And he went. Maybe he would have survived that Czech jail if he hadn't been destroyed by the camps . . .'

'And you know who made sure he was sentenced for life in Prague, by the communists? Franz, of course. Franz was so jealous of him. You know Natasha, Franz had charisma, I told you that, but he had no real talent. He was empty inside. He could feed off others, but he didn't really believe in anything. And in Terezìn, where people were always fighting and arguing among themselves, Pavel Miller had the status of an angel. No one would touch him. Remember I told you about that little article he wrote, about Zionism? Well, Franz got it out of him, but it was meant to be a satire, a parody. Not a serious thing at all. And everyone knew that. But after the war – I was already in America – Franz needed to save his own skin. His position was precarious.

'Did you hear that he was a soldier in Svoboda's army in Russia? He had been in Russia before the war, for a sports event, and then just stayed there, and eventually joined the Czech unit. There were many Jews in that unit, and many communists among them. That's where he became one, or at least pretended to. I never really knew with him. So he volunteered for parachutist's training, to be parachuted from Russia back to Czechoslovakia, on a secret mission. He and four others flew, in 1941; do you know what Franz once confided in me? He told me he had no interest whatsoever in fighting with the Czech brigade; all he wanted was to get back to Prague, to see his mother!! He was insanely dedicated to his mother, who lived alone in Prague. This was his way of deserting the army, really . . . What he didn't know was that Czech Jews were being rounded up and sent to camps and ghettos. The other four were actually caught by the Germans, who didn't know about Franz. And Franz did make it to Prague, found his mother – only to discover that she was already in Terezìn, and that he was bound to join her there.'

'So that's how he ended up being both a soldier and a camp inmate,' said Natasha. Her voice echoed and reverberated against the rough, grey walls of the cellar. She wanted to get out of there, but Alice seemed to want to finish their conversation in that dark, damp place.

'Yes. But after the war, after 1948, when Czechoslovakia became a communist country, Franz was in trouble, because his "desertion" became suspect to those who had known him in Russia.'

'But didn't he live in England, right after the war?'

'Briefly. That's when he established the contact with me. Begged me to keep supplying him with some information. He said it would save his life in Prague, to have something to give them. That's how he became a proper . . . agent. Secret agent, I mean. Denouncing Pavel Miller – giving them "evidence" that he was a "Zionist agent", on the basis of that little article he wrote – helped Franz get out of the jam he was in, because of his desertion. After that, he was free to move to England. As a secret agent, of course. But he wasn't allowed to take his mother along. The deal was that he could visit her, from London, by travelling under assumed names. He often changed his name by deed poll for that purpose, by the way.'

'That would explain all his travels . . . But what about the magazine?'

Alice suddenly burst out laughing.

'Natashka, the magazine was a cover. Financed by the Czech secret service and the KGB. Isn't that hilarious? That was his way into so many things . . . and safe, too, because it was on the fringe, and inconspicuous.'

'God. You mean, the way *Encounter* was financed by the CIA?'

'Exactly. Except, this being Eastern European money, it didn't go very far. That's why it was such a poor little shoestring operation . . . Still . . . not bad, under the circumstances.'

'And none of the trustees had a clue?'

'I'm not sure. Not sure at all. Who knows . . .'

'Mom, you knew this the whole time, why didn't you tell me when I first got this fucking job?' Natasha was genuinely outraged.

'Because, my darling, you were having such fun with it. I didn't want to spoil it for you. Not until the trial came up, and I had to tell you all this. And also, you started snooping around yourself . . .'

'Let's get out of here,' said Natasha. 'I need some light.'

Out on the street again, Natasha looked at the almost decomposed picture of the young man in the locket. Unlike Held's portrait, it seemed to hold no mystery.

They walked back, and saw, in one of the buildings that was now a museum, some sort of class in progress. Natasha, nosy as ever, peeked in, and heard a lecture about the history of Theresienstadt being given in German to a group of young kids. The teacher turned towards her and Alice and reprimanded them sharply: 'You are disturbing us. Please go away.' Natasha wanted to tell the bitch that her students could all learn more from her mother, who had really been there, but Alice pulled her away. 'Let's go. We'll miss the bus,' she said, softly.

Back in London, Alice packed her suitcase and prepared to leave. She had a few days left and intended to spend them all with Erica. This suited Natasha, who had to throw together her last issue of *The Nose*, whose publication was now to be financed by the small collection Zygmunt Levy-Newman had organized among the trustees.

She knew exactly what she would put in her last issue. She sat down and recorded everything her mother told her about Franz Held. *Everything*. The truth had to be known, finally. And she didn't care what anyone thought. She typed furiously for two days, until she had written down every word of her mother's account, and every detail of her own investigation. This included the information – offered by Alice and verified by Natasha – that Franz Held had in fact committed suicide, when, after the Prague Velvet Revolution of 1989, the secret files gradually became accessible to the public and his history was in danger of being revealed. He shot himself in Prague, behind his mother's old house. Natasha would add the picture she had of Held, and the tiny one, enlarged, of Pavel Miller. And after a moment's thought, she decided also to add a photo of Alice.

Then she phoned Karl Spitzer. 'Karl . . . change of plans.'

'Oh, I know my dear. I didn't for a minute assume that we could continue . . .'

'I don't mean that. Though that, too, of course, now that you mention it. Shall we say that you and I . . . that we're . . . history?' They both laughed, Karl a little sadly.

'I mean the issue. No Jews and crime, please, I have new material for you. Can you take care of it, as a matter of some urgency?'

'Of course, Natasha.'

'Good.'

That done, she suddenly remembered that she was married. To Tim. A good, kind, solid man who never really talked about anything. She remembered how, after a good few moments in bed, she had once asked him: Tim, was this nice? Yes, he'd answered. But how? Why? What was nice about it? Can't you tell me? No, he'd said, without even thinking about it. Why should I? It was just – nice. That's all.

And now she was dying to see him. She felt free – free of the magazine, free of all the mysteries, free of history and histories . . . Tim was her hero, she suddenly realized. A real one. Not one of those insanely complicated twisted characters, busy spying and living ridiculously complex undercover lives. Screw all that. She wanted her own, simple life back. Now.

She tried to locate him, and was told he might actually be on his way back to base from duty. If she took the tube now, she could surprise him at his office. That would be fun. Erica was with her mother, and she and Tim could go out in the city. She would love to show off to the whole world that her 'date' was a British Transport cop.

Sitting in the train, Natasha fantasized about how amazed and pleased Tim would be to see her. She was so tired and relaxed, she nodded off.

She was fast asleep when, somewhere near King's Cross, in the narrow confines of the Piccadilly Line underground tunnel, the half-empty train was suddenly torn apart by a violent explosion. It hadn't been an accident. Tim and Ian were on the scene almost instantly, as they'd received a warning from John White, a member of 'The Group of '33', through Charlie Darwin, that a terrorist attack on a tube train carrying the editor of a 'kike journal' was imminent.

*

After several long meetings, the trustees went ahead and published Natasha's last issue anyway, leaving it to Karl Spitzer to decide what it should look like. Karl followed Natasha's instructions to the letter: he included the biographical material on Franz Held, the contents of Hoffmann's file, as translated by Alice, the photos, and even a poem by Nigel Pearce, entitled 'The Jewish Fate'. When Charles Sugarman sent in his prepared obituary, however, Spitzer put his foot down and wrote his own, brief one.

It read:

> Natasha Kaplan edited *The Nose* for only one year. In her last issue, she presents a complete demystification of our founding editor, Franz Held, and an apology to our loyal reader Nigel Pearce, whose poem she felt we ought to have published a long time ago. Unfortunately, Natasha Kaplan herself remains a complete mystery to us. Perhaps it must be left to a future editor of *The Nose* to tell us who she was.

Acknowledgements

I am extremely grateful to British Transport Police at Euston Road Police Station in London for letting me watch them work and for answering, very patiently, *all* of my FSQs; in particular, I must thank Chief Inspector David Breen, Chief Inspector Bob Pacey, PC Rob Gifford and PC Carl Jones.

I have also had the privilege of benefitting, in different ways, from the help and experience of George Avakian; Vered Berman; my brother, Maxim Biller; my father, Semjon Biller; Ruth Bondy; Jiri Franek; Eva Herrmannova; Elana Jorden; my husband, Shalom Lappin; my daughter, Shira; Anthony Lerman; and David Margolick.

My very special thanks to my agent, Gill Coleridge, for her generous support and wisdom.